THE SWEET SKULL

MANUEL RUIZ

CONTENTS

Get your Free Starter Library

Sign up for the no-spam newsletter and get a NOVEL, NOVELLAS, and SHORT STORIES, plus more exclusive content, all for free.

Additional details can be found at the end of this book.

Get your free Starter Library here:
manuelruiz3.com

DEDICATION

Dedicated to everyone that was part of the actual events that inspired some of the craziest scenes in this story.

Daisy
Jenny
Rocky
Jessica
Erica

CHAPTER ONE

GABBY TRIED TO MAKE A CLEAN SLICE AROUND THE LATERAL rectus, but her blade was dull and the eyeball was stuck.

She eased her finger between the muscles that control eye movement and pulled the blade up slightly but with precision. There was a squishing sound as the eyeball popped forward.

She was off her game.

Normally she could slice out an eyeball and put it back together within three minutes. Two minutes was her personal record.

She reached down to the dangling eyeball. She was going to need a sharper blade.

"Everything okay, Gabby?"

The voice made her jump. She was so focused she didn't notice her boss standing behind her.

"I need to head out. Are you okay to stay alone?"

"I'm good."

Some people might dread the thought of sharing a room with a bunch of dead bodies, but Gabby was used to it.

"Don't worry, Mr. Bernard."

"Ed, Gabby. Mister is way too formal. Please."

"I'm sorry, Mr... Edward. Ed. It's hard after calling you Mr. Bernard since I was ten."

"It's okay." He smiled. "Have a good night. I'll see you tomorrow afternoon."

He left, and she was alone with the four other bodies in the room.

The display she was working on is The Diver, a man standing with his arms straight out, parallel to the floor with his knees bent, preparing to leap off a diving board. Someone had damaged his eye. People are curious, and many overzealous patrons ignore the signs. The instructions are simple: DO NOT TOUCH.

She walked back to the repair area, better known as the office Emergency Room. The exhibits were difficult to break, but certain parts were more fragile than others. Someone had placed their fingers into The Diver earlier in the day during one of the tours.

Gabby walked straight to the medical supply drawers, found a scalpel, and inspected the blade. She was able to tell right away that it was in better shape than the one she had been using.

She returned to the main showroom. The Diver's eyeball was still dangling, hanging on by strands of the six muscles connected to a human eyeball. When she was done, no one would be able to tell it had ever been disturbed.

She looked straight into The Diver's eyeball as she lifted it.

A small shiver ran up her neck. That happened from time to time. Even though she had been around bodies and displays like this for years with her mother, every so often the creep factor made an appearance. As long as she didn't think about it too long, she'd be okay.

She went back to the lateral rectus, and it sliced through

easily. She positioned the eyeball and started the reat-tachment.

She pulled out her glass cement glue and spread it around the muscles of the eye, ensuring it covered all the necessary parts. It left a bright and reflective look. The shine would diminish somewhat once it had time to set and dry.

She heard something move in the adjacent room.

"Mr. Bernard? Ed?"

Nothing.

She put the cement glue back down and picked up the scalpel before walking into her least favorite place at work: The Baby Room. It was the darkest of the exhibit rooms, which was necessary so the displays, which consisted of transparent cylinders and glass boxes, could illuminate their contents, that included fetuses in various states of develop-ment as well as body parts showing nervous systems and bone development. Fortunately, she didn't have to visit the room too often since the bulk of her responsibilities were with the actual body exhibits.

She looked around, passing some of the baby displays. Some were still in the placenta. She tried everything she could not to think of Ally, but couldn't help it. She was over-come with the realization of how lucky she was that her daughter was healthy and didn't suffer the fate of these babies on display for the public's consumption. She upped her pace and passed through the next section, which held Informational Displays and showcased smaller sections of bodies and body systems with explanations on the Plastina-tion process that allowed the human body displays to remain so well preserved. Some called it the Reading Room. She rushed past into the final section used for storage and major body repairs, but more importantly, held their Archives. She took a few quick glances around, trying to avoid the spare body parts laid out in various areas of the room. She didn't find anyone.

Probably just the air conditioner or something that came from the hall.

She returned to the showroom and, out of her peripheral vision, noticed something bright and out of place to her left.

The Runner. One of the displays that depicted a runner in a full sprint stride. Someone had painted her face.

She turned slowly and saw a mix of colors on the skeletal muscles. The Runner's anatomy exposed her legs and arms to show how the muscles moved when in motion. Her face was multicolored. The eyes were white and odd-colored patterns covered half of her face. It was a mix of black and pink flowers, but it didn't look like paint.

She reached toward the flowers with her finger and felt the coarse material. She looked at the cheek and then back to her fingertip, then brought it up to her lips. She licked it.

Sugar.

That's what it was. The Runner's face looked like the type of skulls that appear around Halloween or the Day of the Dead. *Calaveras.* Sugar skulls.

The hair on the back of her neck rose.

Then she thought of Ally.

She pulled out her phone and quickly hit speed dial #2.

It rang. Then again. After four rings, it went to voicemail.

Gabby looked back at The Runner's sugar decorated face and then turned back to her phone. She broke into her own sprint.

She felt the sweat pouring down her back as she blew past the main door and didn't even consider locking it behind her.

She rushed down the hall, threw open the exit door, and ran down the stairwell to the first floor. One of her heels flew off mid-stride as she picked up her pace, but instead of turning around to pick it up, she kicked off the other one. She was panting as she reached the door marked "LOVE DAYCARE" and panicked when no one was at the front desk.

She hit the bell twice before deciding to head into the hallway.

"Gabby, what's going on?" a woman walked into the hall.

"Ally?" was all Gabby could get out.

"She's fine. I was just in the room. Two babies threw up at the same time, so they needed me to help. Did you need to pick her up?"

Gabby tried to catch her breath.

"You're sure, Donna?"

"Take a look yourself. She's in one of the play pens having a great time."

Gabby took a few more bare steps toward the door and looked in. Ally was standing and smiling while she looked at the few kids who were still there. Most parents picked their kids up by 5, but Ally was one of the last kids picked up since Gabby usually wasn't out until right before closing.

Gabby shook her head.

"Are you sure you're okay, Gabby? What happened to your shoes?"

Gabby turned and smiled through her flushed cheeks.

"It's okay—just mom paranoia. I'll be back in a little while to get her. I need to go finish up."

Donna nodded as Gabby walked back down the hall. She took the stairs back up instead of the elevator to grab her shoes. Although she exercised on her home elliptical at least four times a week, she was breathing hard as she made her way back up to the office's front door. Fear and adrenaline mixed with sprinting the fastest she'd run in years weren't kind to her body, even though it was a healthy one.

Gabby entered the room and The Runner was in the same spot, wearing its colored sugar mask. She grabbed a towel and a water sprayer and touched the display's chin.

"I hope you don't think I'm a coward just because someone decorated your face. If this is just an office prank, I'll find out who it is."

She raised her voice at the end of the sentence as she soaked some water on the cloth and dabbed The Runner's cheek. Fortunately, the sugar wasn't glued or embedded, and within a few minutes, its entire face was clean.

She returned to The Diver, feeling calmer and foolish. The staff sometimes played pranks on each other, but it hadn't happened since she first started. Jimmy Foreman from marketing was the office prankster and had rigged an old, damaged body in the ER to raise its arm as Gabby walked by, scaring her so badly she fell to the floor. It was a newbie ritual, and Gabby had gotten a kick out of it, her scream turning into crying laughter. It was something her friends would have done.

Even so, how good would someone have to be to make up the face so quickly? Maybe that's why only half The Runner's face was decorated. Gabby closed her mind off and concentrated on The Diver's eye repair. This time, she was able to get it fixed on the first try. The glue would dry within an hour but would take up to 24 to dry completely. Once it looked normal, she walked back to the ER to put away her items. She placed her old scalpel in the repair box so that it could be sharpened later. She walked back out to move The Diver back into his place.

She entered the room and stopped cold.

The Diver and The Runner were in the center of the Showroom, facing each other with each of their faces fully decorated in sugar designs.

Gabby let out a piercing scream as each of their heads turned to face her and smiled.

CHAPTER TWO

GABBY FLIPPED AROUND AND RAN, GRABBING HER PURSE ON HER way out without bothering to lock the office.

She was halfway out the front building doors when she stopped, gasping for breath.

"Ally!"

Her arms were shaking as she raised her palms to her face to calm herself down. She rushed back into the daycare and got Ally out as fast as she could.

Once in her car, she fumbled to issue a voice command to her Bluetooth.

"Call Angie."

"Calling Angie," her car's voice echoed.

"Hey, Gabs. What's going on?"

"Angie, can you and Ree come by for dinner? Something happened. I'm not even sure what it was, but I need to know I'm sane."

"Of course. I talked to Ree earlier. Let me see if he can make it. Are you sure you're okay?"

"I'll tell you all about it when you come over. You'll have new material to make fun of me if it's just stress."

"Already worth it. I'll see you in a little while."

Ally squealed and Gabby looked into her rear-view mirror. Her daughter smiled when she saw her eyes through the reflection.

"Your momma may be losing it, Love."

Ally didn't seem to think so as her hands shook in delight at her mom's attention and pointed at her.

"Mama!"

By the time Angie and Ree arrived, Gabby had the delivered Chinese food set out in three places on her kitchen island.

They each sat and started eating without saying much. They knew the food from Fortune Cookie didn't taste the same cold.

"So, what happened with you today, Gabby?" Ree asked as he finished up his last egg roll. "Angie said you sounded pretty shaky on the phone."

"You'll think I'm losing it, but it really freaked me out."

"You work around dead bodies almost every single day," Ree said. "No surprise there."

"It's not like she hasn't seen them since she was little," Angie said.

Ree nodded. "Okay, Gabs. Spill."

Gabby told them everything that had transpired after her boss left.

"It doesn't surprise me," Angie said. "You have Ally to take care of at night, then work and grad school during the day. Not to mention the studying in between it all. You've got to be tired."

"That's what I think, too, but it was so real. I'm positive I didn't move either display. I mean, sometimes I get into my work and forget what I was doing an hour before, but nothing like that."

"Yeah, but you haven't had to do so much alone either,"

Angie said. "Losing Michael was difficult enough, but losing him and your mom within two years? I can't believe you're right back into it. Eventually, it's all going to catch up with you."

"You know you have your two best friends," Ree said.

"Don't forget who the number one BEST friend is, though," Angie said.

"Ignore the Petty Queen. You know I'd be happy to come watch Ally a few hours just so you can get some rest. I keep offering and you have yet to ask."

"You've both already done so much," Gabby said.

"Between your sister and the two of us, you should be able to get at least one night to yourself just to recharge," Ree said.

"I hate to leave her," Gabby said. "You know that."

"Yes, and I understand, but you can't keep doing this. You're obviously stressing. You never expected to be a twenty-three-year-old widow with a toddler. That's too much for almost anyone to handle, no matter how strong you might be."

Gabby nodded. Her friends and sister Teri had been incredible after Michael's passing. They had brought food and company during those first two months after the funeral. Gabby and Michael had been married less than two years with Ally on the way when he died, but she knew she would never give up school. Her future and Ally's were too important.

Nine months earlier, just as she was throwing herself into a normal routine, her mom had passed.

"And for the hundredth time, Gabby, you should let your sister watch her one night so the three of us can go out. Maybe you just need to let loose a little," Ree said.

"For once, I agree with Ree," Angie said. "I'm not saying go party all night, but just come out and don't let yourself worry. Let your sis keep her overnight and you can sleep in. Say yes for once!"

Gabby thought about it. "Maybe. But what about this thing at work? What if it happens again?"

"Look," Angie said. "Jenna's brother Jay is all into the occult and attends seances. At first I thought he was a lemming poseur, wearing black t-shirts and eyeliner just to look the part. Jenna says she thinks he's legit and they have some family history that she doesn't really like to talk about. And you know that says a lot coming from Jenna."

"Yes, your girlfriend tries SO hard to be lame," Ree said.

"At least I have someone, unless Blow Up Cheerleaders count."

"It was one time on a dare FIVE years ago after way too much tequila!"

"Do you still have her?"

"That's not the point!"

Angie smiled as she continued. "I haven't hung out with Jay much outside of their family events, but once when we went club-hopping with him and an old girlfriend, he seemed to know what he's talking about. Claims he knows people that have seen haunted houses, that kind of thing. If anything happens again, I'll contact him and he can check it out."

"Ghosts? Oh, now you believe?" Ree said.

"Not really," Angie said. "But Jenna keeps an open mind, and although she tries to keep her family's offbeat history quiet, I know she believes. I don't buy into all that supernatural stuff, but if it helps."

"Don't buy into all the supernatural stuff? Really, Angie? You know what happened to me when I was little!"

Both women groaned.

Angie put her hand on Ree's shoulder. "Please don't tell that story again."

"I know what I saw!" Ree said. "And my cousin was with

me. Whatever it was floated across my backyard and then stopped and looked right at us. My dog wouldn't go outside for a week. That ghost wore a really outdated white dress, and it wasn't just a poor fashion choice. My cousin pissed himself!"

"I don't think we have ghosts at the exhibit, Ree," Gabby said.

"Those bodies were once alive. You have dead babies in there, Gabby! Maybe you just need to get the place blessed or something."

Gabby thought about it. They received the bodies from a private overseas company and had little verifiable background information on many of the bodies used in their exhibits.

"Okay, Ree. If something happens, I'll have Angie contact Jenna's brother. I still think I'm just tired and seeing things."

"Okay, then," Ree said. "If something else happens, take a picture or video before you leave the room. Maybe you can show us something and we can decide if you're bonkers or not."

That sounded reasonable enough.

"Gabby, since we met, I've never known you to be superstitious. Don't let Ree's supernatural stories freak you out."

"There you go again," Ree said. "Just because I didn't move here until high school, you get the final word."

"I am her bestest, number one friend," Angie said.

"I'll always be number two. I get it. Why do you have to rub it in? Just because my best friend moved away after graduation, I get stuck with you two. Lucky me."

"You know you love us," Gabby said.

"That I do," Ree said, smiling.

CHAPTER THREE

GABBY GOT THROUGH HER MORNING CLASSES AND WAS BACK AT work after lunch. As soon as she walked in, Mr. Bernard greeted her.

"We had some vandals during one of the class visits this morning," he said. "I've already had the display pulled aside."

He led her into the Emergency Room and The Gymnast waited for her. The body was in a bridge pose, with her hands and feet on the floor while her front formed an upward arch. One of the back legs was bent like someone had kicked in the metal bar that held her leg up.

"Did you find out who did it?"

"A few pre-teens. One pushed another into the display and ran off. Didn't want to cause a stir. That school is one of our steadiest customers and they were just being kids."

She sighed. This was going to take some time compared to yesterday.

Not only was the bar bent, but the back leg muscles down to the Achilles were smashed in. She would have to repair much more than she expected.

Her phone dinged. It was a text from Ree.

"Take pics." He followed up with a ghost emoji.

She smiled, then took a snapshot of the ripped up leg and sent it to Ree and Angie. "Vandal repair. Before."

"You have a disgusting job," Ree replied.

"I'm already gagging. Thanks, Gabs." Angie didn't have much of a stomach for the dead bodies Gabby worked with.

Gabby got settled in and started to work. She had to replace the bar first so she could work on the muscle repair. The bars were sectioned and fortunately only one section was bent inwards. There were so many class visits this time of year, minor damage was expected. She could see the sneaker mark on the muscle.

She pulled out a screwdriver and tools to help pull the bar free. It was bent almost 40 degrees, but the base and connecting bar above it were mostly intact. She was able to get it off without a major effort. The top connecting bar was also slightly bent, but she was able to reset it with her hand.

Gabby started working on the muscle. The display was too heavy to lift, so she alternated sitting and squatting positions as she commenced with her repairs. After an hour, she felt a twinge in her left quad.

"Ooh, cramp," she said aloud.

Gabby stood up, massaged her quad for a few seconds, then left for the break room to fill her water bottle. She noticed more groups in the exhibit than normal, but from what she could tell, they were being civil. She returned from the break room and as she entered the ER, she noticed something was off.

The body was still intact, but there was something. She lifted her phone to take another picture of the area.

She sat at the repair table and took a few chugs from her water bottle.

Then she saw it. One of the computer monitors nearest her

was blinking. It flashed in orange bursts, like it was in sleep mode or not fully connected. Normally, there was a screen saver with turtles swimming in water, but the screen was blank now. She hit the keyboard and the lock screen popped up.

Ed or somebody else must have come to check on something during my break.

The screen wouldn't typically just lock up like that.

She unlocked the screen, and the turtles were swimming again after a few more seconds. That was more comfortable to her than a dark screen.

She returned to her task and had the back calf muscle repaired within thirty minutes and moved to the ankle and Achilles. This was going to be more uncomfortable since she would have to do it from her stomach or back.

The perks of this job are never-ending.

She lowered herself down to start her work. There were some minor tears and one big slice. Before digging in, she posed with the severed muscles pieces beside her. She pretended like she was going to stick a piece in her mouth as she snapped it.

"I will never kiss you again," Angie said with a smiley face.

Gabby got into it and before she realized it, a few more hours had passed. It was almost closing time.

The door opened and Ed popped in, noticing her on her back.

"Hey, Gabby, looks like you're fixing something under a car."

She laughed. "Yeah, this one is a little awkward."

"I am going to leave in a few. If you need to finish this tomorrow, you can."

"No, it's okay. I should be done in another 15-20 minutes.

I'd rather finish it now than have to pull out all these tools again tomorrow."

"Just like your mother," Ed said. "She never could leave anything unfinished."

"Have a good night," Gabby said.

Ed looked at her for a few moments but didn't say anything at first.

"Everything okay, Ed?" she asked.

He looked up like he was startled from a daydream. "No, no. It's fine. Just thinking about your mother."

"Yeah, I do that sometimes."

"It's just that when I see you, it's uncanny how much you remind me of her. I'm sorry she won't be around to see Ally grow up."

"Me, too, Ed. I'm glad she was able to meet and enjoy her for her first year, at least. Have a good evening."

He smiled, hesitated like he was going to say something else, then walked out.

Gabby returned to her work and finished up.

Once she was done, she walked to the bathroom to wash her face. She had built up a sweat and her hands were sore. She hadn't really felt it until she ran her hands under the cold water. She was going to pick up Ally, have a light dinner, and hit the books. She had a big test coming up and was behind a few chapters.

Her phone dinged.

Ree sent a group message to the long-standing trio of friends.

"Anything mysterious happening today? Where's the after picture?"

Gabby smiled.

She walked back toward the room. She held her camera ready as she opened the door. She lifted her camera and as she started to press the button to snap the picture, she jumped back.

The Gymnast was on the table. It had been lifted four feet onto one of the bare tables, facing her. She screamed as she ran. She already had her purse around her shoulder and almost dropped her phone.

She was still shaking when she got to the daycare downstairs to pick up Ally. She assured Donna she was fine, even though she knew her quivering voice showed otherwise. Donna was about to ask more questions, but decided not to press.

After arriving home, she fed Ally and tried to distract herself. A little after nine, there was a knock at her door.

Ree and Angie were waiting. Her face must have looked bad because Angie rushed in through the door as soon as she saw her.

"I texted you three times!" Ree said.

Angie looked at her best friend's face. "Are you okay?"

Gabby nodded.

"Phone?" Ree said.

Gabby hadn't even checked her phone. She had seen Ree and Angie's texts and missed calls, but was too shaken up to answer.

"I was waiting for your picture!" Ree said. "What happened?"

"I'm not sure," she said. "The display model I had just finished working on was on the floor. I left the room for just a couple of minutes and came back to take the picture when I saw it. I'm not even sure if it took any."

"Saw what?" Ree asked.

Gabby tried to explain but couldn't.

Angie picked up Gabby's phone and entered her password. There weren't many secrets among them.

"Oh my God," Angie said.

Ree looked and grabbed the phone. He flipped through screens.

"Is there something there?" Gabby asked.

Ree turned the phone back to her.

"You took a burst of pictures, but I can see why."

The Gymnast was staring straight back into the camera and was most definitely on top of the table.

"I was gone for no more than four or five minutes," Gabby said. "I just went to the bathroom to wash up."

"How much do these things weigh?" Ree asked.

"At least 200 pounds, depending on the display weight. It would take at least two people to lift that. It's too awkward to lift alone, even if you were strong enough."

"And you're sure no one was in the office trying to play a prank on you?"

Gabby shook her head. "No one was there, and I saw everyone leave for the day. It was so quiet I would have heard the chime if someone had walked back in. Ed always locks the door, and it was still locked when I ran out."

"What do you think it is?" Angie said.

"I don't know. Maybe someone was in there the whole time, but why go through all that just to scare me? All I know is I don't think I've ever been more terrified than I am right now."

"What do you want to do?" Angie asked.

"Ang, can you contact Jenna's brother? I need to know what's going on and I'm not going to tell my boss anything until I know for sure. I need this job and if this turns out to be nothing, I don't want to make it sound like I'm losing my mind."

Angie nodded and stepped away as she dialed her phone.

"We'll figure out what it is, Gabs," Ree said. "It's okay."

She hugged him and still felt herself shaking. "Hopefully it's just a sick joke."

CHAPTER FOUR

WHEN GABBY ARRIVED AT WORK THE NEXT DAY, MR. BERNARD immediately walked up to her.

"Gabby, who did you get to help you pick that up? Good job on it. Can't even tell anything was wrong just yesterday. It took three of us to get it down and back in place earlier."

"I saw some of the guys from the law office down the hall and they were able to help me. Just needed to get some detail on the lower part of the heel."

He nodded and didn't question any further.

Gabby enjoyed two quiet days at work. No more unusual activity, and Gabby was grateful. She didn't think she could be in another room alone with the bodies. She told Mr. Bernard she had to leave early, and it wasn't a lie. She had to catch up on her studies and the next day she was meeting with Jenna's brother. She didn't want Ally around it, so she spoke to her sister Teri about watching her.

Gabby arrived at her sister's house late Thursday afternoon. Teri was an accountant for a few select clients, which allowed her to work from home most of the time so she could be around for her kids. Her husband, John, was a lawyer who worked long hours, so Teri's job flexibility kept her close with the children.

"Thanks for watching, Ally, sis," Gabby said. "I know you're busy."

"No, it's fine. John's working late, anyway. He has a big case he's preparing for. You might pick up Ally before he even gets here. I love seeing my only niece."

"Aunt Gabby!" a yell came from another room as two young girls came running in.

"Hey, Grace! Linda!" Gabby said as they rushed up for a hug. "What are you up to?"

They both started talking over each other about coloring, a dog, and something about a crash.

"Nick! Jess!" Teri yelled.

Two older kids came in. Nick had on his headphones and Jess, the fourteen-year-old, had a book in her hand.

"Hey, Aunt Gabby!" They both came and hugged her.

"I don't know how you do it," Gabby said. "Two teenagers and two little ones. I can barely keep my head on straight with Ally, and she's barely 21 months old."

"Miss you, Aunt Gabby," Jess said. "How are you?"

"Good, sorry I haven't been around the last few weeks. My classes are getting pretty intense. Semester ends soon."

"I get you," Nick said. "I can't wait to be out of 8th grade. This Algebra class is killing me."

The ten-year age gap between Gabby and her sister was sometimes awkward. Gabby always wished they had been closer in age, like Jess and Nick, who were only a year apart. Even Grace and Linda, who were four and six, had each other. Teri had married at 21 when Gabby was just ten. Gabby had insisted she'd never get married that young, but once she found Michael, all that changed. It hadn't lasted long, but she had Ally. That kept her sane most of the time.

"So what do you have going on tonight?" Teri asked.

"Ree, Angie, and Angie's future brother-in-law are coming over. I don't really know the brother-in-law and really didn't want Ally around. I know you've been bugging me to come over and I'm sorry I've missed the last few Sunday dinners. Hopefully Ally will be enough for today?"

"I'll take a few hours with her over nothing, but you need to promise to try to make it over here sometime soon."

"I will definitely try. I promise things will be better once the semester's over."

"Okay, well head on out before you get stuck in traffic. I know it's only a few miles, but it'll take you over an hour if you wait too long."

Gabby knew she was right. She didn't like stretching the truth by leaving out why Angie was bringing Jay, but didn't want to worry Teri if it turned out to be nothing. She kissed Ally and her nieces and nephew and headed out to meet a paranormalist for the first time in her life.

CHAPTER FIVE

GABBY GOT BACK TO HER HOUSE TO SET UP. SHE WASN'T SURE what to expect, so she threw herself into preparing dinner.

Ree arrived about 6:30, and Angie was there a few minutes later with Jay.

"Jenna's not coming?" Gabby asked.

"No, she had some work to finish up, plus it gives me a chance to get some alone time with this brother of hers. Jay, this is my dear friend Gabby."

They sat down to eat and get to know each other before diving into what had been going on with Gabby.

Jay seemed like a decent enough guy. A little heavy on the eyeliner and a little into himself, but wasn't overly arrogant. He took his fascination with the occult seriously. Angie wasn't kidding when she said he was into it.

When everyone was almost finished with the main course, Gabby decided to get the conversation started.

"Jay, I'm not sure how much Angie's told you. What do you need to know?"

"I asked her not to give me too many details so I could form my own opinion," Jay said. "First, please explain to me about your job. Angie mentioned something about dead bodies?"

"I work at an exhibit that uses actual human bodies to demonstrate the inner and outer workings of our anatomy. It's my job to prepare and maintain the fully posed bodies. I also help create themes for our exhibits to not only attract investors but also keep our regular customers coming back."

"Wow," Jay said. "The ultimate show and tell."

"That's a great way of putting it."

"So the best way to start is to tell me everything," Jay said. "Please don't hold back."

Gabby went into the details and finished the story by showing him before and after pictures. She was expecting him to say it was haunted, but he took some time before speaking.

"I know you don't know me well, but this is something that's fascinated me since I was young. I won't immediately assume it's something supernatural or ghostly, but the story doesn't add up, and Angie tells me you're not the type of person who would claim something like this unless you really believed it's what happened. The main thing is to determine if this is simply an elaborate prank. I know it doesn't seem like the people at your work would do this, but could it be a jealous co-worker trying to run you out, maybe? I'd really have to see your work area to get a better feel. Any chance I could come over sometime to check it out?"

Gabby considered it. "Yes, we could go tonight if you have the time. I have the key and with my daughter gone, the timing couldn't be any better. I need to know what's going on."

They all looked at each other.

"I don't see why not," Jay said.

They finished their meals and then headed out the door.

"I'll drive," Angie said to Gabby. "Your car seat makes things a little cramped."

They arrived at the office within twenty minutes. Gabby led them to the second floor and Jay checked out the logo on the door.

"The Body Parade," Jay said. "Good name for an exhibit like this."

"Angie's been here before and Ree once, so prepare yourself, Jay. It's a little jarring at first."

She unlocked the door and they entered. She flipped on the lights and led them to the Showroom, revealing the full body exhibits as well as skeletal and multiple smaller displays, some of which featured blood vessels and nervous systems of various body parts.

"These are the three that I was working on when all this started," Gabby said. "These displays are called The Diver, The Runner, and The Gymnast."

Jay took some time to take the visual in before Gabby led them to another part of the Showroom.

"We have seven full displays. These other four are The Swimmer, The Cyclist, The Dancer, and finally Mother and Child, which is my favorite."

She pointed to the display, which depicted a mother kneeling and reaching out to her daughter as she tried to run from her mommy.

"Wow," was all Jay said as he walked around, inspecting each model. Gabby led them into several of the other rooms.

"Did you say there was a Baby Room?" Jay asked Angie.

Gabby had been hoping to avoid that one.

"I guess you get the full tour," Gabby said.

She pointed him into the Baby Room but only took one full step in. Ree joined Jay, but Angie stood behind Gabby.

"I'd love to be anywhere else right now," Angie said. "This place has always freaked me out."

"I know. I'm not a big fan of being here at night myself," Gabby said as she glanced around the room and tried not to make direct eye contact with any of the baby displays.

"Anything?" she asked.

"Not yet, but this is fascinating," Jay said. He was staring at the anatomy of a fetus in its second trimester.

Gabby turned back to Angie.

"Have you been sleeping?" Angie asked.

"Yes, but keep waking up every few hours. If it's not Ally, I'm thinking about these exhibits. How bad do I look?"

Angie pulled out a compact from her purse and opened up the mirror. "You're still gorgeous, but your eyes are saggy and not like they normally look when you're studying too much."

Gabby took a look. Angie was right. She had dark patches under her eyes and looked like she hadn't slept in days.

"Gabby!" Jay yelled. "Come here."

Gabby ran in. Angie stared into the room but didn't follow.

"What is it?" Gabby asked.

"Did you hear or sense anything just now?"

Gabby had felt fine and shook her head.

"I felt something. Let me see that first display you were working on again."

She took him back to The Diver in the Showroom. She showed him the eyeball area she had repaired a few days before.

"Nothing here. What about the repair area?"

Gabby took him to the ER. The four of them entered and Jay studied the table.

"Did anything happen that seemed unusual or out of the ordinary on either day?"

"You mean other than moving around and one ending up on the table?"

"Yes, I mean something small. Something minor."

Gabby remembered the blinking monitor and mentioned it to him.

"Which machine?"

Gabby pointed to it and started it up.

They stared at their reflections on the black screen before it came on.

"You into computers, too?" Gabby asked.

"Just a little," he said. "I'm no expert, but just wondering if there was some kind of glitch. I just want to run a quick diagnostic."

He gestured toward the computer. "May I?"

Gabby logged in. Jay clicked through the machine and started to run something.

He let it process a few minutes then turned it off.

"Nothing definitive here," Jay said. "The computer seems fine, but I did sense something in that Baby Room, though. I'm not ruling anything out based on just that."

"What do you mean, sense?" Gabby asked.

He looked at Angie.

"He claims to be kind of gifted," Angie said.

"Claims?" he said.

"Jenna told me he is."

"Gifted how, exactly?" Ree asked.

"I can sometimes sense when something's not right. Supernatural stuff, that is. It's only happened four or five times in my life, but in each case I felt or saw something. In three cases, so did others."

"Like you can see spirits?" Gabby asked.

"I've seen a few since I was young," Jay said. "But I can sometimes sense something's around, even when I don't see anything."

"Did you sense it in there?"

"I'm not sure. It was so quick I couldn't get a grasp on it.

Could have just been a cold draft. I think you need my number, Gabby. I have a group of people who can do this right if it gets that far. I can't say one way or another. Unfortunately, that means you'll have to wait and see if anything else happens. This place already lends itself to disturbing feelings of curiosity and fear, so it could just be the remnants of visitors' emotions I'm picking up. We'll just need to keep ready if anything else does happen. I'll see if I can do some research on this building, but I've never heard of anything in this general area. Doesn't mean much, though. Big world out there. Can I go see the babies again?"

Gabby nodded. She hoped nothing more would happen and this would be the end of it. Her life was crazy enough.

CHAPTER SIX

EVERYTHING RETURNED TO NORMAL THE FOLLOWING WEEK AT work. Gabby hadn't seen or heard anything and there were no new vandalism incidents. The timing worked out as the long planned thespian themed exhibit was in full preparation mode. Two boxes of body and display props had arrived with more to come.

Gabby had made the suggestion to Ed several months before when they were trying to decide on a new exhibit theme. The current athletic decor had been in place for more than three years and needed an injection of something fresh. The body displays would remain the same since once they underwent the complex plastination process, they couldn't be repositioned, but they could be redecorated.

Gabby already knew what she would do with The Diver. She was basing this display on Hamlet and planned to use one of The Diver's outstretched hands to place the skull that Hamlet talks to in the bard's play. The clothing was the key to each display, but she also wanted to adorn the throat and tongue muscles with various colors to emphasize speaking and performing lines. The bodies would have masks, hats and props to keep with the look.

Gabby had come up with the idea one day when she was thinking about her mother, who acted in high school theater and after a long drought, also performed in a local theater for a few years before her job started taking up more of her time. She even put Gabby in a few productions when she was a child. Teri never took to the theater. She was a swimmer and involved in multiple sports. Gabby played volleyball during her high school years and performed in a few plays as well.

It was a Friday and Gabby was thinking of her nephew and nieces she'd seen the previous week and how she'd promised to try harder to see them. She also thought she might do something for her sister at the same time.

She texted Angie during a quick break. "Hey Angie, can you watch Ally tomorrow? Overnight, possibly?"

Angie replied quickly. "Big date?"

"No, nothing that juicy. I want to spend the weekend with my sister's kids. It's a first step to the night out I promised you and Ree."

"In that case, I'm in. Didn't have any set plans for Saturday. Jenna's out of town all weekend for work. Maybe I can get Ree to come over, too."

"Thanks, Angie. I'll talk to Teri and let you know for sure."

Ed walked in, holding a box. "How's it going with the new model?"

"It's been great so far, Ed."

She turned as she replied and hit the box with her shoulder, knocking it to the floor. Several items fell out.

Gabby reached to help pick the mess up.

"No, I got it!"

Gabby already had a few items in her hands. She looked down and saw a picture of her mother.

She looked at her boss and back at the document.

"What's this?"

"I'm sorry, Gabby. I would rather you hadn't seen that. I still had some of your mother's old paperwork in one of my office drawers. I saw it and was moving it to the Archives."

Gabby stared at the picture. She remembered it. Mom was holding Gabby and Teri was in the background, refusing to smile for the picture and giving the photographer an angry look.

"I had forgotten about this picture. She had it in her office in a frame."

"Yes, it was there up until she died," Ed said. "I was going to separate the non-work items and get them to you when I had some time."

"Can I keep this one now?"

"Yes, of course," he said. "One of my favorites."

She put the rest of the papers back in the box.

"Thank you, Ed."

He smiled, hesitated a few seconds, and then walked back to his office instead of heading toward the Archives. Gabby noticed but just thought he didn't want her to feel bad, although she didn't. This was a good memory. It made her think of the times she would visit Mom at work and admire the framed family picture with other loose ones around the desk or on a corkboard. It made her feel at peace. She laughed when she saw how Teri looked. She remembered her and Mom fighting sometimes when Teri was in high school, but it was never too serious as far as she remembered. Typical teenage stuff, like wanting to go out with her boyfriend. Considering that boyfriend was now her husband, it all worked out.

It must have run in the family. Mom, Teri, and Gabby had all married men they'd met in high school or college.

Ed came back out. "I'm leaving for the evening, Gabby. Have a good night."

He shuffled out quickly and barely made eye contact. She sensed he was embarrassed, but there was no need. She was a little happier than she had been just before she had planned to call her sister.

Sister.

She shifted back to her phone and dialed.

"Hey, Teri. I know I've been MIA lately and want to thank you for watching Ally the other night. Do the kids have anything going on Saturday? I'd like to pick them up and bring them over for the night. Maybe take them to eat and watch a movie, then hang out at the house. I'd like them to stay overnight if you're okay with it."

"Are you sure, Gabby?"

"Yes, Sister. I'm trying to heed the advice from you and my friends. I need to take more time with the people important to me and not have everything just be about school and Ally. You and John can have a night out all to yourselves."

"Night out? I think I'll send him on a night out with his friends and just stay home, take a nap, a bubble bath, and binge-watch murder shows. Do you know how long it's been since I've had a night to myself? I need a break from everybody and will absolutely take you up on your offer. Thanks, Gabby."

They hung up and Gabby sighed.

As she hung up her phone, she didn't see the yellow eyes reflecting off the black computer screen as it locked.

CHAPTER SEVEN

GABBY WAS AT ANGIE'S BY 10 AM WITH ALLY. ANGIE WAS A morning person and had already been up three hours. Gabby would sleep until she had to get up but was a night owl by necessity. Studying late, Ally, the job, and squeezing in all the little things bred that environment.

Gabby took a long look at Ally and kissed her. Besides daycare, she hadn't left her with anyone but Teri since her mom had died. Ally smiled, then ran toward Angie, raised her arms, and let Angie pick her up. So much for crying as Gabby left, which she hoped wouldn't happen, but at the same time, wouldn't have minded a tear or two.

The kids were all dressed up and ready with their back-packs when Gabby arrived at her sister's house. Linda and Grace were messing with Nick's hair and Jessica had her headphones on, listening to music and occasionally flipping back to her phone screen to exchange texts and scan social media.

Teri was in her Wonder Woman jammies already.

"You ready for them to go?" Gabby said, smiling.

"Thank you, Gabs. You don't know how badly I need this.

I recorded a marathon of murder shows last night and when those run out, I'm streaming that food truck battle show I'm already five episodes behind on. Priorities."

Gabby turned back to the kids.

"So, did we agree on a movie?" Gabby asked.

She figured the latest Disney movie was the most likely candidate, but Nick said, "*Cyborg Detective, Part 3!*"

Gabby looked at Teri. "You're okay with this?"

"He showed the girls parts 1 and 2 last week. I was upset, but the girls didn't cry or have nightmares. They actually want to see this one."

"Yeah, and would she have ever let me or Nick see that when we were four? Or six, even? I don't think so," Jessica said without hiding her contempt.

Teri always monitored their movies and shows. Gabby raised her eyebrows at her sister, both in surprise and awaiting confirmation.

"I don't care today," Teri said. "I'd let them watch *The Exorcist* at this point if it meant I have a day and night to myself. Go before my mom gene kicks back in and I call this whole thing off."

Gabby gathered the kids, put in the car seats for Grace and Linda, and they were off. They reached the theater with time to spare, and Gabby splurged. She ordered three refillable buckets of popcorn, four pickles, and each kid got their drink and choice of candy with the option for more. They would be nice and wired by the time they got home.

Gabby thought the movie was okay, but the kids enjoyed it, so she had a better time than she might have watching it alone. It was mindless fighting and car chases with a cyborg killer on the loose that only a Cyborg Detective could stop. Fortunately, there was only one partially nude scene and Gabby was quick to cover Grace's eyes and Nick had already covered Linda's.

They laughed and yelled and jumped and just had a great time. No one was crying, which was always a good thing.

Once the movie was over, it was time for a late lunch. Gabby called Angie to check on Ally and got one "Mama" out of her before she ignored the phone and went back to playing with Ree.

"Where do y'all feel like eating?"

"Pizza!" Grace, Linda, and Nick yelled at the same time. Jessica didn't yell, but issued a thumbs up once she heard their choice. It was unanimous.

Gabby realized she was low on gas, so she pulled into the first gas station she found.

"I'll put the gas in, Aunt Gabby," Jessica said.

Gabby was confused since Jess had barely lifted her head from her phone but went with it.

"Okay, here's my gas card."

She lowered the windows as Jessica got out and got the gas pump going.

Grace and Linda were still talking about the movie.

"What was your favorite part?" Gabby asked.

Grace looked upwards as she thought about it. "Where the police dog ate the bad man's metal ear!"

Linda followed with, "I liked where the man with the black glasses broke that guy's finger."

Gabby stared. "That was the bad guy breaking that poor nerd's fingers. You liked that part? Why?"

"Because that boy looks like Bobby in my class. He makes fun of me and pulled my hair."

"So you want someone to break his fingers?" Gabby asked.

"If it makes him stop pulling my hair, then yes. Maybe even two fingers."

Nick gave her a high-five. "Good call, Sis."

Gabby wanted to protest but started laughing instead.

"Aunt Gabby, check this out," Jess said.

Gabby looked up. Jessica was staring at the gas pump, but she didn't see why.

"What is it?"

"I let it fill up until it clicked. Check out the total," she said.

The numbers were $6.66.

Gabby stared at the total for a few seconds.

Has to be a coincidence.

"I had less than a quarter tank," Gabby finally said. "It should take more than that."

Jess pulled on the pump handle and the numbers moved up until it clicked.

"That was weird, right Aunt Gabby?" Jess said as she put the handle away.

Gabby didn't want to dwell on it with the children there, so she just nodded.

The kids wanted to pick up rather than eat in, so Gabby returned to her house loaded with pizza boxes. She bought enough to cover dinner and leftovers. She had already bought drinks earlier for the kids. Juice boxes, soda, and sweet tea covered it. It was a rare treat for them since Teri limited their sugar intake. Gabby figured they'd have more sugar and fast food in them this weekend than they had in the last month or two combined.

The kids didn't seem to mind.

They sat at the table and island and ate, still talking about the movie. They were all laughing, and even Jessica had a smile on her face.

"What do you all want to do next? I have games, more movies, or you can hook up to my stereo and play music."

The kids took a few moments to discuss.

"Games first," Nick said, who was apparently the assigned Sibling Spokesperson.

"Then something we can all play," Gabby said.

"There's a cool online trivia game," Nick said. "You can put in the ages for everybody and it'll ask age-appropriate questions."

"I know more than you," Grace yelled.

"I'm sure you do, Grace, but how about you and I team up?"

"Okay, Aunt Gabby.

"Linda can be on our team, too!"

"No, I want to play by myself," Linda said. "I'm in first grade, you know."

Okay, sounds good.

Nick pulled out his handheld gaming machine and hooked it up to Gabby's television. They played for the next few hours and enjoyed it. The age appropriate questions kept Nick and Jess from winning every game.

After losing twice in a row, Linda looked up. "I don't wanna play this anymore."

It was time to move on.

"What kind of movies do you have?" Nick asked.

"Go look in the cabinet under the TV. I have streaming, too. What do you have in mind?"

"Scary movies!" Grace and Linda cried.

"Your mom is gonna kill me!"

"She said it was okay!"

Teri had said she didn't care, which translates to let them watch whatever they wanted.

"Fine, just nothing with a bunch of nudity!"

"What's noddity?" Grace asked.

"Naked people with boobies and wieners," Linda answered

"You don't even know what you're talking about," Jessica said, unable to contain her smile as her little sisters giggled.

Nick was in the cabinet and Jessica was on her phone checking what was streaming.

"*Halloween? The Blair Witch Project? The Exorcist?*" Jessica asked.

"Despite what your mom said, not *The Exorcist*," Gabby said. "That one still scares me."

They agreed on *Halloween.*

"I know there's at least one part with boobies in that," Gabby said. "I'm covering your eyes on that part, but that works. Snacks or cold pizza?"

"Both!" Linda and Grace yelled simultaneously.

"I have more popcorn and s'mores," Gabby said.

"Popcorn!"

"S'mores!"

"Pizza!"

"I guess we'll just have to have them all," Gabby said and was met with cheers.

Gabby went back to the kitchen and put the first bag of popcorn in the microwave. The s'mores would take more time.

She turned on the gas oven.

"It's hot, Auntie Gabby," Grace said.

"She's always hot!" Linda said.

"Do you want me to turn the temperature down?" Gabby asked.

"Just get her a fan," Jess said. "She'll complain no matter how cold it is in here. She's part Eskimo."

Gabby went to the other room to grab a fan. By the time she returned, little Michael Myers was already killing his sister. Linda had one eye covered, but the little one's eyes were big.

"That's fake!" Grace said.

"How many scary movies have you seen?" Gabby asked as she set up the fan.

"Two. *Elmo's Halloween* and this one."

Cyber Detective was child's play compared to this.

"I think Nick and Jess have been showing you movies that Mom doesn't know about. Am I right?"

Linda stared at Gabby and her face froze, but then she slowly opened her mouth. "We're not supposed to tell Mommy, but Nick and Jessica give us candy to be quiet."

"That's not being quiet," Nick said.

It was Gabby's turn to make a decision. Cool Aunt or Snitch?

"I won't say anything if you don't tell her I let you watch *Halloween* or whatever else we see tonight," Gabby said, smiling. Linda's look of panic subsided.

Gabby went back to the kitchen as the movie went on. She gave them more popcorn and drinks as they picked through the pizza boxes, then decided to start on the s'mores.

She had a fresh bag of marshmallows and decided to roast them off the stove flame.

As she put the first batch of marshmallows over the fire, a loud alarm went off. At first Gabby thought it was the fire alarm, but after a second she realized it was their phones. Nick and Jessica looked at their phones and then back at Gabby.

"What is it?"

"Check your phone, Aunt Gabby," Jess said.

It was an Amber alert. The missing child's name was Ally, followed by two lines of 6's. Nothing else.

"That's odd, right?" Jess said.

Gabby quickly forwarded it to Angie.

"Hey, did you get this, too?" she texted.

Gabby went back to the s'mores as the kids got back into the movie.

They reached a part where Michael Myers jumped out at a victim and they all yelled.

Gabby looked up as they started to laugh at each other, and then something popped. The kids jumped and Gabby ran over.

"What happened?"

The fan was knocked over and sparks were shooting out of it. The plastic burst into a small flame.

Gabby picked it up by the base and ran toward the kitchen. The cord flew out of the wall and hit her on the back of the leg, but she ignored it as she rushed toward the sink and threw the fan in it. She flipped the water on and doused the flame when she felt a burst of heat behind her.

The kids screamed as Gabby turned. The flame from the stove shot up three feet. Gabby felt the heat on her face.

She jumped back, and the flame doubled its intensity and shot out even higher, nearly reaching the top shelf.

As soon as the flame dipped, Gabby reached over and turned the knob off.

The kids were hiding behind the couch with their eyes just over to see what was happening. Even Jessica had pulled off her headphones and looked terrified.

Gabby's phone dinged and made her jump. It was Angie. "No, is that some kind of bad joke someone sent you? Ally's fine and fast asleep right here next to me."

Gabby looked at the kids and back around the room as Michael Myers was stalking a victim in the background. Fear. She felt genuine fear.

"I gotta go, Ang."

The TV flickered. The kids didn't see the screen go dark. Gabby saw something. A face, but not a complete face. It was looking out of the television screen. She wanted to scream but saw the fear in her nieces' and nephew's eyes. She swallowed as the screen flicked again and Mike Myers continued his rampage.

Gabby looked back at the stove and around the house. She didn't see anything else.

"Aunt Gabby," a soft voice said from behind the couch. Grace's eyes were saucers and wet.

"My bedroom. Under the covers. Now!"

The kids picked up on the sense of fear and got up screaming, running into her bedroom.

By the time Gabby hit her king-sized bed, the kids had wrapped themselves under the covers. Nick and Jessica were each holding one of their younger sisters. Gabby jumped between them and they all grabbed onto her.

"It's okay. I think it's okay now," Gabby tried to reassure them, but her quivering voice made it hard to sell.

"What happened, Aunt Gabby?" Nick asked.

"I don't know," Gabby said.

"Is the house haunted?"

"No, it never was. Nothing like that's ever happened. Maybe a coincidence."

"No way that was a coincidence," Jessica said. "Maybe we caused whatever happened by watching that movie."

"We didn't ask for anything like that," Nick said.

"So we have to decide on whether we need to call your mom and get you all home or stay here and hope the rest of the night is quiet."

"If we tell Mom, she'll never let us stay here again," Jessica said. "Plus, even though I'm about ready to shit myself, this may be one of the coolest things to ever happen to me."

Grace gasped. "You're not supposed to say shit! Mom said!"

"You just said it, too! So if you rat me out, I'm taking you down with me!"

Grace closed her mouth.

They all caught their breath with the cussing distraction.

"I'm okay to stay here as long as we all stay in the same room," Jessica said.

The five of them stayed under the covers with the light on for the next twenty minutes.

"I think we're okay," Gabby said. "How about we just watch the TV in here? Disney or *Halloween*?"

"Disney!" Nick said. "I'll take *Snow White*. Just skip the witch parts."

"Definitely," Jessica said.

Gabby found a streaming version of the movie and started it. No one slept and they tried to concentrate on the movie, but Gabby saw something no one else noticed. Something was staring at her from the TV screen that wasn't part of the movie. The kids didn't say anything, so she hoped this was fear-induced hysteria, but inside she felt like it was the beginning of something much worse.

THE KIDS WERE ASLEEP BY 2 AM. THEY SAW ALMOST TWO FULL movies before sleep took over their fears. Gabby tried to wait until Jessica, the last one awake, was asleep before she even tried to lay her head down. For all her teenage angst, Jess kept hugging her younger sisters and even hugged her brother.

Just when Gabby thought Jess was falling, she looked up at Gabby and smiled. "I know you're trying to be protective and show us that you're not scared, but it's okay. I'm scared, too."

"Thanks, Jess. I am still trembling a little."

"Is this the first time something like this has happened?"

Gabby hesitated to answer.

"It's okay, Aunt Gabby. I don't think you've ever lied to us, but I don't think I can get more scared than I did earlier.

It's more excitement right now. I just want to know you're okay."

Gabby looked at her niece in an entirely new light. She stared at her face and maybe it was the shadows in the room, even though the main light was turned on and would stay that way until after the sun came up, that gave her niece a different look. For the first time, Gabby was seeing her as a young woman and not as the sweet little girl she usually pictured in her head. She was older and in high school now.

"Some odd things have been going on. It started at work and has been happening for a couple of weeks. Nothing like this, though. Displays moving, seeing things. Didn't think it would happen here. In fact, nothing's happened before today. Nothing this obvious."

"What are you going to do?"

"I've already talked to Angie's soon-to-be brother-in-law, who knows about supernatural things. At least he seems to. I'll need to talk to him again. I don't know why this is happening, but he's my best chance right now at finding out why. I need to know for Ally's sake and for all of you if you ever come back again. You think Grace and Linda will keep this from your mom?"

Jessica shook her head. "Linda couldn't keep a secret if a lifetime supply of sour gummies was at stake."

"I'll deal with that when I have to," Gabby said. "Pointless right now. I need to get to the bottom of this. No matter what happened tonight, I'm glad we got to talk. Even if it took a shit-scaring event to get us there."

CHAPTER EIGHT

G ABBY FELL ASLEEP LAST AND WOKE UP FIRST. S HE SLEPT ABOUT four hours. She eased out of the bed and checked around the house, but nothing stood out. Everything looked back to normal. She checked the refrigerator and behind the couch, sneaking looks toward the bedroom to make sure the kids were still asleep. She approached the stove and reached over to turn a burner on, but hesitated.

"Cold cereal and leftover pizza for breakfast today," she said to the stove.

Grace and Linda woke up first and their older siblings dragged out about thirty minutes later. Gabby fed them and the kids talked about the previous night and the excitement of it now that the fear had subsided.

"This was one of the best nights ever, Aunt Gabby!" Grace said. Her sisters and brother agreed.

At least it was a memorable one.

Gabby dropped them off by noon.

"How did it go?" Teri asked.

They all looked at each other. Jessica was the first to reply.

"We had a great time, Mom. We played games, watched scary movies, and then slept in Aunt Gabby's big bed. It was fun."

The other kids just nodded. Linda was biting her lip.

This secret will be out by tomorrow, tops, Gabby thought to herself.

"How was your night, Sis?" Gabby asked.

"I can't remember the last time I had a relaxing night. I even made John sleep in Nick's room. Thank you, Gabby."

"You're welcome. Sorry, I got the kids a little riled up with movies and candy."

"It's okay. This weekend was a break for all of us. Back to the routine tomorrow, but just going to enjoy the rest of the day."

Gabby hugged the kids then was off to get Ally. On the way, she pulled Angie and Ree into a conference call from her car's Bluetooth.

"Gabba-Gabby, hey!" Ree said. The classic song reference used to annoy her, but it got charming after a few years. "We had a great time with your little one last night over at Angie's. What's up?"

"Angie's on, too, Ree."

"Oh, the group thing."

"You wish," Angie said.

Gabby chose to ignore him. "Angie, I need to see your potential brother-in-law again. A bunch of strange stuff happened last night, and the kids were with me. It was kind of exciting, to be honest, but I also know it could have been devastatingly worse. Could have burned the house down now that I think about it."

"What happened?" Angie asked.

"I'll tell you everything in person. Just let me know when Jay can come over. The sooner the better. If my stove's not possessed, I'll even make dinner."

"I take it you'll explain what that means when you get here. I'll check with him."

"Thanks, Ang."

They hung up and Gabby arrived at Angie's apartment a few minutes later. She was greeted by a smiling Ally, who started twisting her wrists in a waving motion as she ran into Gabby's waiting arms.

"So you did miss Mommy?" Gabby asked as she picked her up and kissed her all over.

"Mama!" Ally squealed, followed by mumbling mixed in with a few small words in between, like she was telling her an exciting story.

"How was she, Ang?"

"She was a doll. Slept most of the night. She had a ball with Ree. He made her laugh for like an hour straight."

Angie's phone dinged.

"Jay said he's free Tuesday after six. Will that work?"

"Tell him that'll be fine. I'll text Ree while you let Jay know."

Ree confirmed seconds after Gabby hit Send.

"He's in. Can you make it for dinner Tuesday night, Ang?"

"Yes, I'll be there. Gabby, so last night. At least give me the Cliff's Notes."

"It was a crazy night," Gabby said. "The kids are all riled up and will probably remember it for the rest of their lives, but I know it's going to hit the fan once Teri finds out. I just hope they don't have nightmares."

Gabby proceeded to fill her in on the event highlights of the night before. Angie's eyes were wide with fear.

"What is going on, Gabs?"

"I wish I knew, but there's no denying it now. First work and now the house. I don't know what it means, but if Jay can't help, I may have to look for another source."

"I doubt the Ghostbusters are still in business," Angie said.

Gabby smiled. "Ghosts. Not sure what this is, but I hope it's not anything that crazy. Are you sure you're still willing to come over?"

"I'm completely terrified of even the thought of something haunting you!"

"So you'll be there by 5:30 to help me set up?"

"Your friendship and my stomach supersede any fear I am currently experiencing. Of course."

CHAPTER NINE

Tuesday night, Gabby prepared a dinner of enchiladas and rice with a store-bought cake she picked up on the way home for dessert. Angie arrived early, as promised, to help.

Ally was in her room asleep when Ree arrived. Jay showed up five minutes later, carrying a large duffel bag.

They sat at the kitchen table and went straight to the food. Gabby explained the weekend events with her nieces and nephew in as much detail as she could remember. She was still feeling drained from the lack of sleep, but retelling the story wired her up with adrenaline.

Jay looked around the house as he finished his food, then moved to his duffel bag he had set on the couch and opened it. He pulled out a small object no one recognized.

"What is that?" Gabby asked.

"It's an electromagnetic fields sensor, or EMF for short," Jay said.

"Electromagnetic fields?" Ree said. "How do electromagnetic fields deal with the supernatural?"

"If there's an unexplained spike in the field, it could mean there's some kind of supernatural being there that we can't see otherwise."

"Do you just assume that's what it means?"

"Not by itself, usually. If I sense something and this goes off, then it makes me a little more confident it could be a spirit or something unexplainable."

"Let him work, Ree," Gabby said.

"I'm just curious!"

"It's okay," Jay said. "I prefer to tell you what I'm doing so you don't think I just grabbed a funky looking remote and am putting on a show."

Jay walked around the kitchen. He put his hand on the refrigerator and checked his EMF, then moved to the stove.

"Which burner?"

Gabby pointed to the front left one that had been a bonfire just a few nights before.

He felt around the burner before flipping the switch and starting the flame.

It took Gabby a moment to realize she was holding her breath.

No bursts this time around.

He felt around the stove and even laid his hand over the flame for a few seconds.

"The fan?"

Gabby walked into the pantry and brought it out.

"I had it in the trash but decided to take it out and wash it once I knew you were coming."

Jay picked up the fan and then moved to plug it in. He flipped it on. It didn't start spinning, but within seconds an electronic burning smell permeated their noses. He flipped it off but kept feeling around. He eventually put it down and then walked over to the television. He was about to ask for the remote but saw it on the couch. He put his hands around the TV and moved his EMF box around it. He flipped the TV on and changed a few channels.

"What station were you watching?"

"It was HBO On-Demand. *Halloween*," Gabby said. "Channel 500."

He flipped to channel 500 and again moved the EMF around the screen and behind it. His eyes squinted like he was searching for a hidden serial number.

He moved around the house a little more.

"You're killing us, Jay," Angie finally blurted out. "Did you find anything?"

"Yes, just give me a few more minutes."

He walked into the bedroom but quickly came out.

"I get a weak sense and nothing major on the EMF, but I feel like there was definitely something here," he said. "It's not anymore, so I don't think you're being haunted. At least your house isn't. The thing is, everything started at work, right?"

Gabby nodded.

"Did it always happen in the afternoon when you were alone?"

Gabby hadn't thought about it. "Yes, right after my boss left and I was alone."

"Since that's where it all started and strange things have happened more than once, I think we need to go back, but closer to the same time instead of going as late as we did before. Is there a way you can get me in when you are alone?"

"Most days my boss is gone before five and I'm there until at least 5:30 and that time would match some of these incidents. I have until 6:30 before I have to pick up Ally. Other than a late meeting we have now and then, I think any day this week would work since I'm usually the last one there. What's your schedule?"

"I'm pretty open," he said, looking over at Angie.

"By that, he means he's a modern day Bohemian," Angie said. "At least that's what Jenna says. Still, he's growing on me."

"I'm like a fungus," Jay said.

"Some days you look like one, too."

Jay laughed as he turned back to Gabby. "Actually, contrary to Angie's Bohemian comment, I can't meet tomorrow, but any other day will work this week or next."

"Magic tournament?" Angie asked as she folded her arms.

"Dungeons and Dragons, if you must know."

Gabby turned to her best friends. "Ree, Angie, you're both welcome to come."

"I work late Thursday," Angie said. "Just please keep me updated."

"I think I got my fill of dead bodies last time," Ree said. "But I'll go if you want me to."

"No, it's okay, Ree. The sun will still be out if we don't go too long."

"Thank you!"

Gabby turned back to Jay. "Let me just give you my number. Maybe it will be better if we're not a big group like last time, anyway."

"And don't try anything crazy," Angie warned.

"Hey, I'm a safe fungus."

"Besides, I'll have Jenna beat you if you step out of line."

Jay smiled. "You aren't kidding. She's a lively one."

"Thursday's fine," Gabby said. "No one typically works late besides me, but if that changes, I'll let you know so we can reschedule. Hopefully not, because I want to get to the bottom of this as soon as possible. I'm getting worried about Ally and me being here alone. Thank you."

They called it a night, and Gabby had a hard time shutting off her mind. Ally was kind enough to sleep through the night, and Gabby finally shut her eyes and dozed off around 3 am, mainly from pure exhaustion.

As expected, Ed left a little after 4:45 on Thursday and everyone else cleared out by 5. Gabby texted Jay that they were clear. He arrived within ten minutes. He was already down the street having coffee.

"So what's different from last time?" she asked as she let him inside.

"Now that I'm pretty certain something out of the ordinary's going on, I'm going to try to entice it to come out."

"How are you going to do that?"

"I want you to just go about your business. Ignore the fact that I'm here. I'm going to move to another room and see if maybe something happens. Hopefully, my EMF will register something."

"Okay, I actually do have that new exhibit to work on."

A new set of clothes and props were delivered earlier for the Thespian display. This one was going on The Gymnast. In addition to her costume of blue wool and lace, strategically cut to reveal the body and muscles, Gabby planned to add a prop sword in her hand and place a script of one of Shakespeare's plays on her stomach.

Gabby walked into one of the back rooms and left the door open. The models had to be relocated away from the Showroom no more than two at a time in order for her to prepare them and still keep the Showroom displays open for business. All she could think about was what Jay might be doing, so she started sorting the clothing and props to keep distracted. She started to picture the best way to place the accessories. The model's plastination process made them impossible to readjust on a grand scale, but Gabby had free rein to decorate and dress them however she saw fit. She tried to set the sword prop first, but it didn't fit easily. She'd have to add a wire or some type of fastener to keep it in place.

Then she moved toward The Runner. She reached into a box of supplies and pulled out a scarf. This one would be a musical pose. She wanted to show off the intricacies of the mouth muscles, displaying a voice box and vocal cords with a small magnifying glass that would help expand on the details. She was trying her best to position the scarf, got it where she wanted and then turned back to the box, but it wasn't in the same spot. She looked around and the box had moved back and to her right by at least two feet. She knew she hadn't pushed it that far.

She stared back at the display, but nothing was moving.

Jay had been waiting outside the room and his EMF started to react. The digital numbers increased by 7 and then randomly jumped back down and up for several seconds. He pulled out his phone, ready to take a video if anything happened.

Jay eased into the room and Gabby was looking back and forth from the display to her supply box. Then Jay saw something.

The computer monitor. The one Gabby had seen the light on previously. The screen looked like it was on a screensaver, but it was the oddest screensaver he'd ever seen. It was gray and looked like scales, maybe a gray skinned snake. Then it moved and was gone. Gabby's phone, which was on the nearby desk, lit up. Whatever image had been on the monitor was now on her phone. Jay started to lift his own phone to record, but he couldn't take his eyes off what he was seeing. He realized her phone was face down. The image was coming off the back cover. He stepped closer. Gabby looked up and saw him walking in slowly with his mouth wide open. Jay moved his thumb to hit record, but his hand was shaking.

"What is it?" Gabby asked.

She saw his eyes focused behind her. The hair on the back of her neck went up immediately. She turned slowly to try to see what Jay was looking at, but she didn't notice anything.

Jay stared as the gray blur shifted off her phone case. He couldn't see anything at first, but then something glittered behind Gabby's head. She was wearing a ponytail and the metal holder was shimmering. He moved closer, and the blurred image was on the metallic fastener. The image flipped in a circle, but Gabby's head hadn't moved. A full shadow passed over the display, which he was about two feet from. Jay hit the record button a few times and then his screen locked. The gray scales filled his phone, then bright yellow eyes opened from the center of the image, revealing part of a face. The face shook and then a crooked smile emerged, revealing dripping, pointed teeth. The mouth seemed to jump from the screen like it was trying to leap at his face.

Jay dropped his phone and his box and screamed.

"Ohshitohshitohshitohshit!" he yelled over and over, unable to move. His entire face was filled with sweat.

Gabby jumped up. "What?"

"You didn't see that?" he asked, gasping for air.

"What did you see?"

"Something... something jumped from the computer around the room. It was on your metal ponytail thing! Then it was... Then it was on my phone screen. Oh my God. I think I'm gonna pass out."

"I thought you were all into this stuff?" Gabby yelled at him. "You're supposed to be the brave one!"

"Gabby, I have a light sensitivity to things, but I haven't seen anything that real since I was a kid. Back then it was a slow moving, white entity. This was a big scary face, and it was all over. That was aggressive, and it was taunting me."

"If that scared you, what the hell am I supposed to do?"

His mouth was quivering as he tried to speak.

Gabby shook her head and walked to the small refrigerator in the room and took out a water bottle and popped the cap off.

"Drink this. It's gone, and I didn't see anything, just the scarf and box move. Why would it come right at you but hide from me?"

"I don't think it's been hiding. You were probably so caught up in your work that you didn't notice. This could have been happening every day."

Now Gabby was flushed. That wasn't a comfortable realization.

"Tell me exactly what you saw, Jay."

"It was part of a face. I couldn't tell what it was. Just looked like a shadow or something, but once it got to my phone, I saw eyes and teeth. Then dripping fangs. Then it looked like it was trying to jump out of my phone screen. Wait! I may have gotten video!"

Jay picked up his phone, then decided he didn't want to look. He tried to face it twice when Gabby took it from his hands.

"There's nothing there, Jay. It's okay. Calm down." She flipped the unlock screen and a password screen came up.

"Unlock it," Gabby said.

"No, I'm good. The code is 2490."

She pressed the code and saw his camera gallery was up. She checked the first blurry image. She went back. There were three pictures, but they were all smears of yellow and gray.

She showed him his phone. "No video. Just a few blurry pics."

He finally grabbed his phone. "No! It must have scared me so bad I switched to camera."

He stared at the pictures a little longer and went through

each. "I might be able to fix this, but that yellow part. That's its eyes."

"It looks like a yellow line of light," Gabby said. "I can't make out eyes or anything. So what do I do? If this thing did this to you with one look, what chance do I have?"

"Reinforcements," Jay said. "I know people who do this on a more regular basis. If I can fix this picture, show them my EMF data, one of them may agree to help. Something's hovering over you, Gabby. I can tell you that. It is watching you."

"Why?"

"I have no idea, but we need to find out. This thing is strong to be shifting around you this way. It followed you from here and possibly to your home, causing these strange events with your family. It can't wait. I'll find someone, I promise. I need to go. And please don't tell Angie what happened."

"You know I'm not lying to her, but I'll explain the situation. If Ree were here, he would have probably busted his head open after passing out, so don't feel too bad."

"I need to get out of here. I'll call my contacts tonight, and I'll get back to you as soon as I can."

"Okay."

Jay turned around and started to walk away.

"Hey, you're not leaving me here alone after that!" Gabby said.

His head shook up and down. "I'm sorry. Just a little freaked still. Please hurry."

They exited at a frantic pace together. Gabby didn't bother to turn the lights off. She just wanted out.

CHAPTER TEN

AFTER THE EVENTS OF THAT NIGHT, GABBY HAD DIFFICULTY clearing her head and tried to keep focused at work and during class. She was happy the next two days were uneventful and looking forward to the weekend.

Saturday brought an optional class that would be part field trip.

The optional classes were a special treat for Gabby as a first year physical therapy graduate student. Professor Gordon, in her Clinical Med II class, announced that the class would be meeting three times during the semester at a private medical practice, a hospital, and an ER to understand how physical therapists interact in different environments with patients. Today they were meeting at the Baylor Scott and White All Saints Medical Center ER in Fort Worth.

Gabby was excited for the distraction and didn't want to think about the strangeness that had overtaken her life. The private practice visit had happened two weeks prior and although Gabby enjoyed it, it just didn't compare to the anticipation of visiting an Emergency Room.

She didn't have many close class friends yet but was part

of a small study group that consisted of seven to ten students who had become her closest acquaintances.

Gabby arrived at the ER just before 11 am. Although she normally worked most Saturday mornings, Body Parade's busiest exhibit day, she had taken today off for the class visit. Weekends were when the exhibit received the most public visitors, while weekdays were limited hours for schools and special events, and she was able to get much more done.

The ER visit was supposed to last two hours, but Professor Gordon told the class they could stay longer if their schedule allowed. The students met in the lobby, signed in, and a doctor in scrubs was waiting for them with two other people by her side.

The class of 14 students stood in a group while the doctor addressed them.

"Good morning, I'm Doctor Janice Green. I'm the attending physician today and just wanted to welcome you. Over the years, one wouldn't expect physical therapists to be involved directly in an Emergency Room. However, that paradigm has shifted in the last few years. We are one of the few ERs in the DFW area to have in-house PT personnel. This has helped better prepare our patients, especially the older ones, to understand how to care for themselves once they leave us. We have seen a decrease in repeated injuries and return visits. Overall, we receive positive feedback from our patients as a whole. So, we welcome any prospective physical therapists with open arms. Although I am the attending physician and typically call the final shots, it is Charge Nurse Leanne Harden who runs the show."

Doctor Green gestured toward the woman next to her.

"Thank you for your time, and I hope you have a great visit. Good luck to you all."

The students applauded as Dr. Green walked away, and Nurse Harden stepped forward. She wasn't smiling.

"Hello. The first thing I want to make clear is that this is my ER. I have to ensure that patients, doctors, and staff are all working together to give everyone the care they need and deserve. I will not allow anyone to hinder that process. Before I turn it over to Doctor Vargas, our lead physical therapist here at Baylor Scott & White, I just want to set a few ground rules. The ER is sometimes quiet and sometimes chaotic. We're kind of right between that today, so please listen to Doctor Vargas closely. If we need you to relocate or exit the ER at a moment's notice, please be quick about it and don't ask questions. We are a little short staffed, so if I seem rude or a little rough around the edges, know that it is due to necessity. This ER was ranked first in patient care the last three years in a row and we earned that by being efficient, considering our patients our top priority, and making sure everyone respects the chain of authority. Even though you are all guests, I still expect the same level of respect for our philosophy. Doctor Vargas runs the PT show, so do what he says and we won't have a problem. I am still the Ringmaster, so do what I say or we WILL have a problem. I have no qualms about embarrassing someone by having them forcibly removed. I'm sure that's not something any of you want while here with a professor who controls your grades. Everybody clear?"

The students nodded. Nurse Harden did not seem like someone you wanted to cross.

"Great. Enjoy your visit. I need to get back in there."

Doctor Vargas then stood front and center. "Hello, my name is Doctor Robert Vargas. Professor Gordon and I go way back. We actually went to undergrad together and have remained great friends for years. I love having her classes come in and hope today won't discourage any of you from your chosen profession. I love my job and I especially love the chaos of an ER. We never know what to expect most days and although some of it may seem routine, it's best to always expect the unexpected."

Doctor Vargas led them into the ER. There were already a few doctors and nurses running in and out of rooms. "A lot of folks in here today, but we're going to enter this room and meet one of my patients."

As they entered, an older man in his mid-60s was sitting up on the bed.

"Mr. Byron, how are you today?"

"Doing a little better."

"Can you let these students know why you're here with us?"

"I was cleaning out my gutters and fell. I thought I shattered my kneecap, but it turns out I just twisted and bruised it up pretty bad. After patching me up, they want me to get some physical therapy in quick before letting me go."

"That is correct. Even with Mr. Byron's age, it's key to begin therapy as soon as possible without harming his knee but getting the healing process started as soon as possible. As Doctor Green mentioned, having PTs in the ER working directly with patients before they leave has helped ensure better patient care and satisfaction. Previously, patients would leave the ER with instructions to follow up with their doctor and arrange physical therapy, but would either never do it or would wait too long, causing more serious injury. Those percentages have diminished by over sixty percent since we started this program."

Doctor Vargas turned to Mr. Byron. "Someone will be coming down for you in just a few minutes, Mr. Byron. Good luck!"

"Yeah, easy for you to say. Good luck to all you students."

They moved on and saw a few more patients, and within thirty minutes, the ER seemed to be busier. At the end of the two hours, most of the students left to either study or enjoy the rest of their weekend, but Gabby and four others stayed on.

Barry Morgan, one of her study partners, was one of the four and smiled at her. "Glad to see a familiar face."

Gabby smiled. Barry had been nice enough during their classes.

"You think you'd want to work in an ER someday?"

Gabby nodded. "I think it would be exciting."

"Eh, not too exciting now."

On cue, a loud scream emanated from the other side of the ER.

"Lockdown! All non-essentials get in a room and take cover!" It was Nurse Harden. "We have a situation. Move now!"

There was a loud ruckus and sounds of people yelling and something falling.

"Let's move!" Doctor Vargas said.

Everyone rushed for cover. Professor Gordon left with Doctor Vargas to see if she could help. Gabby, Barry, and another classmate named Laura ran into a nearby room and huddled together.

"What do you think's happening?" Gabby asked.

Barry shook his head. "No idea, but it has to be big for them to lockdown."

There was a loud booming sound followed by what sounded like gunshots.

"What's going on?" Laura yelled.

The door flew open, and there was a loud thump. It was Mr. Byron. He was on the ground, trying to crawl in.

He groaned.

"Mr. Byron," Gabby said. "Did you fall? What's wrong?"

Laura and Barry looked at him wide-eyed. The patient in the room they had run into, a woman in her mid-30s, was knocked out and didn't react.

Mr. Byron tried to answer, but he looked up at them, struggling to breathe.

Barry reached over and helped pull him fully into the room as his legs were still hanging out the door. As he pulled, a streak of blood followed him.

"Oh, my God!" Laura yelled.

Barry pulled him in and set him on his back.

He checked where the blood was coming from.

"I think he's been shot!"

Laura froze, and Barry looked at her.

"We need a doctor," Laura said.

"There's someone out there with a gun," Gabby said. "We need to stay locked down!"

"We have an active shooter!" A faceless voice said over the intercom. "Remember: Run, Hide, Fight. Keep your heads down."

A gunshot rang out. Barry and Laura ran to the back of the room and huddled in a corner, but Gabby didn't move.

"No one's coming," Gabby said.

"Get over here, Gabby," Barry said. "It's not safe!"

Gabby looked back at her classmates and then at Mr. Byron. Mr. Byron groaned. "You have to help me."

"A doctor should be here soon, Mr. Byron."

"I can't breathe. Please."

Gabby looked at her classmates. Laura was sweating in terror, and Barry was shaking his head.

Gabby looked back at Mr. Byron. He was in serious pain. She lifted his gown.

"I'll do what I can," she said. "Is that okay with you?"

"Yes, yes. It hurts."

She looked at his wound. He was bleeding steadily. She set her hands over the wound and applied pressure, but the blood seeped through her fingers.

"You have to get the bullet out," a soft voice said from behind her.

She looked up. An older man in a white coat was staring at her.

"You're a doctor?"

"Yes, but I can't help him."

He raised both his arms and thick gauze was wrapped around his hands. "You need to do this or he'll die right here."

"I'm not a doctor."

"I will walk you through it. You can do this."

"How? I don't have any instruments."

The doctor moved a little closer and kneeled, looking at the wound.

"Use your hands to see how deep the bullet is. It doesn't look that bad, but you need to feel for it."

"You want me to stick my bare fingers in there?"

"Yes, and I'd suggest you hurry. He doesn't have much time."

Gabby looked back at Barry and Laura, but they were just staring back at her, motionless.

"Please," Mr. Byron said. "I don't want to die here."

Gabby took in a deep breath and used her index and middle finger to feel along the outside of the wound.

Mr. Byron gasped.

"I'm sorry. This is going to hurt."

"Just do what you have to, don't mind me."

She eased her index finger in, feeling around. Her experience with the body exhibit and her medical classes helped her understand where certain muscles and bones were, but the outer flesh of a living, breathing human was an entirely different experience.

"Do you feel it?" the doctor asked.

"No, just wetness and flesh. How will I know?"

"You'll know. The bullet will feel foreign. Just ease your finger in a little more and inch it down."

Gabby's pulse started to race higher. She looked at Mr. Byron's terrified face and knew she had to calm down. She pictured her late grandfather, took in a breath, and exhaled.

She pushed her finger in further, this time ignoring Mr. Byron's scream just before he passed out. She pushed in a little deeper, then pulled down and felt the metal.

"It's there. I can feel part of it."

"Okay, now you know where it is. Just pull it out. You'll have to use two fingers."

Gabby moved her middle finger to join in and spread the hole to make room. As she tried to get them both around the bullet, the piece shifted and she lost it. She had to dig deeper, but finally got it between her digits.

"I have it!"

"Be careful. It's wet and slippery. Just hold on to it firmly, not too tight, and ease it out."

Gabby pulled her fingers backward at a steady pace, wanting to avoid pulling too fast and risk losing it.

There was a wet pop as her fingers exited, and she looked at the bloody piece of metal in her hands.

"Excellent. You need to clean and stuff that wound until one of the other doctors can get here. Go to that second drawer."

The doctor pointed to a metal drawer and Gabby moved toward it and pulled it open. She grabbed gauze, tape and some antiseptic, then returned to Mr. Byron, who was still passed out.

"This is just temporary. We need to slow that blood flow down. Pour some of that antiseptic into the wound. Be generous."

She did as instructed, and the cut fizzled with white bubbles.

"That's good. Now put in the gauze, and be generous. Pack it in. Fill the wound so no blood can escape."

"Okay, okay."

She took several strips of gauze and stacked them into a thick ball. She placed it in the wound and once again let her fingers enter the bullet hole until the gauze felt like it was tightly packed. She grabbed more and added to it.

"How's that?"

She looked up, but the doctor was gone. She started to look out the door, thinking he had rushed out.

Mr. Byron groaned as he came to.

"Thank you," he whispered. "Bless you."

Gabby smiled. "Just keep your head down. I'm sure another doctor will be here soon."

Gabby turned to Barry. "Where did he go?"

"Where did who go?"

"The doctor?"

"I'm sure he's still dealing with this shooter."

She looked at him oddly.

"But why would he just rush out?"

Barry looked at her, and a wrinkle formed between his brows. "How did you know what to do?"

"I didn't. The doctor walked me through it."

Barry's head tilted. "What doctor?"

"Lockdown lifted!" Nurse Green announced over the intercom. "The threat is over. If anyone was injured, please get our attention."

Laura rushed out of the room and screamed, "Someone was shot!"

She didn't stop and ran out of the hospital.

"Who yelled about someone being shot?" a voice echoed from the hall.

"Over here!" Gabby screamed.

The door opened. Doctor Green entered with a male nurse by her side.

"What happened?" Doctor Green asked.

"He was shot and bleeding. The bullet's out."

Doctor Green examined Mr. Byron. "Who did this?"

"She did," Barry said, pointing to Gabby. "It was incredible."

Doctor Green turned to Gabby. "What is your name?"

"Gabby."

"Gabby, do you have emergency medical training?"

"No, but the other doctor guided me. The older male."

"There was another doctor here? Why didn't he do this himself?"

"His hands were bandaged. He said he couldn't help."

The nurse's eyes widened, and he looked up at Doctor Green.

"Normally, I'd reprimand you and ban you from performing any kind of procedure in my ER without a medical license. However, these circumstances were unforeseen. We'll get Mr. Byron into the OR as soon as possible to be sure there's no internal bleeding, but I think you saved this man's life. The threat's been neutralized. An angry father tried to shoot the man who killed his daughter in a hit and run this morning. The suspect was injured in the crash, but nothing life threatening. Not that it matters. He's dead now."

Gabby nodded.

"Do you mind waiting for a few minutes? I'll need to get a report of what happened. With everything going on, I'll have Nurse Lao here get your information so we can get a hold of you later to complete an incident report."

Doctor Green looked over at the nurse and nodded. They left and within a couple of minutes, Nurse Lao returned with another nurse and a gurney. They loaded Mr. Byron onto the gurney, and the new nurse wheeled him out.

Nurse Lao remained and looked at Barry. "Excuse me, can you give us a minute? I need to talk to Gabby."

Barry nodded, still in a daze, and walked out.

"Gabby? As Doctor Green said, I'm Nurse Lao Chen."

He handed Gabby an index card and a pen.

"Can you please put your information here? Name, number, and address are sufficient. Someone will probably call you by tonight. What you did was extremely brave."

"I couldn't have done it without that doctor's help," Gabby said as she filled out the card.

Lao took in a sharp breath. "You said he had bandaged hands?"

Gabby nodded.

"What did he look like?"

"He was tall, older, fit and had gray hair. His nose was a little crooked, and he had a scar just to the right of it."

"Yes, he broke his nose in a bad fall when he was a teenager. That was Doctor William Hartman."

"Oh, is he still around? I'd like to thank him. Has he worked here a long time?"

"That's just it. He worked here for a ridiculously long time. Over forty years, until he burned his hands in a fire that destroyed part of the hospital about ten years back."

"So, he still works here but can't help patients?" Gabby hesitated. "Wait, why were his hands still bandaged?"

"Here's the thing, Gabby. He died in that fire. He burned his hands pulling patients from the building, but the roof collapsed and killed him."

Gabby stammered. "Are you saying the ghost of a long dead doctor just helped me save Mr. Byron's life?"

"Many of the staff have seen him before. He tends to show up during surgeries or when it's extra chaotic. I've seen him a couple of times, but from a distance. I've only heard of him speaking and interacting with someone maybe once. I don't know whether you believe it, but I'd recommend maybe leaving that out of the conversation when you get called."

Gabby wasn't sure how to react. "The look Doctor Green gave you. That's what that was about, wasn't it?"

"You're very observant, and yes. We all know about him, but we can't put that on anything official. Can you just say you just went on instinct?"

"Yes, I can improvise."

"Thank you. It'll make things a lot easier. The fact that you had a full interactive experience with him is impressive. And frightening."

"That's why my classmates looked at me the way they did. Great, now I'll be the crazy student if they spread this around."

"That's exactly why we don't put these incidents in anything official. Just talk to them. It was an intense situation and maybe they'll just think it was the stress of it."

"I hope so."

Lao left the room and Gabby stood there for a moment. The last few days had already been odd, but now she had a ghost doctor instructing her on how to save a life?

Gabby left in a daze, not understanding what was happening to her.

She spent Sunday alone with Ally, unable to shake the image and conversation with the ghost doctor. She kept her texts and calls short, using studying as her excuse to avoid everyone. She hoped a better week was coming, but her pending sense of dread carried into a sleepless night.

CHAPTER ELEVEN

GABBY WENT THROUGH THE MOTIONS MONDAY AT SCHOOL, doing her best to avoid eye contact with Barry and Laura and praying no one would ask her about the ER visit. Although only five students were around when it happened, the shooting made the news and she was sure students were talking about it. She worked to use her body language to tell anyone that might want to chit chat she wasn't in the mood. She rushed to her car after classes were over.

Her mood carried into the afternoon at work. Ed walked up to her about an hour into her shift.

"Are you feeling okay, Gabby? You look a little out of sorts."

Gabby tried to force a smile.

"Just a tough day in class."

Ed nodded but held her gaze an extra second before moving on, and Gabby realized she wasn't doing a great job of hiding how shaken she still was. She didn't work late and left right at 5 for once.

She was on her way home a few minutes later with Ally

screaming in the background. Donna from the daycare said she had been good but got cranky toward the afternoon.

Gabby was flipping through the radio and a Celine Dion song came on. Ally stopped yelling. It was a slower song and with each long note, Ally cooed along.

"Thank you, Celine," Gabby whispered.

Her phone rang. It was her sister calling. Gabby's stomach churned. She knew it was only a matter of time. Not much got past Teri.

Gabby answered it through her car's Bluetooth.

"Hey, Sis."

"Gabby, did something happen when you took the kids last week?"

She paused, trying to think how best to answer. "Can you be more specific?"

"I know something happened. I know my kids. They've been acting weird, and last night Grace and Linda both woke up in the middle of the night and ran down to sleep with me and John. They only do that when there's a thunderstorm or they're scared, and it's been dry for days. Linda said something about fire and Michael Myers. I asked the kids together what had happened, and they looked at each other like they're keeping a military secret. So I'll ask again, what happened?"

Ally was listening to her aunt's voice and squealed.

"You're in the car?"

"Yes."

"Then come over for dinner. The kids and John are eating now. I have to take Nick to a UIL math competition practice and go shopping until he's done, so we had to eat early. I need to leave in about an hour. I'll wait for you and we can talk."

"Okay, Teri. I'll be there. I'll tell you everything."

Gabby was overcome with a need to let it go. Although

Angie and Ree knew what was going on, she'd have to be careful how she told Angie about what happened with Jay because she might get overwhelmed and have a panic attack. Ree would just make a joke to show he wasn't scared.

Gabby needed to talk, and she knew her sister needed to know what happened with the kids, even if it meant risking her future access to her nieces and nephew. Teri would be brutally honest, for better or worse.

Gabby used her satellite radio's memory to jump back to Celine. They heard it five times in a row by the time they reached Teri's house.

Teri greeted her at the door. As Gabby walked in, the older kids were on the couch. The younger ones came out. Jessica pointed at Linda. Her little head was down and she wouldn't look at her Aunt Gabby.

"Hey, guys, it's okay." Gabby moved to hug them all. As she embraced Jessica, her niece whispered, "I told you Linda couldn't keep a secret, but she tried."

Teri led her to the table where the food was already sitting. Spaghetti and meatballs with French bread. Gabby placed Ally on the chair next to her, but Jess came up to grab her and took her to the living room.

They took a few bites. Teri stared at her but didn't ask.

"Okay," Gabby finally broke the silence. "What I'm going to tell you is going to freak you out, and I have more to say. May want to send Grace and Linda out of the room."

Teri turned to her youngest children. "Go with Dad to the bedroom. He's watching a baseball game."

The girls ran off. They'd make him change it to the Disney Channel within the first five minutes.

Gabby motioned to Nick and Jess. "Come here, guys."

Jess was still carrying Ally as she and her brother moved to the table and sat with them.

"I'm not sure when it started, but I can tell you when I first noticed it."

Gabby proceeded to tell her everything. Teri broke in.

"So the house could have caught fire with my kids there?"

"Mom," Jessica said. "We're all fine. What if Aunt Gabby and Ally had been there alone? At least we were all there to see it. You always say how things can always be worse."

Teri gave her a look, not quite angry but not happy her own words were used against her.

"Keep going."

"Something else has happened since. You remember Jenna, Angie's girlfriend?"

Terri nodded.

"Jenna has a brother named Jay who is into this kind of thing and he came to my house and also to the office. He saw a lot more than I have, but I'm usually there alone. So whatever this thing is, it may have been around me longer than I even realized. I haven't seen anything directly. I'm scared. I'm sorry the kids tried to hide it from you. I was going to tell you, but I wanted to know if it was just exhaustion, paranoia or something else before I brought it up. And now, I can say that I think it seems like it is something."

"Are you sure this guy wasn't just trying to scare you or scam you for money?"

"No, Sis. If you would have seen how scared he was, you'd know it wasn't fake. I think I saw a wet spot on his pants but didn't want to make him feel worse."

The kids started laughing.

"That is a family secret!" Gabby said. "Not to be repeated. Remember how scared you all were when the fire shot up?"

They both looked down.

"I was scared, too," Gabby said. "It's easier to laugh afterward, especially when it's not you."

She looked back at her sister.

"Then something happened this past weekend. Something concrete. My class met at an ER in Fort Worth on Saturday and I saw and spoke to a ghost doctor in the middle of a shootout."

The kids stopped laughing.

"Are you serious, Aunt Gabby?" Nick asked.

"Yes, and he helped me save the life of a gunshot victim. I had no idea until a nurse told me about it after everything was over. He looked as real and as solid as all of you are to me now."

"Wow," Jess said. "That's insane."

"That's pretty much everything, Teri. I don't know what to do. I'm surprisingly not that scared right now, but I think my need to know what's really happening is stronger than my fear. At least for now."

Teri soaked it in and took a few seconds to compose herself. "Ever since you were little, you wanted to know how and why things worked, so that doesn't surprise me at all. You're hyper-focused on your work. Even a ghost or whatever this thing is that seems to be haunting or stalking you isn't enough to deter you. It was good this guy Jay went over. So what now?"

"He admitted it was too much for him. He's trying to find someone who has more experience that might be able to help. He truly wants to find out what's going on, but I swear he was more scared than the kids were. Have the little ones really been okay?"

"Other than the nightmares I told you about, as far as I know, they're fine."

Teri turned toward her oldest children. "But these two wouldn't tell me if they weren't okay without me pushing it. So?"

Nick and Jess looked down. "I've been a little shaken up some nights," Nick said. "I jumped when I looked in the mirror earlier, but it was just Jessica standing behind me before she combed her hair."

Jess hit him on the leg. Ally noticed and swatted at him, too. "Jerk. I've been okay. I'm more worried about Aunt Gabby."

"So what's going through your head now that you know everything?" Gabby asked.

Teri hesitated and picked up her cup of tea.

"It's still sinking in. As you told your story, I was trying to process if I could simply believe all this without question, but from what I've seen with the kids and what they've just told me, I think that now…"

"Now what, Mom?" Jessica asked, like she knew what was coming.

"I don't think the kids should be at your house or alone with you until this is resolved," she said, almost in a whisper.

"No, Mom! You can't do that!" Jessica said, raising her voice.

Nick just shook his head. "We can help her, Mom."

"How? How can you help her? Now I'm thinking about what COULD have happened. What if one of you was near the stove? Or maybe the TV could have fallen? What if the house had caught fire? This could have been much, much worse. So why invite it?"

"Mom, would you turn your back on any of us?" Jessica asked.

"No, of course not."

"Then how can you turn your back on your sister?"

"Gabby," Teri said. "You are welcome to leave Ally or the both of you can come over anytime as long as I'm here."

"That really sucks, Mom," Jess said.

"No," Gabby said, turning to her niece and nephew. "Put yourselves in her position. I'm doing that now. If this was Ally, I'd want to protect her over anything. That's what I'm trying to do now. I'm letting strangers come into my house to help me figure out what's going on. Your mom has every right to feel how she feels. She's scared for you, and considering I don't know how deep or dangerous this could be, I can't blame her."

Jess started to tear up. "That means we won't see you, Aunt Gabby!"

"I promise you will. In fact, with everything going on, I may use you all a little more to watch Ally. I don't think I want her in the house if I have people there looking into this stuff. What happens if something attacks me when Ally is near?"

"Gabs, maybe you should finally let me watch her long term. I know you always wanted her near you at work, but it seems this started at your work and hasn't let up. I can watch her during the day, and she can stay here any night you need her to stay."

Gabby had always resisted her sister's offers to watch Ally permanently. She would never say it out loud, but she always feared Ally might grow more attached to her. She knew Teri was a good mom, and Gabby was still trying to get her life together as a single mother. Plus, Teri had always been the one that did everything right growing up. Right now, however, she felt shame for even thinking that.

"I don't know, Teri. You already have so much on your plate."

"You know we all love her. And if that's how I can help, then I will. The sooner you resolve this, the better for everyone. Then we can get back to normal."

Teri put her head down as Jessica was still giving her an evil stare.

"Thank you," Gabby said. "And it's okay. Don't feel bad. If you can protect your kids and Ally, then that's what you should do. Thank you."

"Don't thank me," Teri said. "I feel horrible already banning the kids from hanging out with you. If anything similar were ever to happen to me, I hope you'd have sense enough to take them away from me as well."

"I'd like to think I would," Gabby said.

Gabby's phone rang. She looked at the screen. It was Jay. Gabby walked away from the table and into the hall, then finally answered.

"Jay?"

"I found someone," is all he said.

"Who?"

"One of the most gifted paranormalists in the state. I told him what happened, and he was able to read something off my phone and EMF. He wants to help you. This is something he's never seen before and wants to know more."

"How soon can he meet?"

"He won't be able to meet until Thursday. Can you wait a few more days?"

"Is he really that good?" Gabby asked.

"His name is Benjamin Jordan," Jay said. "Just look him up. He should pop up pretty quickly. Read up on him, then let me know. He is the best, and I guarantee you he won't be a trembling coward like I was."

"I will look him up, but for now, let's keep the Thursday date. Let's see what happens between now and then."

"Okay, I'll let him know. He'll be worth it. I promise."

She hung up and returned to the table. "It was Jay. He found someone. We'll get together later this week. I need to go."

Gabby hugged Nick and Jess and Teri made Grace and Linda come out, too. She realized the next time she saw them it would be an officially supervised visit with Teri around. Even if it practically wouldn't be much different than her visit now, simply knowing it would have stipulations would make it awkward.

Gabby hugged the little ones and said she'd see them soon.

"You look sad, Aunt Gabby," Grace said.

"I'm a little sad that I'm leaving, but I'll see y'all soon."

"Okay, Auntie Gabby," Grace said. "Make sure you look out in case Michael Myers or fire are trying to sneak up on you."

She cringed, not wanting to make eye contact, but was okay. Grace had proved the point. They were affected by it.

Jess handed Ally back to Gabby and everyone took turns kissing her goodbye. Gabby checked her phone once she was back in the car and had several missed calls from Angie and Ree.

She called Angie back first.

"Hey," Angie said as she answered.

"I knew she would call you first!" Ree yelled in the background. "I'm always the bridesmaid."

"You're still loved," Gabby said. "What's up?"

"I just spoke to Jay and he told me some of what happened and that he and some new guy are supposed to meet you again on Thursday. We want to hear it from you. Also, there's a concert Wednesday night. Let's go!"

"Who would be worth seeing on a Wednesday night?"

"What is the one 90s band we kept talking about seeing but never did, and then they broke up?"

Gabby's eyes widened. "No! The Black Crowes?"

"The one and only," Angie said. "The brothers are back together and touring. I know it's a weeknight, but maybe your sister can watch Ally."

Gabby considered it, but shook her head. "Guys, that's sweet, and I do have more to tell you, but…"

"No buts!" Ree's voice shot up as Angie switched to

speaker phone. "Everything's crazy for you, and now you have someone coming to your house to evaluate a possible spirit following you around. Let's do something kind of normal. The concert ends by 11, so it won't be too late. We want to take you out to forget about everything for a while. One of us will drive! Just dress up and let's go let loose a little."

Gabby had to admit the thought was enticing.

"Gabby. It's the Black Crowes." Angie said.

Gabby caved. "Okay, I'm in."

"Don't you have to ask your sister first?"

"Just leaving her house. I can already tell you she'll say yes."

CHAPTER TWELVE

Barry walked up to Gabby after class the next day. She had hoped to avoid him and was happy Laura had a different Wednesday schedule.

"Hey, Gabby."

Gabby nodded toward him, unsure of what to expect.

"Do you have lunch plans?"

Gabby hesitated before answering, trying to figure out his motive.

"I was just going to eat a sandwich before I headed into work."

"Let me take you to lunch. Maybe we can talk a little more about what happened at the hospital."

Gabby's mouth opened. She had picked up on the subtle flirtation between them during some study sessions but didn't think it was anything close to serious.

"You mean like a date?"

His hands started to fidget. "If that's okay with you, I'd like it to be."

"Now?"

"Yes, so you don't have too much time to think about it."

Gabby looked down at her jeans and Daisy Duck tee shirt. "I'm not dressed for anything nice."

"Nothing fancy," Barry said, pointing to his Dallas Cowboys shirt. "We're both dressed fine."

Gabby hadn't been asked out in a long time. She was flattered and her head was suddenly filled with Angie and Ree, who had been telling her for months she needed to start going out. Ree's phrasing was "You need to get laid, Gabby!" but he meant it nicely. Gabby had no desire to go on a first date without prep time, but her curiosity was piqued.

She looked back at Barry and his face dropped as if he was already expecting to be let down. Before she could overthink it, she blurted out, "Okay. A date. But not now. Not like this."

"How about tonight or tomorrow?"

The concert was tomorrow, and she was already anxious to know what Barry wanted to discuss.

"Tonight would be better," Gabby said. "I need to confirm a babysitter, but I think I'm covered."

She knew full well Angie or Ree would jump at the chance to help her.

"Then maybe we can do a little fancy. How about Dragon Steakhouse?"

Gabby loved that place, but it had been more than three years since she'd been there. It didn't require formal attire, but was definitely business casual.

"Okay, Dragon it is."

"Does 7 pm work for you? I can pick you up."

"No," Gabby said. "I'll meet you there, just in case something comes up with my daughter."

"Then it's a date."

Barry smiled as he gathered his backpack and walked out with a little extra bounce in his step.

Gabby laughed at the unexpected turn of events and quickly texted her friends. She didn't want to overburden Teri with Ally since she was already watching her for the concert and would only go to her if Angie or Ree couldn't do it. Within thirty seconds, both replied.

"Holy shit! Yes!" Angie texted.

"GABBY MIGHT FINALLY GET LAID!" was Ree's response.

GABBY FINISHED HER SHIFT, THEN HEADED HOME AND DRESSED UP for the night. She gave Angie and Ree the full details of the Ghost Doctor and the awkward date setup when she dropped Ally off. Her friends decided to co-babysit, but truth was they loved spending time with Ally. They could play with her and have fun, and if she got out of hand, they got to leave her with Mommy at the end of the night.

The story took longer than expected, and Gabby arrived at the restaurant two minutes late. Barry was already waiting. He wore a nice dark shirt and slacks, which was a nice alternative to the casual look she was used to seeing. Gabby wore a light black and white sundress.

Barry smiled when she walked in and stood up to give her a hug.

"I was afraid you might have gotten cold feet," he said.

"It's only a couple of minutes!"

"I know, but you know. First date jitters. I haven't been on a date in over a year."

"Really?" As handsome as he was, she found it hard to believe. "Why is that?"

"Bad breakup and with this school year, just haven't found the time."

"Then why now?"

"You know, we've gotten to know each other a little better. I'm comfortable with you and we're kind of going through this together. Plus that thing you did the other day in the hospital. Talk about a serious turn on."

Gabby laughed. She wondered if he'd feel the same if he knew a large part of her agreeing to the date was to find out if he'd told anyone and how he interpreted the whole ghost doctor situation.

"Sorry, was that too forward?"

"No, not at all. Just surprised me. I'm not sure if you know I'm a widow. Haven't really been on a date since my husband died. Just wasn't sure if I was ready, and like you said, school makes things tougher. Plus, working part-time and being a mom keeps me pretty busy."

They spent the next half hour talking freely, stopping only to order their food. Gabby was feeling unusually comfortable with the conversation and having a difficult time working in her planned uncomfortable questions. The first real pause was Barry clearing his throat.

"I don't want to ruin this conversation, but there's something I have to ask you."

Gabby felt a sense of relief that she wouldn't have to ask first. "What is it?"

"The hospital. How did you do what you did? That was so brave. Laura was terrified, and I was trying to keep her calm, but when I looked over, I swear you were talking to yourself, but then it seemed like you were looking up at nobody. Is that some kind of protective device when you're scared or under pressure?"

"Not really," Gabby said, overthinking her next words. "Something odd happened."

She wanted to stop, but for whatever reason, she couldn't and kept going.

"This may not be first date level conversation, but remember you asked. There was a doctor there that was guiding me through the process."

"What doctor? I never saw anyone."

"Yeah, apparently only I did. That nurse that came in told me afterward there's some doctor that haunts that hospital and a few people have seen him over the years, but my situation was unique. He appeared to me and helped me save Mr. Byron's life. I can't take full credit for it."

Barry sat there, convinced she was messing with him, but the way she said it had no sense of humor to it.

"That's really what happened?"

"Really? You believe that right off the bat?"

"The little I know of your demeanor in class and in study group is that you're pretty honest and open when you're being funny. I don't think you'd joke about something like that."

"Do you believe in that kind of stuff?"

"I don't know. I guess not, but nothing like that's ever happened to me. I've never really had to think about it, but do I think there are things out there we can't explain? Sure. I've heard stories and figure they have to come from somewhere and can't all be just wild imaginations. This is cool."

Gabby felt a sense of tightness in her chest ease. Barry laughed and asked for more. Gabby proceeded to tell him every detail she could remember.

"Has anything like this happened before? I mean, have you ever seen a ghost?"

Gabby hesitated, since just a few weeks ago the answer would have been no.

"Not exactly," she finally decided to say.

"Meaning?"

"I've never had any kind of experience like that until just recently."

"What kind of experience?"

She thought carefully about what to tell him. She didn't

want to bring up her family, so she started explaining the moving displays at work.

Barry's eyes were big and he didn't blink. "That's frightening, Gabby. I hope it's nothing bad."

Gabby felt something vibrate. "Sorry."

She reached into her purse for her phone, just in case it was Angie or Ree.

No calls or texts.

She looked down at the table to see if it was Barry's phone, but nothing. The table stopped.

"You feel that?"

"What?"

"The table was vibrating. I thought it was my phone."

"I didn't notice anything, but could just be a passing truck."

She looked at her wine glass and the red wine had something in it.

"You see that?" Gabby asked. "There's something in my wine."

He looked at her drink. "Did they drop an olive or something in there?"

Gabby looked closer. There was something floating in her glass. It wasn't an olive, and she felt a sense of relief that she hadn't taken a drink since her last refill.

"I'll get the waiter to bring you another glass."

Barry lifted the drink and as he brought it to his face for a closer look, the object turned in the wine and flattened against the glass. A pulpy eyeball stared back at him.

Barry jumped out of his seat and the wine glass shattered, throwing glass and red wine all over him and the table.

"What's wrong?"

"Was this a joke? You tell me the ghost story, then slip an eyeball from that Body Parade place where you work to scare and embarrass me? What's wrong with you?"

"Barry, I didn't do anything! What eyeball?"

She looked around the floor but only saw glass shards and spilled wine. Whatever she had glimpsed before wasn't on the table or under it.

A few patrons were staring, and some were laughing.

"This isn't funny," Barry said, his tone completely changed.

He grabbed a napkin and headed to the bathroom.

Gabby didn't know what to do or say as a waiter rushed to the table to clean up.

"I'm so sorry, ma'am. May have just been a bad glass. I'll get this cleaned up."

As the waiter crouched down to clean up the chair and pick up the broken pieces, Gabby looked at Barry's still intact wine glass and a pair of yellow slitted eyes appeared for just a moment, then faded away, making the hair on Gabby's arms rise. She looked around, but none of the people still staring in her direction seemed to notice.

Barry returned to the table as the waiter was still cleaning.

"You okay?" Gabby asked.

He put some cash down on the table. "I don't appreciate what you did, Gabby. I guess I don't know your sense of humor after all, but I didn't come here to be humiliated. Have a good night."

"Wait," Gabby protested, but sat back down. She wasn't about to explain what had happened. He was scared and embarrassed, and anything she tried to say now would be pointless.

Way to go, Gabby. I guess it was too good to be true after all. Should have kept your big mouth shut.

The first date was a disaster, but without a doubt, a memorable one.

CHAPTER THIRTEEN

GABBY SPENT AN HOUR TALKING TO REE AND ANGIE AFTER arriving earlier than expected to pick up Ally.

"I'm sorry, Gabby," Ree said. "This craziness is invading your love life."

"Love life?" Gabby said. "It's just another disaster. Not like it was great before I started seeing ghosts."

"The concert's tomorrow," Angie said. "We can forget about dating, ghosts, and weird stuff for one night. Just hang in there."

Gabby agreed. She needed this more than ever.

The next day's morning classes turned out to be uneventful. Although Barry wasn't in any of her classes and no study group was scheduled, she stressed about seeing him or possibly getting awkward stares from classmates he or Laura may have spoken to. Fortunately, none of that happened, but she still found it difficult to concentrate.

Her afternoon at work was mostly quiet, but Gabby found herself avoiding her computer monitor and kept her phone covered. If she felt even the possibility of something or someone near her, she refused to turn and face it.

Gabby hoped to leave as early as she could so she wouldn't be alone. She just wanted to go to the concert and away from the crazy for one full day and night.

She worked as fast as she could.

"Gabby, I'm heading out," Ed said from behind her.

She jumped at the sound of his voice and dropped her scalpel.

"Gabby, I'm so sorry! I didn't mean to scare you."

"It's okay Ed. I'll be finishing soon."

"Have fun with your friends tonight. I don't mean to pry, but are you okay?"

She hadn't told him anything.

"Why?"

"You've seemed distracted the last few days, and I've never seen you jump like that."

She tried to offer a sincere smile but felt her cheeks tightening as she did.

"Just haven't been able to sleep lately. School is busy and Ally's been a little fussy."

"I hope she's not sick," he said, smiling. "Just let me know if you need a little time off."

She could use a few days off, but she needed to keep working. It was keeping her mind occupied.

"I'm sure I'll be fine, Ed. I'm hoping to get some rest this weekend. I'm not even sure I want to go to this concert tonight, but my friends insisted."

"Try to have a good time, and I hope you feel better."

He left, and she heard the door lock as she returned to her display. She tried to make changes and concentrate, but was suddenly aware that she was alone. Jay had sensed what was around her when she couldn't and she felt sweat forming down the back of her neck as she was overcome with thoughts of being surrounded by unseen forces.

Her hand was trembling as she tried to add some glue to the hand of the display.

She sensed something to her left. Something staring at her. She could feel it. Or was she just letting her paranoia get the best of her?

"Damn it. Get yourself together, Gabby," she whispered. "There's nothing there. She swallowed and turned quickly to be sure.

Two yellow, menacing eyes filled the computer screen. It looked fake and she couldn't distinguish if it was part of a different screen saver or just a still picture meant to scare her. Her fear subsided as she was overcome with curiosity. She leaned forward to look closer. The eyes blinked and were gone. She looked around the room and something moved behind her. She caught the movement as she turned, and one of the frames on the wall had one yellow eye. Then, to her right, she saw another flash of yellow eyes reflecting off the metal logo of the copy machine. Then they all blinked simultaneously. It was like the entire wall was staring at her.

She grabbed her purse, dropped her scalpel and glue, and rushed out. She was afraid the fear would overtake her if she ran, so she walked as fast as she could without breaking into a jog.

She was breathing hard as she arrived at the daycare to pick up Ally.

"Gabby, seriously dear," Donna said. "Have you been to the doctor? You look more and more pale every day."

"I just have a small cold." She could feel her own voice trembling and tried to calm herself. "I just need some fluids and to eat. Also, Ally may not come in for a few days. My sister misses her, so I might let her stay there a bit."

"Okay, do you know how long so I can update her records?"

"I'd say at least a week, but I'll let you know."

Donna nodded but stared at her with concern.

She and Ally got home. Gabby took a shower and got ready with Ally seated with some toys on the bathroom floor, like she usually was when Gabby got cleaned up. Once she was ready, they took off to her sister's house.

"Thanks for watching her," Gabby said.

"It's okay. Maybe this night out will help."

Gabby waited for her to ask if anything was happening. She didn't, but Gabby saw it in her eyes. She wanted to ask but was afraid to. Gabby didn't want to talk about what had happened earlier, so she changed the subject.

"Teri, I think I'm going to take you up on your offer to watch Ally while I'm at school and work. At least for the next week, if that's okay."

Teri's face changed from concern to a smile. "Of course. She can stay with me as long as she likes."

"Thanks, Sis. I'm going to leave my car here. Angie's driving. She was already here when I pulled up, so she's waiting on me. I'll try not to be too late."

"It's okay. You sure you don't want to just leave Ally overnight in case you're running late?"

"No, I'll come get her. If anything changes, I'll call you. I'll have my phone on me the entire time and will be checking it in case it's too loud. Please call or text me if anything happens."

Gabby left and got into Angie's car. Ree was in the backseat. Gabby hadn't mentioned the earlier incident at work and didn't intend to. Not tonight.

They got to the concert about 30 minutes early and made sure that they bought concert shirts early so they wouldn't miss any part of the show. Ree and Angie wanted to make it a supernatural free night, so they didn't ask her anything, even though she knew she looked out of sorts.

There were two mediocre opening bands, but The Black

Crowes were worth the wait. The trio of friends were all singing at the top of their lungs midway through the concert and the plan for a distraction was working. Gabby thought about videos, music, and how much she loved the songs. She would periodically check her phone, but there were no calls from Teri for the first two hours. Gabby sent a text after the second opener, asking how it was going, and Teri replied that the kids were all playing with Ally and making her laugh. That gave her enough comfort to enjoy the rest of the show.

After two encores, it was over.

They spent the entire walk to the parking lot talking about the songs and the stage show. They especially loved the pyrotechnics and all agreed their favorite part was the singer being lifted over the stage onto a platform in the back section, landing only two rows in front of their seats. He was so close they felt like they could almost touch him.

They got to the car and headed out with the line of cars fighting to get out first. They were still raving about the concert as they left the parking lot when Ree broke the conversation.

"Let's get something to eat. I'm famished,"

Gabby looked at her watch. It was a little past eleven.

"Don't worry about the time! You know your sister's up late. Just real quick," Ree said. "There's a sports bar with great wings that's open late on weekdays."

Gabby thought for a moment but wanted to keep the night going. "Okay, but we have to be quick."

"Angie, turn right at the next light. I know a back way."

Angie did as instructed. They went through a busy neighborhood and were soon passing through some unlit fields of corn.

"Are you sure you know where you're going, Ree? Gabs, check your GPS on your phone."

She lifted her phone, but Ree's hand blocked her screen.

"No GPS! I demand your ultimate trust. It's only a few miles away, and this way is better. No traffic, no lights! Once we pass this small bridge coming up, it'll just be a few more minutes."

Gabby put her phone down. They looked around the darkness as large fields of corn were on their right and empty fields to their left.

"Man, wouldn't it suck to have a blowout here in the middle of nowhere?" Ree said, laughing.

BOOM!

The car swerved and Angie slammed on her brakes. Everyone screamed, with Ree's being the loudest.

They skidded and finally came to a stop. Angie had managed to move the car a few feet off to the side.

Angie turned to Ree and started hitting him. "Why would you say something like that, you jackass!"

Gabby looked around the car.

"Did you hit something?" she asked.

"I don't know. Ree, you get to check since you decided to mess with karma."

Ree looked out. "Do you have a flashlight? My battery's low and don't want to use my phone."

"Yes, it's in the trunk," Angie said. "My dad always reminds me to keep a rescue kit in the back."

Ree got out and Angie popped the trunk. He found the flashlight and already saw the car was leaning. He hoped it was just stuck in the grass or some mud, but the driver's side back tire was missing. It looked like it had exploded.

He returned to the driver's side window and Angie looked up at him in anticipation.

"What is it?"

"Tire flew off. Is your spare beneath all your stuff in the trunk or underneath the car?"

"It's in the trunk."

Ree went back and moved Angie's assorted mess, mostly clothes and some bags, aside and lifted the carpeted spare tire cover. The compartment was empty.

"Angie, where is your spare?"

Angie thought for a moment. "Oh, I had to use it last year, and it got damaged. I was going to replace it, but I guess I never got around to it."

"Isn't your dad always telling you to make sure you always have a fully filled spare?"

"Yes, he is. So don't tell him. Or Jenna. I told them both I bought one months ago."

"What do we do now?" Ree asked.

"Let's just call someone to come get us," Gabby said. "Do you have a towing service?"

"Oh, yes! The car warranty gives me free towing within 50 miles."

Angie made the call. "They'll be here in less than 60 minutes."

"Then let's go eat and wait for them!" Ree said.

"How? We have to be here for the tow."

"Just call them and have them pick us up wherever we are. It's just about two miles down to get back to civilization and the sports bar. We can get there in like fifteen minutes. It'll be an adventure."

Angie looked at Gabby. "May not be the best option."

Gabby thought. "It's dark, but we have a flashlight and I have to admit I'm hungry and don't really want to wait another hour. Plus, we've gone jogging when it was darker."

Angie shook her head. "Not middle-of-nowhere dark!"

"Come on, Ang. I'm starving!" Ree said.

Angie called the towing service back and told them where they'd be. She offered a nice tip if he'd come by and get them. He agreed.

They started walking, using the flashlight to guide each

step. They stayed on the edge of the road in case a car came by, but none had.

"How about the new guitar player?" Angie asked, trying to break up the silence.

They had only walked a few minutes, but it seemed like it had gotten darker.

"Maybe this wasn't such a great idea," Angie said. "I'm getting creeped out."

They approached a part of the farm road with the sign, "Willow Bridge." They started to cross and looked down at the creek the bridge was built over.

Gabby tried not to look down. The bridge was only about 20 yards long, and as they reached halfway across, something bright appeared to their left.

It moved across the center of the bridge. It was a dull white, just bright enough to stand out. They froze. Ree pulled the light up toward it, but nothing was there. As he lowered the light, the bright image moved toward them and turned. It was a woman. She was in a long dress, with something covering her face. There was also a darker shape next to her. It looked like another person. They took a step closer. It was a man dressed in a nice suit.

All three froze and Ree dropped the flashlight. It fell facing to one side so they could see the two images clearly. The pair stood next to each other and moved forward.

The male stepped toward Gabby and Angie and the woman came straight at Ree. Angie crouched down and covered her eyes but still couldn't make a sound.

The couple moved within inches of them. Their faces were pale white and their eyes were wide open and didn't blink.

Gabby was trembling, and Ree had tears coming out of his eyes. The pale couple stood there for a moment, then leaned their faces in closer. Their lips pursed, and the woman moved toward Ree and the man crouched down toward Angie, who had her eyes shut tight. They each felt cold air and wetness against their lips. Then the woman turned to Gabby and gave her a cold kiss. Just as Angie let out a gasp, the couple disappeared.

"Oh, my God!" Ree finally let out.

Ree started running. Gabby grabbed Angie by the shoulder and Angie screamed.

"Run!" is all Gabby could get out and without realizing it, her legs were flying. Angie opened her eyes and saw Gabby with a head start and took off, leaving the fallen flashlight.

Ree was a good thirty yards ahead of them and didn't stop.

As they ran, scared to look behind them, the ground started to rumble. Everything around them was shaking. Something big was coming, and it was off to their left on the opposite side of the road. A light swept over their faces and as they turned, a loud whistle announced a train flying by them. They hadn't noticed any tracks, and all screamed as it roared by. It was only about fifteen cars and just as soon as they noticed it, it passed. They kept running and finally saw some light ahead as they neared a populated area, which revealed a slick road from earlier rain—the first in weeks. Ree finally slowed down enough for the women to almost catch up to him, but didn't stop moving. As they ran through several puddles, Gabby saw something. Two big yellow eyes, fangs and a dark gray face, smiling and making a guttural, repeating sound like it was trying to laugh.

Ree almost fell, and Gabby pushed him forward before he lost his balance. They passed the puddle and kept going.

Within a few minutes, brighter lights surrounded them, revealing a few outdoor shopping centers. The "Sammy's Sportsbar" sign was the only one lit up brightly, although there were closed establishments with dimmer lights on. Ree didn't stop until he reached the parking lot, and Gabby and Angie were only a few steps behind him.

Angie grabbed onto Ree to stop her momentum. They were all bent over and breathing hard.

"Oh, my God," Angie said. "What was that? What was that? Is it still behind us?"

Ree had his face buried in his hands. "I don't know, I don't know..."

Gabby forced herself to turn, and all she saw behind her was the road.

"Nothing's there. Maybe the lights helped."

"I'm never taking a back road again," Angie said. "Ree, you hear me!"

"If you had a spare, none of this would have happened!" he yelled back.

"If you hadn't said that stupid thing about how it would suck to have a blowout in the middle of nowhere, this would have never happened!"

He started to fight back but looked down. "You're right. That was stupid."

"Let get inside. I don't want to be out here anymore," Gabby said.

They were sweating and shaken. As they entered the sports bar, the 15 or so patrons looked up at them but went right back to their games and conversations.

They walked to a nearby table, and the bartender showed up a few seconds later.

"You looking for something off the grill?"

Angie looked at Ree. "You got us here. The food better be worth what just happened."

"Yes, the grilled wings would be fine," Ree said. "Three orders with fries."

"Sounds good."

"And some drinks," Angie said. "We have a tow truck

coming soon, and I think we all need something to settle us down before he gets here."

The bartender took their drink orders and before she turned, she started to ask something, then stopped herself. She stepped away and returned with their drinks a few minutes later. She took an extra few moments to stare at each of her new customer's faces.

"I'm sorry, but I have to ask. Where did your car break down?"

"About 2 miles back," Ree said. "Just before Willow Creek bridge."

"Did something happen?"

"Why would you ask that?"

"Something did happen, didn't it?"

The looks they gave each other were enough to convince her.

"You saw them, didn't you?" the bartender asked.

"Who?"

"The married couple on the bridge."

Their eyes all bulged.

"We saw something," Gabby said. "I take it there's a story behind that couple?"

"Yes, but I don't want to scare you more than you all already appear to be."

"No, please," Gabby said. "I need to know."

"I don't," Angie said as she covered her ears. "Tell me later."

"Please, tell us," Gabby said.

Ree closed his eyes. "Yes, tell us."

"Well, about 30 years ago, a couple who had just married was on the way to their honeymoon. They crashed on that bridge and died. People have said they've had strange things happen on or around that bridge. Some hear their voices or see them in their wedding clothes, walking around. What did you all see?"

Ree and Gabby looked at each other. Ree opened his mouth, but nothing came out.

"We had to cross the bridge," Gabby said. "We saw them walk across. Then they kissed us."

"OH, awesome!" the girl said. "The wedding kiss! I've never met anyone that's actually happened to, but my boss told me about it. I think it's been over ten years. He's going to love this story!"

"Have you seen them?" Gabby asked.

"Oh, hell no. If I'm working a late shift, I go a different way home, and that road is a major shortcut to my place. I would probably cover my eyes and fly off that bridge if anything happened. I'm a big scaredy-cat, but I love a good story. I've never heard about them purposely hurting anyone, but there have been a few crashes just because people got so scared. Boss says he only knows about two people that died. I'm glad you're all okay."

"I wouldn't say completely okay," Gabby said. "That train made it worse. While we were running, it flew by and scared the crap out of us."

"What train?" the bartender asked.

"The one on the east side of the road. It passed by quickly."

"There aren't any train tracks there."

"What do you mean?"

"I mean, there are no train tracks. I've lived here my whole life and have worked here for five years. This is new. I'll be right back."

Angie let her ears go. "What happened?"

"Do you really want to know?" Ree asked.

"No. I mean, yes. No. Yes, tell me, but don't make a scary voice or anything."

Ree told her and slammed his hand on the table as he said, "First time in TEN years someone got kissed!"

Angie jumped and smacked him on the shoulder. "Asshole!"

The bartender came back with the food about fifteen minutes later.

"So, some news. I talked to Sammy and our night manager, Suzanne. Suzanne's worked in this area for over forty years and knows a lot more about its history than anyone I know. She said there used to be tracks here, built back in the 1800s. However, there was a bad derailing in the late 70s and those tracks were shifted to the outside of town a few years later. I never even knew that, and this is the first time I've heard anything about a train. She said the same thing. You must be the first to experience a ghost train."

"Ghost train?" Ree asked. "Lucky us."

"You aren't kidding. Dinner's on the house. That's the best story we've had in a long time, and the train just added even more spice to it. The Boss loved it. Can I take your picture? He wants to keep it so he can put faces to the story he said he'll be telling for years."

They were in no mood to pose, but Ree perked up. "Yes! Go ahead."

Angie didn't look directly at the bartender's phone camera, and Gabby tried to force a smile. They may not have wanted to take the picture, but were grateful for the free meal.

"Thank you!" the bartender said.

"Glad we could oblige," Gabby said. "Please thank Sammy and Suzanne for us."

The bartender smiled as she returned to the bar.

The wings were plump and steaming, and they realized how hungry they were. They ate, and it helped calm them down. With all the running and adrenaline, the food was a welcome distraction.

"These wings are pretty good, Ree," Gabby said.

"Hell of a night," Angie said, feeling calmer with each bite. "Sorry I freaked out. I don't even know what to think."

"This is my fault," Gabby said. "Maybe you both need to stay away from me for a while."

"Nonsense," Ree said. "That may be the most scared I've been in my life, even worse than the woman I saw with my cousin, but we won't abandon you. What kind of ass would I be if I did that?"

"The same kind of ass who took off running and left us behind to possibly die," Angie said.

"Nobody told you to wear the hooker pumps!" Ree said. "That's a disadvantage you chose and I should not be punished for."

"My eyes were covered!" Angie said.

"Another bad decision!" he yelled.

"You ditched us, Ree," Gabby said. "We know you'll abandon us first if the Apocalypse ever happens."

"I'll speak well of you both since I'll be the one that survives," Ree said. "And tell everyone I tried to save you."

"Just for that, you're letting me borrow your spare tire once we get my car home," Angie said.

"It's not borrowing if you keep it!" Ree said. "But I accept my punishment. My spare's not in great shape, so get a new tire tomorrow, or I will tell your dad."

"Fine!" Angie said as her phone dinged.

"Tow truck's here."

They thanked the bartender again and rode in the tow truck to get the car.

They all stayed in the truck as the driver hooked up Angie's vehicle and got it ready for the tow. They didn't want to be there any longer than they had to be. The flashlight was still on the ground, and Angie nodded when the tow truck guy picked it up to show it to her.

On the way to Angie's house, Gabby called her sister.

"Hey, Teri. We had a blowout and got delayed. Were you still up?"

"Yes, it's still early for me. You can leave Ally if you'd like. She's fast asleep."

"No, I'll have Ree take me home once we get to Angie's. Maybe another thirty minutes."

Gabby knew it would be best to leave her but wanted to get home as soon as possible and her car was still at her sister's.

"Just stay with me," Angie said. "Jenna's still out of town for work and I don't want to be alone. I'll be able to take you early tomorrow once Ree puts his spare on my car."

Gabby thought about it and nodded. "Never mind, Sis. I'm going to stay at Angie's. I'll leave her tonight. Thanks."

They got back to Angie's place.

Ree didn't want to go home or sleep in separate rooms. Gabby and Angie slept on the king size bed and Ree threw a pillow on the floor.

"Get your bailing-ass up here," Angie said. "There's plenty of room. I'll put a pillow between you and me so you can keep your parts to yourself. Jenna might get jealous."

They talked for a little while. Once they were convinced it was going to be a quiet rest of the night, it only took two hours for them to fall asleep. Ree was the first one to crash. Angie turned to look at Gabby.

"I'm afraid to be the last one to go to sleep," Angie said.

"Then let's go to sleep now," Gabby said.

Angie was down within five minutes. Gabby closed her eyes and pretended she had, too, but her mind was racing. She kept thinking about how this was her fault and wanted to know why it was happening to her. What had she done? That face. At work and now on their night out. Was that thing in her house with her and Ally? She didn't even know she was being watched at work until Jay showed up. So how long had it been happening? She was thinking about the upcoming visit from this so called expert and just hoped he could help.

It was the last thing she thought about before she finally fell asleep.

CHAPTER FOURTEEN

GABBY DRAGGED ALL DAY. AFTER GETTING HER CAR AND TAKING Ally some extra clothes and supplies for her first official day with Teri, she made it to her class and crammed her homework in after getting there an hour early. Fortunately, she had read up on some of it a few days before. Barry was in a couple of her classes, but they sat on opposite sides of the room and avoided each other. Even so, Gabby was too tired to care.

Once she got to work, Ed didn't mention the mess she left the day before, so she picked up right where she left off. Since she had finished most of her adjustments before she ran out, it didn't take her long. She left the door open all day and covered the computer monitor with a cloth.

Ed came by later.

"Gabby, everything good? Have a good time last night?"

"Yes, is something wrong? Meeting?"

He rarely spoke to her when she was working. Typically, he would only come by just before he left for the day, unless there was a meeting or something unexpected.

"No, everything's fine." He looked around and made an odd face when he saw the computers.

"Is something wrong with the computer screen?" he asked.

"Oh, no, it's fine. The screensaver was bothering me, so I covered it."

"Oh, okay. Maybe you can change it before you leave to something less distracting."

"I'll try to do that," she said.

He looked at the monitor again and then back. "The Thespian display is coming together nicely. Just a few more pieces to set up and you can put it all together for the big Donor Showcase. I'm excited to see it. We should be getting the new signs and flyers, and we'll send out press releases once it's ready for the public. I have a photographer coming in as soon as you give the word."

"If all goes well, they may be ready for pictures by next week. Still need one more supply order after this one. I checked the shipment and it should be here by Friday at the latest. Plenty of time before the donors get their sneak peek."

"Excellent. I think this will be a nice shot in the arm for our exhibit. It's looking great so far. Just like your mother, you have some excellent ideas."

She smiled as she thought of her mom. "Thank you, Ed. I hope it works out."

"I'm sure it will. I'll let you get back to work."

He left, and she finished up the final touches. She was done in under two hours. She looked back at the covered monitor, realizing now she had to change the screen saver or he'd know something was up.

She got on the machine and started to sweat a little as she went in to modify the display settings. She chose a beach setting. Sand, a palm tree and water. No, not water. She looked around and found one with just sand. She wanted nothing reflective. Although she knew the entire screen was reflective and it made no sense, fear outweighed her logic.

Gabby kept herself busy with forms and some paperwork so she wouldn't start something she couldn't finish. She left five minutes after five. The paranormal expert was coming tonight, and she wanted to be prepared. She was cooking. Jay, Ree, and the expert would be there.

Her phone dinged. It was Angie.

"Hey, Gabby. I'll be there tonight."

"You don't have to, Angie. Really."

"Ally is going to be home, right?"

Teri had school events with the kids and couldn't watch her.

"Yes, she'll be in her room or with me if she's fussy."

"I'll be designated babysitter if she gets rowdy," Angie said. "I can't guarantee I'll watch the festivities, but I'll do my best."

"Okay," Gabby replied. "That actually would help. I'm making lasagna."

"That is a big motivator but has no bearing on why I'll be there."

"With banana pudding as a side."

"That's not fair. That does have a bearing. See you at 7."

Gabby got Ally settled in her playpen and started cooking as soon as she got home. She had cooked more in the last weeks for these paranormalists than she had in ages. She learned to cook from her mother and grandmother, but typically only had time to make quick meals for herself. She was too busy to spend time cooking, but she had enjoyed preparing the last few guest meals. She concentrated on the recipes and the ingredients, taking her mind off what was going on.

Everyone arrived a few minutes before 7. Ree drove with Angie. Jay and the expert arrived together.

The expert walked in and looked around the house. He wore a black short-sleeve button-up shirt and she could see several tattoos along his upper arms. Nothing familiar.

"Gabby, this is Benji," Jay said. "He was the one I was hoping I could get to come. He's sought after for things like this and when I told him your story, it intrigued him enough to reply. We're really fortunate to have him."

"Yes," Benji said. "If what Jay's told and shown me is true, I'm definitely intrigued."

"Do you do this full time?" Gabby asked.

"I spend a significant amount of time with it. My full-time job is working at my family's funeral home."

"Funeral home?"

"Yes, my family's owned one for three generations. That's where I first learned I had the ability to see and sense things. I've spoken to dead spirits that linger around the funeral home, but I've seen so much more. I also occasionally help the authorities. Unofficially, of course. I do private readings when it's interesting. There are so many people that think a plumbing leak in their kitchen is a dead spirit haunting them and causing them to act crazy. Usually they are just seeking an excuse for abhorrent behavior. I know what exists, but also know that human nature often makes people see or hear what's usually not there and believe with limited to no evidence. Even though I know there's more than our visible world, I am the ultimate skeptic. Don't get me wrong, I've witnessed plenty of legitimate issues, but they are rare."

"So, what are we doing tonight?" Gabby asked.

"I understand you've made dinner. That wasn't necessary."

"Well, Jay said you wouldn't charge for tonight, so I felt I had to thank you both somehow."

"I appreciate it. Let's talk as we eat. I'd like to get to know you and understand what's been happening. Straight from you."

They sat down to eat with Ally in her high chair. They took a few bites before Benji turned to her.

"Start with when you first noticed anything was amiss. Even the smallest thing."

Gabby thought about it. "Some odd things at work. I work with dead bodies used in scientific exhibits."

"A fair feeding ground for something paranormal," he said.

"Do you always talk like that?" Angie asked.

"What do you mean?"

"You sound medieval."

"My apologies. There is a bit of morbid show involved in what I do, but do not mistake that for lack of sincerity."

Gabby got to the point leading up to the night before.

"Everything seemed to have calmed down for a short time, but now it's been consistent up through last night's concert. Up until then, everything that had happened had been around work or the house. Well, except for the gas station incident. That was outside the house but could have just been a coincidence."

"You were in your vehicle with your family, correct?"

Gabby nodded.

"Please tell me what happened the night of the concert."

Angie got up. "I'll go eat with Ally in her room."

She picked up Ally and carried her in one arm while taking their food in the other. It was too soon for her to hear this story again.

Gabby started with the concert and described how they were having a good time and how relieved she was not thinking about what was happening for a little while. Then detailed how the blowout occurred at the exact moment that Ree uttered his words. Then she told them about the married couple, the train, and the story the bartender shared with them at dinner.

Benji sat and thought for a long moment. He extended his hands, one in front of Gabby and another for Ree.

"What? Why do you need my hand?" Ree asked.

"Apparently, you were the trigger that started the events of that night. I want to sense what you both felt if I am able."

Ree looked at Gabby and she nodded.

"I'm in," she said as she placed her palm on Benji's.

"I think I should get bonus friend points over Angie for this," he said as he took Benji's hand.

Benji closed his eyes. There were no crystal balls or flashes of light, just Benji swaying his head and squeezing their hands intermittently. His neck craned back like he had a back spasm and the chair squealed as it shot backward. Everyone at the table jumped.

Benji breathed in several times. Deep, heaving breaths, then opened his eyes.

He gently let go of their hands.

"What did you see?" Gabby asked.

"I saw and sensed some of what you described. I felt the sense of fear that something was behind you and can tell you that most of the time, it was there. What happened to you all that night, though, that was different. There are two phases you've experienced. The first is seeing whatever is stalking you, and I don't believe it's a ghost. I've sensed spirits and ghosts before, but their signatures are unique. Similar to smelling an orange. If you were blindfolded and someone put an orange near your nostrils, you would know it's an orange. That's how I see death and spirits. This is no orange. It's darker and has a distinct scent. I've caught minor whiffs of darkness in my years of doing this but have never been able to hold a solid grasp long enough to know what it truly is. This was the first strong scent I felt throughout. Whatever has singled you out is not a ghost. That I can tell you definitively."

He paused.

"What is it?" Gabby asked.

"I'm not sure. I can tell you what it isn't, which may not sound like much help, but it is important. This scent has gotten stronger and stronger with each passing day and each passing event. At first, I imagine it was confined to your work or wherever it may have originated. It then was strong enough to follow you into your home and then with your family in your car. It's gaining more and more strength, and then this night with your friends. That is the most peculiar. It's fresh, so I get a stronger sense of what you both experienced, but based on what the bartender told you, the events with the married couple and the train stood out. Those were old hauntings and old paranormal memories. The ghost couple has been spotted by others and they are a local legend. That train a distant memory. However, you saw the face of this creature in the reflection on the ground in between."

Gabby felt her face flush and her head throb. "What does that mean?"

"I don't know. I need more time. I need to determine the origin, but what makes sense is that whatever this thing is has gotten so powerful that as it followed you last night, it spurred on other paranormal phenomena in its vicinity. The energy it created was like a catalyst to other otherworldly phenomena and stirred them awake. I think if there had been a Civil War battle site nearby, soldiers for the Blue and the Gray would have come out fighting as you passed by. The train and married couple are not related to what is happening with you but were coaxed by the unexpected surge of energy that was released at that moment."

"Why?" Gabby asked. "Why me?"

"There is never an easy answer to that, Gabby. It could be something peculiar about your soul or your environment. If it was a true haunting of you as a person, I'd most likely know the answer, but whatever is after you is far more powerful than a pesky ghost. There are several things it could be, but none are good, I'm afraid. I will need to go to your work to see if we can find the origin. Jay mentioned he didn't get far during his visit. If that is truly where everything started, I might be able to determine that and hopefully narrow down what caused this to come to you and your world. It's permeating not only your essence but things around you. The first step to finding a solution is finding the source."

They stopped talking for a minute as they let it all sink in.

"So what do we do now? Do we go to my work tonight or tomorrow?"

"For now," he said. "I would love to finish this incredible food. It's the best meal I've had in ages."

"After what you just told me, should we go tonight?"

"No, not tonight. I need preparation time."

"And what will this cost?"

"Nothing. This is an exceptional event. I just want permission to share my findings if there is anything of substance. Having an opportunity to zero in on this scent is worth more to me than money. Then again, it could lead to more money later, to be fully forthcoming. I will need your help, Jay. This is beyond a one-man job."

"How much time do you need?" Gabby asked.

"I would set aside at least a couple of hours for setup, implementation and cleanup."

"Cleanup?" Gabby asked.

"Could get messy when you poke at beasts from the other side. Can you arrange tomorrow?"

"Yes, I think so."

"Then tomorrow we shall continue."

He stopped talking and finished his meal.

Dinner tonight, poking at beasts tomorrow. Gabby's calendar was getting stranger by the day.

CHAPTER FIFTEEN

As Gabby walked out of class, she pulled out her phone and saw a voicemail notification from a number she didn't recognize. Her first thought was a telemarketer, but with everything that was going on, she didn't want to risk missing something important.

"Hello, Gabby? I'm really sorry to call you, but this is Rhonda over at Steeplechase Apartments. I know you'd be happy to never hear from us again, but we found something that I think belongs to you. Feel free to call me back anytime. If you don't, I'll understand, but looks like something you may want back. Again, I'm sorry to have to call, but had to try."

Rhonda left the return number and there was a short gasp like she took in a breath to say something else, but then she hung up.

Gabby got to her car and sat in it for a minute, trying to decide whether to call.

She stared at her phone and dialed. It went to voicemail.

"Rhonda, this is Gabby. I just got your message. I can head over now."

She drove to the apartments, taking a route she had avoided for a long time. Whenever she neared the main road that led to the complex, she typically turned right to avoid having to pass anywhere near the former home she shared with her husband for two years.

She kept on the path and as she neared it, she realized the complex, which had a green theme when she lived there, had been repainted a golden brown. She pulled in and the main office was in the same location. Other than the new coat of paint, it looked exactly the same.

Gabby entered and recognized her former apartment manager immediately. She was short, with a full body and thick, strong legs. Her long nails, which used to sport various bright neon colors, didn't disappoint. They were bright orange and stood out from her dark pantsuit.

She was on the phone and didn't recognize Gabby at first, but as she got within a few feet of the desk, she looked up and her smile straightened in an unsure horizontal line. She motioned for Gabby to sit as she finished up her call.

"I understand. I'll follow up and I'll get back to you before the end of the day. I promise."

She hung up, then tried hard to smile.

"You look good, Gabby. I'm so sorry you had to come back here."

Gabby nodded. "It's okay, Rhonda. It's not as bad as I thought it might be. Not yet, at least. Your message. You said you found something of mine?"

Rhonda reached into her desk and pulled something out, holding it in her fingers.

"I have a great memory when it comes to certain things. Nails, watches, but especially jewelry. I am pretty sure I saw you wear this back when you lived here."

She held out an earring. A gold earring with a one-carat,

brilliant diamond in a teardrop shape. Seeing it triggered Gabby's memory. A second anniversary gift.

Gabby reached out and took it.

"You are observant," she said. "This is definitely mine. I have the other one in a jewelry box at home."

"I thought so. Can you just sign for it? I'm sure you don't want to be here longer than you have to."

"Where did you find it?" Gabby asked.

Rhonda paused. "We found it in your old apartment."

"After two years?"

"Yes, we were getting some repairs done and one of the drywall folks found it."

"It was never found by the people that moved in after us?"

"Well, sort of."

"What do you mean?"

"Are you sure you want to hear this?"

"Please, it's okay. I really want to know."

"After what happened with your…"

"My late husband," Gabby said. "You don't have to sugar coat it. After my husband died in the apartment."

Rhonda cleared her throat.

"After your husband died in the apartment, it was difficult to rent. We had to disclose there had been a death in the place. We finally rented it a little over a year later to a couple that cared more about the discount than the history. They just moved out last week and did some minor damage that had to be repaired."

Gabby stared at the earring. She remembered looking and looking for it but couldn't remember why and was overcome with a need to know more.

"Can you show me where it was found?"

"Gabby, are you sure?"

"Yes, Rhonda. Please. For some reason, I can't remember how I lost it. I want to see if the room will jog a memory."

"Do you want more memories coming up?"

"Nothing can be worse than that night," Gabby said. "Maybe I just want to check if I'm really past it."

Rhonda picked up her phone. "Jony? Can you cover me? I need to escort a guest to one of the apartments."

Two minutes later, a young woman walked in to relieve her and Rhonda led Gabby outside. The apartment was located in the second building on the third floor. Gabby walked up the flights of steps and the memories of heading up and down, especially when she had been pregnant, filled her head.

They got to the room and Rhonda opened it up.

Gabby entered and felt her breath suck in. The apartment was empty, but she immediately pictured their couch and coffee table in their original places in the living room.

It didn't hit her as hard as she thought it might. She was relieved that she didn't immediately break down and run out of the room, which is what she figured Rhonda was expecting.

Rhonda moved forward and into what had been their bedroom. It was a two bedroom, single bath apartment and the master bedroom was generous. It was the main reason they had picked this layout.

Rhonda moved to the wall nearest the closet. The room smelled like wet paint.

"There," Rhonda said, pointing to the lower wall between the closet and the bedroom door. "There was a crack in this section of the wall and our repairman had to cut out a piece of the drywall and replace it. The earring was inside."

Gabby stared for a moment, then felt her knees give. She lost her balance and fell onto the carpet, kneeling as her left leg went numb.

"Gabby, are you okay?"

Gabby held up her hand, holding her off. "Yes, I just need a minute."

"Take as much time as you need," Rhonda said. "I'm sure this can't be easy."

"That's the thing," Gabby said. "I was starting to believe it might be."

Rhonda put her hand on Gabby's shoulder and gave her a look of sympathy.

"Do you mind giving me a few minutes alone?" Gabby asked. "I want to get beyond this. The therapist I used to see taught me how to face things head on, but I wasn't too good at that. I mean, I never came back here."

"Sure," Rhonda said. "Just lock the door behind you and come see me when you're done. No one is scheduled to be here the rest of the day."

"Thank you," Gabby said, giving in to her wobbly leg and taking a seat on the carpeted floor.

Rhonda walked out.

Gabby stared at the wall. How could she have forgotten? She had just come home after one of her undergraduate classes was canceled at the last minute. She arrived about thirty minutes earlier than usual and passed a blonde woman coming down the stairs as she was on her way up. She looked familiar, and then Gabby remembered who she was. Nicole. She worked with her husband.

Once she recognized her, she rushed up the stairs and entered her place and found the door unlocked. Her husband yelled from the bedroom, "You forget something? Hurry up. She'll be here in less than an hour."

Gabby entered the bedroom, her tears already falling. The elation of finding out she was pregnant only five weeks prior was still fresh and carrying her through her toughest class days, but the elation ended the moment she opened the door.

"You were a shitty husband," Gabby said out loud.

"Was I?" someone said.

She looked up from where she was seated and Michael was standing in the bedroom doorway, staring at her. She crawled back from the sight of her long-dead husband, dropping her purse as she dragged her bottom against the carpet to move away.

"What? How?"

"Reminiscing?" he asked in his deep, condescending voice.

Gabby flashed back to her therapy session where Dr. Mora talked to her about her vivid memories and nightmares of Michael after his death. He looked so real, but the therapist assured Gabby it was just her mind's way of dealing with the pain of her marriage and losing her husband. The visit to the apartment must have triggered it. She hadn't seen him this clearly while awake since three months after Michael was buried.

"I know you're not here, Michael," Gabby said, breathing rapidly. "Just my way of dealing with the hell you put me through."

Gabby's dead husband took a step into the room and looked back at the spot she had been fixated on.

"The wall? Why would you come back here and look at that wall?"

Her old therapist's instructions kicked in.

Don't fear what you see. Confront it. Deal with it. Control it or it will always control you.

Gabby stared at her purse. It was close to Michael and out of her reach. She had never owned a gun in her life, but bought one after her marriage ended and still kept it in her purse. In her head, she knew he wasn't real, yet the desire to grab the gun was still there.

"Don't keep me in suspense, Gabby. What's with the wall?"

Gabby decided to engage.

"My earring. The earrings you bought me the first time I caught you cheating. I thought it was over, but that day I came home early and found Nicole leaving our place. That was the day you went from being a cheater to being a wife-beater. You remember that, coward?"

Michael smiled at her.

"Yes, I remember. I held back for so long, thinking about hurting you all the time, but to have my fantasy actually come to fruition? It was exhilarating."

"You slammed my head through that wall, you worthless bastard. I must have blocked that memory because I didn't remember it until I saw that wall again a few minutes ago. My head hit it so hard that one of the earrings fell inside. They just found it today."

"What a wonderful memory. It's nice to have some activity in this apartment again. I was alone for so long until the new couple moved in. I enjoyed their company. That man was so much worse than I was. You should ask Rhonda."

Gabby shook her head. Her own psyche was playing mind games with her.

"It took knocking me around to make you feel like a real man. I was bleeding, almost passed out, and you still took me. I was so out of it I couldn't say no, but I do remember that being the hardest you'd ever been. It's a miracle that soft, worthless member between your legs was even able to get me pregnant."

Michael rushed her and reached out for her neck. Gabby gasped as his hand went through her and she started to sweat heavily. She crawled backward until her back hit the opposite wall.

Gabby closed her eyes and shook her head. "Come on, Gabby, he's not real."

She opened her eyes and screamed in his direction. "You're not real!"

"I'm as real as you believe I am," Michael said.

"You only knew about Nicole and the first girl, Debbie. You never found out about the others. There were so many, but you were too caught up in wanting to have a baby and finishing school you didn't notice. It was so easy. Why don't you ask Rhonda what she knows? You never realized how many times you slept on a bed that was soiled with the fluids of another woman. It was the greatest feeling seeing you and imagining what had happened on those sheets just a few hours before. You were completely clueless."

"But in the end, you weren't so smart, were you?" Gabby yelled. "You took it too far that one last night. You tried to kill Ally before she was even born. How smart are you if you were stupid enough to lose your life for it? Was that last chance to beat me in order to feel like a man worth it? Because you died, you son of a bitch. And I was happy you did. That may have been one of the best days of my life, watching you let out your last breath. You'll never touch me again."

Her anger took over, and she stood up and ran at him. As she reached him, he disappeared. She lifted her hands to stop her momentum against the closet door.

"Coward," she whispered as she rushed out of the room and returned to the office.

Rhonda was back at her desk.

"You okay?" she asked as she saw Gabby sweating profusely.

"I just had some things to deal with."

"Anything… strange happen?"

Gabby looked at her. "Why would you ask that?"

"No reason."

"Rhonda, be straight with me. Why would you ask that?"

Rhonda shook her head. "I don't want to upset you."

Gabby stared her down until Rhonda was visibly shaking.

"The last couple. They reported hearing and seeing things a few times. Really just the wife. She described Michael to a tee."

Gabby sat down.

Rhonda's eyes widened. "Something did happen, didn't it?"

"I saw him. I thought it was just my mind coping. Hold on. What was the story of this couple?"

"You know I can't tell you that."

"Rhonda, one thing I remember is you never hesitating for some good gossip. Tell me, how many people have you told my story to? The pregnant woman getting beaten and cheated on. If you never repeated that to another tenant, tell me so and I'll leave. If you have, then you at least owe me the courtesy of telling me what happened with this couple."

Rhonda sighed. "They were a couple without any kids. The husband was arrested. He beat her over the head with a pipe. She survived, but he did a number on her."

Gabby waited for more. "Is that it?"

"No. The woman came for her deposit yesterday and said the man she described as Michael was egging him on. Her husband never saw Michael the entire time they lived there, but she said he would show up on nights when her husband decided to beat her. Said he had never touched her until they moved into that apartment."

Gabby covered her face with her hands. "I have another question for you before I go, and I want the truth."

"What is it?"

"Did you sleep with my husband?"

"What? No! Why would you think that?"

"Michael just told me he slept with more women than I realized. He said to ask you what you know."

Rhonda's eyes shifted down and to the side.

"Rhonda. He's dead. I don't give a shit about him or my past. Other than giving me Ally, I wish I'd never married him and I'm glad he's gone. You'll probably never see me again after today, so just tell me."

"We had some rooms being prepped a few years ago and the carpenters and electrician were behind schedule. I decided to drop in and see what the delay was. They were supposed to have been reinstalling a ceiling fan and redoing some wiring. I walked in the room and I found Melinda, my assistant, and Michael having a conversation in the middle of the living room and when Michael saw me, he disappeared."

Gabby closed her eyes and tried to concentrate on her breathing.

"Then it wasn't my mind playing tricks on me. That was Michael's spirit."

"I can't say for sure, Gabby. I've never seen anything like that before that day or since, and the wife is the only one who has ever said anything. And Melinda. I told her the story, and she saw him disappear. She said she found Michael just standing in the room and he started flirting with her. She quit right then and there."

"He knew you knew about one of the women, Rhonda. He said the husband was worse than he was. There's no way I could have known either one of those things. I don't even know who these last tenants were!"

Rhonda cupped her hands over her mouth and didn't know what to say or do.

Gabby thought about what was happening and how this was the second dead man she had seen and spoken to in the last few days. One helped her save a life, and the other was trying to destroy it again.

Dead or not, I'm not giving you the satisfaction.

Gabby stopped shaking. She reached her hand out and dropped the earring. "This was a gift of guilt. One that I accepted as an apology for the sake of my marriage because I was young and scared. I have never considered myself weak, except for those years of hell I was married. Michael will never control me again, not even after his death. Keep this. Sell it. Give it away. I don't care. And thank you."

"Why would you possibly thank me, Gabby? I am so sorry."

"You helped me deal with something I didn't know I still had to deal with. Right now, my anger has overtaken any fear this place used to hold over me. Believe me, the anger is better."

Gabby stood up and left a source of some of her worst memories, knowing she would never return again. As angry as she was and despite what she'd just told Rhonda, there was no denying the fear was still there. It was an undercurrent just below the surface of her anger, begging for release.

CHAPTER SIXTEEN

GABBY TRIED TO SHAKE THE IMAGE OF SEEING MICHAEL AND reliving her worst nightmares. She wanted all of it to stop and was looking forward to Benji's visit later, hoping he could help end this.

Gabby arranged for Teri to keep Ally through the evening so Benji could meet at her work by 7 pm, but she had to talk to Ed first.

She arrived for her shift, went straight to her boss's office, and knocked on the door.

"Gabby! Please, come in."

"I have some friends that were asking about the exhibit, Ed. One has connections that he said might be interested in a sponsorship or donation."

"That sounds like a grand opportunity! Should we wait for your thespian exhibit or invite them to the Donor Showcase?"

"Actually, they're only in town until tonight. I mentioned the exhibit and wanted to give them a behind-the-scenes view of what I've accomplished so far. They don't want a formal introduction and don't want to raise any expectations. Figured I could host them here for a couple of hours."

Ed smiled and nodded his head. "Of course, Gabby. I trust you to do your best. Your mother brought in plenty of donations and investors over her time here. Just let me know how it goes tomorrow."

"Of course, Ed. I will. Thank you. I'll be sure to lock up when we're done."

He smiled as she closed his office door. Everything was set. Now she just had to get through the day without being scared out of her mind. She left her door open as she worked in the Emergency Room, even though there were windows with views to the Showroom and Ed's office. She saw one computer monitor flicker a few times but refused to turn. She heard motions around her and as she tried to position a book into the hands of The Runner display, representing an actor reading their lines, it shook as she placed it. She closed her eyes and swallowed, working hard to maintain her composure. She concentrated on her task and kept going.

Tonight. Just ignore it until tonight.

Her hope in Benji's visit kept her from running out the door and fortunately, the book shaking was the worst thing that happened for the rest of the day.

Gabby slowed down as she hit a stopping point and timed it so she left at the same time as Ed. "I need to get a few things ready, so I'm leaving now."

"No worries at all. Do what you must and good luck," Ed said.

Gabby went straight to Teri's to spend a few minutes with her daughter. She wasn't sure how long the night would take, and Ally's absence from the daycare in her work building was affecting her more than she wanted to admit. The kids greeted her, and then Teri sent them to their rooms.

"You don't usually leave work so early," Teri said. "I guess tonight is important."

"Yes," Gabby said. "Hopefully tonight will shed some light on whatever's happening. The sooner we get past this, the sooner I can visit my nieces and nephew unsupervised."

Teri looked down. "I deserve that but will not apologize for it."

"I know, Sis. It doesn't make it feel any better, but I get it."

"Then I hope whatever you have planned for tonight helps. I'd love for things to get back to normal."

GABBY WENT STRAIGHT BACK TO THE OFFICE AFTER STOPPING TO pick up a salad and ate it in the parking lot. She didn't want too much food in her system. She was already starting to get nervous and the last thing she needed was to cause all that food to come back up if things got crazy again.

Benji, Jay, and Ree all arrived within minutes of each other. Benji carried a large duffle bag and Jay a smaller one. Angie was at home, waiting for an update when it was all over.

Gabby gave Benji a quick tour of the office, emphasizing the Showroom and the ER where most of the activity had occurred so far.

Benji pulled a laptop from his bag and plugged in a USB stick.

Jay pulled out the EMF he had used before, but he also had a few other items she didn't recognize and placed some small boxes in different areas of the large Showroom and ER.

"What is all this?"

"Let's see. This is the EMF I used the other day, but we also have some recording devices. This one is something called an EVP, which stands for Electric Voice Phenomenon.

Sometimes audio recordings, when you listen to them close enough, pick up voices. Voices you may not hear at the time, but some that are trying to have a conversation. I also have digital cameras and digital video cameras. And finally, Benji brought his really nice infrared thermal imaging camera. I have a handheld portable thermal gun that's more in my budget, but they serve the same purpose."

"Wow. I didn't realize so much equipment was involved," Gabby said.

"These are just a set of tools," Benji said, listening in to the conversation. "This represents only a small collection, but even with the more sophisticated equipment, I do not fully depend on or trust it."

"Then why bring it at all?"

"In the event I am unable to pick up anything naturally, this may serve a purpose. I am not infallible. If the equipment picks up enough evidence, I may revisit at a different time. It's not a perfect system, but as I told you initially, I am a skeptic first. How did today go? Were there any incidents?"

"I sensed plenty in the ER," Gabby said. "I didn't acknowledge any of it, but it did shake a book prop I was using and I'm sure there were reflections trying to grab my attention."

"Since you didn't notice much of this activity at first, I asked Jay to place cameras and a few recording devices in some of the additional rooms as well."

After almost thirty minutes, they seemed to be ready.

"That was the last one," Jay said.

"Let's start in the ER," Benji ordered. "Since there is a display as well as computer monitors where you've witnessed activity."

They moved into the room. Benji pulled up a chair.

"Gabby, I need you to begin working on the display, even

if you're not actually doing anything. Please try to mimic a normal, mundane workday."

She found her kit and started to break and readjust some of the settings she had put together earlier. They were just prop related, so she didn't have to damage the display in any way.

Nothing happened for the next five minutes.

"Should I stop?" she asked.

"No, I just wanted to see if there would be any interaction without trying to entice it."

"So how are you going to entice it now?"

"I think whatever it is, it's attempting to conceal itself. The scent is faint, but I feel it may be stronger than it's letting on. I must prove my theory. Know that you are in no danger from me, so I must apologize ahead of time. Please just trust me for the next few minutes."

"Trust you for what?"

Benji put his hand on Gabby's shoulder. "This woman, Gabriella Mendez Alfonso, does not belong to you. You may try to claim her, but she is henceforth MINE to do with as I please. She cannot and will not be claimed by another!"

He was looking up, screaming into the air.

Benji closed his eyes, still shifting around and not letting go of Gabby. He pulled himself closer to her.

"She is mine and you have no claim!"

He pulled her closer and squeezed tight. Gabby grimaced as she attempted to stifle a yell, but one muffled scream escaped.

"Hey!" Ree yelled and tried to enter the room.

"It's okay, Ree," Jay said. "Just trust him."

Ree looked at Gabby. She was wincing but nodded toward him. She was willing to do whatever was needed to figure this out.

Ree took a step back and acknowledged her.

"Do you hear me?" Benji yelled.

He wrapped an arm around Gabby's neck.

"Since you do not wish to dispute my claim, she is mine to do with as I please. I choose to release her soul."

He pulled out a dagger from his jacket. He pulled it up to her neck while he held her down by her shoulder.

Now she was scared. She started to yell, but then Benji gave her a side eye stare and winked at her. She held her scream and bit down on her lower lip, squeezing her fists together to absorb the pain.

"She is MINE!"

Benji raised the dagger and started to bring it down. He was blown back and the dagger went flying. The computer monitor shattered, and The Runner display spun around and fell over. Ree and Jay were slammed back from the doorway.

Benji was on the floor with two cameras and shattered equipment strewn all around him. The dagger he used landed several feet away from him and was standing on the blade tip, spinning.

"Benji!" Jay yelled.

Benji turned as the dagger spun faster. He looked around and picked up the EMF tool and lifted it just as the dagger shot across the room toward him. The blade hit the EMF, which protected Benji a second before it would have speared him between the eyes.

"I yield!" Benji yelled. "I yield! She is yours and yours alone! Accept my resignation to your claim. She is not mine to do with as I please."

The room was quiet. Gabby jumped out of her seat and punched Benji in his face as he still lay on the floor.

"How could you not tell me you were going to do that!"

"They had to sense I was serious," Benji said as he rubbed his bleeding nose. "If your fear was false, they would have sensed it."

"Well, did you at least find something?"

"My senses, yes. That was the most powerful scent I've ever received from this kind of antagonizing test. This presence rescinded itself. It doesn't like that we are here. Its strength, though. It's not just that it was loud, but it was amplified. Amplified enough to fill a sports stadium."

"What does that mean?"

"Let us go through our instruments and tools, assuming they are not all too damaged. I'll know more then. I'll verify what I can here, but will have to return to my place to inspect in greater detail. It may take a day or two."

"Okay," Gabby said.

"I also discovered you have a strong right hook."

"I took a self-defense class when I was an undergrad. You deserved that."

"That I did. Not the first time I've been struck."

"I'm sure you deserved those, too."

She helped Benji up and started to pick up the mess. Ree helped her as Benji and Jay gathered their things.

Benji grabbed his laptop and pulled the USB stick from the machine.

They found a table with some space.

Gabby and Ree moved behind them as Benji started going through the video footage. He synched the cameras and started them from the same beginning point, showing six windows in a two-row panel on the screen. He forwarded through. Underneath each picture was a line that moved up and down. The lines jumped up at times when they had been speaking.

"Is that recorded audio?" Gabby asked.

"Yes, under each video signal is the corresponding audio. One will pick up everything, but this green line below that blue standard line is set to monitor activity outside of the normal human audio spectrum. Such as something dogs might be able to hear that humans cannot."

He forwarded as they were setting up and slowed the speed down as they got closer to the time before Gabby sat in the chair.

The moment Gabby walked into the room there was a spike in activity.

"See that," Benji said. "There was a response the moment you walked in. It was faint, but there."

The activity was almost nil during the initial five minutes or so after Gabby had sat down. Then Benji started yelling. Again, nothing.

Once Benji yelled, "She is MINE," the signal went from flat to filling the entire vertical screen. It fluctuated as he kept speaking. Just before everything went haywire, Benji paused the footage.

"See that?"

He pointed toward the computer monitor.

He shifted back and forth between two frames. The screen from the computer that had shattered had the normal island screen saver one second and just as the software's line ticked up, the computer screen filled with two blurry eyes. Benji paused and then moved forward a few frames at a time. The screen blur grew and shifted into a smoky haze that emanated from the monitor and transformed into a circular cloud. The cloud that they did not notice crept toward them, then picked up momentum. Gabby's hair reacted like a huge burst of wind was blowing behind her, but the cloud simply passed through her and knocked Benji backward. It was like the wind surrounded her, yet left her untouched as it ejected Benji and tossed him away from her. Then something else flashed. Benji went back and forth several times.

"Can either of you distinguish what that might be?" he asked.

"Can you enhance it?" Jay asked.

"Yes, I believe so."

Benji took a screenshot and then opened up Photoshop on a separate screen. From there, he was able to zoom in and sharpen it. He went through three passes until finally it was clearer. There were framed pictures on the wall, a metal coffee mug, a mini-fridge underneath the table and an aluminum soda can that all flashed at the exact same time, revealing reflections of fleshy gray patches, a tooth and part of a yellow eye.

"This is incredible footage," Benji said. "It's like whatever emanated from that monitor moved to the opposite side of the room and knocked us down, all the while sparing Gabby from harm. Whatever this is, it seems there is some visible evidence of its existence that only manifests on reflective surfaces."

"Does that mean anything to you?" Gabby asked.

"Not exactly, but it provides a welcome starting point. I will utilize my resources both at home and within my network to study this further. My senses tell me that this is definitely supernatural, but has some corporealness to it."

"What is that in English?" Ree asked.

"It has some type of physical form, but it is extremely faint. My guess is it strengthens through its interaction with Gabby. However, something still perplexes me."

"What?" Gabby asked.

"This seems too powerful to not be a physical being. I have felt something similar in the past where two people were consumed with evil. They were both murderers. Sociopaths. I was behind the glass of a police interrogation room as the officers interviewed them. One was a serial killer who murdered seven teenage boys over three months. The darkness I felt within him was unique and strong but differs from what I am sensing now. Different but stronger, which tells me it should have a physical body, but it doesn't feel like it is human."

"Do you mean it's too strong?" Gabby asked.

"Not precisely. It may just be that I'm sensing this for the first time and misreading it. This footage will help."

"There is something," Gabby said. "I remembered it when the computer monitor shattered. The first time I actually noticed anything odd wasn't what I told you last night. It was the monitor. I saw a light flashing that I hadn't seen before. I just didn't realize at the time what it meant."

"Is this machine or the others in this room on a network?" Benji asked.

"Yes, the primary machines are in my boss's office, including our two main servers that hook up to the wider network, but all our computers are on the same network."

"Perfect. I need to know if you will grant me permission to access your network."

"Why?"

"I noticed you have at least one security camera and many of these machines have webcams."

"Yes, we use them for virtual meetings."

"I want to perform a deep dive and check if any of the other machines may show similar activity that coincides with what we have already seen and may yet find. There may be something worthwhile. I have a friend who runs in the supernatural circles who is an excellent hacker as well. She would be able to track down any pertinent information or anomalies."

Benji reached down into one of the bags he brought in.

"Just plug this in," he said as he handed her a USB stick.

"What is it?"

"It contains a password crack and some code that will scan all the computers in your network."

"Can we just do this now since no one is here?"

"No, it needs to be installed during a normal workday when most machines are online. We can't log on to machines that are turned off. The more information, the higher the probability of us finding something. As long as there isn't any military level software being used for the passwords, we should be fine."

"I'm pretty sure the security isn't anything complex. It's just entering a single password. Will I need to install this on my boss's computer or the servers in his office? I have access to all the main room keys."

Gabby knew the secret location of the master door keys. Unless Ed had moved them, which she doubted. He probably assumed no one knew, even though she and the office manager Marcy had seen him pull keys out of there more than once. There was a back compartment to one of the upper cabinets in the break room. It was in a box marked as rat poison, but it was an obvious hiding place once you realized that same box had been there almost three years.

"No, as long as his machine and servers are on, any computer on the network will do. Just try to place the USB during your next workday if you're able and ensure as many computers are powered on as possible. You should only need to leave it installed for ten to fifteen minutes and we can gather what we need. Just coordinate with me and I can tell you when to remove it."

"Okay. Today's Friday and the Exhibit will be open all weekend, so it'll have to wait until Monday. But I'll do it."

"That's actually fortuitous. It allows me additional time. Let's move to clean up and I'll continue on this tonight. I'm fascinated. It has been a long time since I had the opportunity to learn something new. Be cautious, Gabby. Although what-ever this is seems to be protecting you, I expect it may be for its own purpose. Something within or around you may be giving it strength or something it needs. Please watch yourself."

They all cleaned up except for Benji, who couldn't leave his computer screen. There were no other disturbances over the next hour. Gabby left a note on the cracked monitor for Ed, stating she accidentally hit it with her tools. It wouldn't be the first time equipment was accidentally damaged and she knew it would be replaced without incident, but she figured she would get ahead of it.

Finally, Benji stood up.

"That is all I am able to do for the evening. I do not want whatever's here to know what I see. Normally, ghosts are none the wiser, but since I don't know what we're dealing with, better to be safe. We will figure this out, Gabby. I promise."

CHAPTER SEVENTEEN

GABBY RETURNED TO WORK LATE ON MONDAY AFTERNOON. Marcy, the Office Manager met her on her way in and Gabby almost jumped out of her shoes.

"Sorry, Gabby! Didn't mean to sneak up on you like that. Just wanted you to know we saw your note. I hope you weren't hurt with the monitor screen!"

"Thank you, Marcy. I'm fine. No cuts or scrapes. I'm so sorry about that. Just lost my balance and smacked the screen with my tools."

"Don't even concern yourself with the machine. You're much more valuable and I'm just glad you're okay. Ed had me switch out the monitor this morning."

Gabby thanked her. She realized how nervous she was and focused diligently on her displays in The Showroom. She worried she might not get an opportunity to get the USB installed since she needed to get to the computer in the ER to avoid prying eyes. She was usually alone when she worked there, but people popped in and out sometimes or walked by. Around 2:45 in the afternoon, activity had slowed and she decided to proceed and texted Benji.

She pulled the USB stick out of her pocket and her hands were shaking.

It took four tries, but she finally got it attached. Just as Benji said, she didn't have to do anything. A red light on the USB stick started blinking and she heard the hard drive spinning.

It felt like a long time and she looked up, but only 30 seconds had passed.

Gabby gripped the stick with her thumb and index finger.

"Come on," she whispered.

"Hey Gabby!"

Gabby jumped as she turned to see Ed smiling at her.

"Sorry, didn't mean to startle you. Everything okay? I was going to ask if you were injured from the cracked monitor but Marcy said you were okay."

"Thanks for taking care of that so quickly, Ed."

"Of course. By the way, aside from the screen, how did it go with the potential investors?"

Gabby felt her breathing quicken as she tried to block Ed's view of the computer.

"Oh, they said they'd get back to me, but they seemed impressed."

She could feel the sweat coming down the side of her face.

"Hopefully you'll hear back from them soon. I'm heading to the coffee shop. Want anything?"

Of course. Ed made an almost daily mid-afternoon trip to the coffee shop downstairs for a drink and snack. He wasn't busting her for what she was doing. At least not yet.

"No thanks, Ed. I'm okay."

He nodded and as he turned to leave, Gabby let out a big breath and turned back to the computer screen.

She texted Benji. "How much longer? My boss just came in."

"Fifteen more minutes, tops."

Gabby wanted to seem less conspicuous but was afraid to leave the machine, so tried to act like she was going through some documents.

Eight minutes later, Ed returned. Gabby was facing the door, so didn't jump this time. He carried a drink carrier and a bag.

"Got you something."

"I didn't want anything," Gabby said, her voice shaking.

"I know. You seem a little jittery today. Figured you have a tough class assignment or maybe Ally was fussy last night. It's your favorite."

He lifted the drink carrier, revealing the sleeve with her name on it. She smiled, grabbed the drink, and took a sip. An iced coffee. Enough caffeine to get her through a tough day and cold enough to shock the system.

"Thank you. You have no idea how much I needed this."

Ed smiled. "Glad I could help."

He returned to his office.

Gabby settled down a little more with each sip and finally returned to watching the screen, relieved. She was only slightly startled when her phone dinged three minutes later.

"It's done," Benji texted. "You can remove it now."

The tension eased from her body as she removed the USB. She put it in her pocket and returned to the Showroom where she worked on The Gymnast. Gabby dove into her work to stay distracted and was still working when everyone had left for the day. She wanted to be gone by 5:30 so she wouldn't have to be alone too long.

As she turned to grab a tool, she was distracted by something on The Diver, directly behind The Gymnast.

She looked closer at The Diver's face. The left eye was looking to the far right and the other eye was looking straight.

"Crap."

She moved closer to the figure to get a better look at the damage.

"Who did that? Need to fix you."

She walked back to grab her tools, pulled out some instruments, and gloved up.

She reached into the eyeball and started to readjust it. She was slow and careful until it faced forward. None of the muscles seemed damaged. She took a step back and stared into the eyes.

Something was shining off each eyeball, like an image reflecting behind her.

She looked back, but there wasn't anyone else in the room.

She stared into the eyeball. There was something in that reflection. A face? A figure?

She moved closer until her own eye was less than an inch from the cadaver's.

Something was moving within the pupil.

"What is that?" she whispered, taking another look behind her. She glanced at the computer to see if that's what was reflecting, but the monitor was off.

She looked back, and the image was clearer. It was Benji, Jay and Ree. Then she saw herself, too. It was an image of them from the night before.

"How?" she thought as she felt her chest tighten.

She gasped and stepped back.

Could there have been a camera in the eye? Is that even possible?

A flash to her right distracted her.

She turned to face The Gymnast. There was a reflection there, too. She backed into the desk behind her and almost fell. Her lips quivered as sweat started to form on her forehead and her neck.

She looked at the other figures in the room. All of their eyes were glistening with motion. She moved away from them, slowly. Her legs wobbled and she almost lost her balance.

Then her vision went black. Her breath sucked in sharply and her body locked as blurry colors returned and started to focus. Something was passing in the front of her eyes, like looking up through a dark piece of dust that had landed on her retina. Something was there, blocking part of her vision. It flashed like an old film reel that was about to break. Dark and bright images alternated in and out of her view. They were only blurs, but she was frozen in a mix of fear and loss of control. She fell on her rear end and tried to make out what she was seeing.

The scrolling images started to slow down, and she found a spot and concentrated on it, holding her eyes still. She waited for the moving images to stop. Each passing slide continued to slow until she was finally able to focus on what it was.

It was Benji looking through his equipment. The moving image became still and Benji took up the entire slide.

Gabby finally let out a breath. The image dissolved and her vision was clear.

She looked up at The Gymnast and then to the other displays in the Showroom. That same image of Benji was now in each of their eyes. A tear of fear rolled down Gabby's cheek and she couldn't react. She was staring into the eyes, wondering what it all meant. Could it have just been her fear or possibly the guilt she felt for placing the USB?

Something popped. Then another pop followed. Gabby screamed as eyeballs flew out of their dead sockets and landed on the floor, all turning directly at her as they landed.

She felt something crack inside her as the reflections all went dark, leaving only the plain eyeballs. Had a bone shattered? No, she felt no pain.

Her breathing was shallow and quick, and she was able to

compose herself after a few minutes passed without any more activity.

She slowly felt around her torso to see what had cracked. She reached into her pocket. The USB was in pieces. Even if she had landed directly on it, it could not have broken into as many chunks as what was in her pocket.

She stared at a larger piece of debris as she pulled herself up.

"This is a warning, isn't it?" she asked aloud, staring at the eyeballs and bodies.

"He'll never come back. I promise. I don't belong to him. Please. Just stop."

There was no reaction, and no reflection returned.

She wanted to rush out of the room and head home, but she knew she couldn't leave the eyeballs on the floor.

"Promise you'll behave. I'll put your eyes back in. Please."

She stood there for more than five minutes before she forced herself to put on a fresh pair of gloves and moved to restore each eyeball. She did each one as quickly as she could, planning to detail them another day and verify each muscle was attached properly. She checked if there was any kind of chip or camera as she reattached them but found nothing.

She replaced them all without incident but still flinched each time she had to look directly into each eyeball.

She planned to heed this warning, but knew she was beyond the point of quitting. If she could deal with the spirit of her dead husband, she wasn't about to let this thing stop her or hurt her friends and family.

I'll find a way to stop this. I have to.

CHAPTER EIGHTEEN

GABBY TRIED TO WALK OUT OF THE OFFICE WITHOUT LOOKING panicked, but her hands were shaking as she set the alarm and locked the doors.

She walked quickly to the car and sat, unable to bring herself to put the car in gear to leave.

Why? Why is this happening to me? Did I do something to bring this on?

She covered her face and her chest started heaving and she found it hard to breathe. The eyeballs were all she could picture in her head. The images. The warning. Putting her family and friends in danger.

"I can't do this anymore. I just want it to stop."

She thought of Ally. Her sweet daughter helped keep her together when she was stressed. A hug and a kiss from this tiny human could soothe everything, but now she feared for her. Was she putting her own daughter in peril? Maybe she would be better off with Teri. Was it selfish to need her?

She finally opened her eyes and looked into the rear-view mirror. She looked cautiously, worried yellow eyes would appear, but she only saw her own eyes looking back at her.

Eyes with dark patches underneath them. Her eyes were red. She needed rest. She needed calm. She couldn't keep doing this.

"For Ally," Gabby said to her reflection. "You're going to figure this out for Ally. She's more important than anything else. Settle down and figure it out, Gabby. For her."

Gabby took in a few deep breaths until she felt better. She wanted to call Benji, but decided to get on the road and settle down some more.

She did some breathing exercises on her way to Teri's house. She didn't make much small talk and Teri didn't pry, although Gabby knew she could tell something was wrong. She also knew her "Don't ask" face.

Gabby wanted to talk to Angie or Ree to settle her nerves but didn't want to get riled up with Ally in the car, so turned up the radio instead.

Ally mumbled and was talking to her stuffed puppy. She was still having an intense conversation with her toy as Gabby carried her into the house.

Gabby set Ally on her high chair at the kitchen table and put her stuff down. She was mostly calm and processing what had happened in the office when Ally let out a small cough.

Gabby put her palm on Ally's chest. Ally didn't look up but coughed once more and then went back to playing with her toy.

"It's about time for you to eat, little girl. Let me get out of these clothes first."

She rushed to her bedroom and stripped off her clothes and got into some sweats and a tee shirt. She moved to the refrigerator and pulled out some cold cuts.

Ally let out a harsher cough. Gabby flipped around and Ally's eyes were staring back at her. She dropped her stuffed puppy as she coughed again, but this one was guttural. More like an adult's hack than a baby's high-pitched cough.

Gabby pulled her from the high chair and picked her up, gently patting her on the back.

"What is it, baby? Are you okay?"

Ally's cough got harder and more frequent. Four back-to-back heaves. Gabby patted her a little harder, hoping to loosen whatever she had stuck in her throat. Then Ally started to gag.

Gabby sat her on the kitchen table and without hesitation, popped her index finger into Ally's throat.

Ally's face started to darken, and she began to wheeze.

"Ally!" Gabby stuck her finger in deeper and scooped around the back of her throat. Something soft was back there. Gabby reached under with her short nail and pulled out a green mass of what she assumed was food. Ally heaved and started turning purple and Gabby scooped again. This time a larger chunk of whatever it was came loose and Ally let out a huge cough, sending green goop flying over Gabby's face. Pieces shot into her mouth and eyes.

Ally cried a little, but her color returned and she hugged her mom.

Gabby comforted her a few more minutes, even as she felt the slimy food, some kind of gelatin, she guessed, drip from her hair. She set Ally back in the high chair and snapped her tray in. She moved to the kitchen and grabbed paper towels to wipe Ally down, but there wasn't much on her skin as most of it was all over her outfit.

"Let's get you out of that."

Gabby pulled off her outfit and left her in her diaper. Ally was already slapping her hands on the high chair tray like nothing had happened. She was hungry. Now.

Gabby looked in her mouth and it appeared to be clear.

She gave her a small piece of turkey and Ally grabbed it and started downing it without complaint.

"Let me go wash up and get you something else to wear, honey. Mommy will be right back."

She ran to the bathroom and flipped on the light, grabbing a towel. She looked in the mirror and it was worse than she thought. The green stuff was all over her hair and green spots covered more than half of her face. After almost two years of motherhood, it didn't faze her at all. She turned on the water and washed off what she could. She looked back and Ally was fine, shaking her head and humming to herself.

Gabby rinsed off her hair and grabbed her face soap from the shower and wiped off all she could. She'd take a full shower once Ally was asleep.

She pinned up her hair in a ponytail and stared back. She could still see small green leftovers in her hair, but it was good enough for now.

She turned around to check on Ally as she left the bathroom. Gabby stopped and gasped.

Ally was sitting on the couch and the high chair tray was on the kitchen table.

Gabby took a quick survey of the room, glancing at every corner or potential hiding spot.

"Who's there? Who's in my house?"

She rushed to the kitchen and reached into her purse, pulling out her Glock, flipping off the safety.

"I have a gun. Who's in here?"

Gabby stood in place for a moment, pointing her gun toward each room. She was trying to decide whether to grab Ally and run or just keep looking.

It couldn't have been more than 30 seconds between the time she had looked back to see Ally humming on the high chair and seeing her on the couch. Still, the water and her eyes closing as she splashed water on and dried her face would have been enough time for someone to move the baby without her hearing, if they were quiet enough. She tried to think about every move she'd made since walking in the door. Had she locked it?

She retreated to the front door and glanced over. The deadbolt was locked, so no one could have come in. If someone was in the house, they were still inside.

She checked behind the kitchen island, then moved toward her bedroom, keeping Ally in her sight. She took fast glances under the beds and closets of each of the bedrooms. It was clear, but she didn't feel safe.

Ally had been silently watching her mommy move around the house with the gun in her hand. Gabby flipped on the safety, set the gun on an end table by the couch, and sat next to her daughter.

She picked up her cell and called Benji. He picked up on the second ring.

"Was planning to call you in a few," Benji said. "Everything looks good on the computer. I spoke to my friend Sheila, and she said she should be able to pull some data in the next day or two. She's pretty swamped."

"Okay," Gabby said, her voice cracking.

"Gabby, everything okay?"

"No. Not okay."

"What happened?"

Gabby gently stroked Ally's hair as she proceeded to tell Benji everything that had happened with the bodies at work and Ally at home. When she was done, the air was silent for a few seconds.

"You're sure everything's okay right now? Do I need to go over?"

"No," Gabby said. "I think this was all a warning. It is upset that you were there. It may have protected me when you pretended to hurt me before, but today I think they were warning me not to do anything like that again. Especially after the images they sent me. But they touched Ally. I can't ever do that again."

"I understand. There's no way to know its true intentions, but I have to agree it makes sense. We'll need to be more careful."

"Yes, I can't risk anything happening to her. Do you understand?"

"Of course. I'll do whatever I can without having to meet in person. The software you downloaded on the computer could help."

"Will you be reading through my boss's personal files?"

"No, not unless there's a reason to. It's the diagnostics I wish to obtain to check if there were any electrical changes or things we can view around the times these interactions were happening. I'll add what happened today. I am hoping some of the computer cameras were on. Do you have any active cameras in the office aside from the obvious security camera in the entrance?"

"I don't know about the computer cameras, but there's at least one other security cam in the Showroom, but I'm not sure how many total."

"Sheila should be able to find out. I promise she won't go through anything personal unless she finds something relevant."

"Good. I've known Ed my entire life. I don't want to invade his personal space. I feel guilty enough."

"Think about Ally," Benji said. "This could help us and keep her from ever being touched again. Do you think you should stay home?"

Gabby looked around the house. She felt an unexpected calmness.

"I can't tell you why, but I think we're okay. The warning's been given. I just need to listen and pay closer attention.

I've been trying so hard to ignore everything. If anything else happens or I feel anything out of the ordinary, we'll head to my sister's place, but I don't want to do that unless it's absolutely necessary."

"Hold on a sec, okay?"

Benji put her on hold and came back on the line three minutes later.

"Hey, I just spoke with Sheila. I provided her a high-level summary. The baby was enough to guarantee me some information by tomorrow. She has a new niece she adores and I am not ashamed to admit I utilized that for our benefit."

"That was devious and manipulative, but I'm not going to complain."

"Do not hesitate to call me if anything else occurs. I'll keep my cell by my side tonight, just in case."

"Thank you, Benji. I just can't thank you enough."

"Haven't done anything yet, but you are most welcome."

"I wouldn't know what to do otherwise," Gabby said. "Just take the thank you. I don't give those out too often."

"Understood."

They hung up. Gabby took Ally into her arms and held her up to face her.

"I'm glad you're staying with Aunt Teri. I think we're okay here, but I need to keep you as far away from my work as possible."

A tear fell as she stared deeper into her daughter's eyes.

"If this gets worse, I may need to keep you away from me."

Gabby squeezed her daughter tight. She didn't want to let go.

CHAPTER NINETEEN

GABBY WAS HAPPY TO BE OFF THE NEXT DAY AND ONLY HAD TO concentrate on her classes. She was in her last class and with about ten minutes to go, she saw her silenced phone flash.

It was a text from Benji.

"Need you to call me ASAP."

Gabby lost her concentration and missed the last minutes of the lecture. She'd e-mail one of her classmates later, but with Barry still not speaking to her, she would have to depend on someone else. Since their crash and burn date, Barry sat on the opposite side of her in every class, making it a point to wait until she took her seat before finding his own. Although he had remained in the one study group meeting since the lockdown, he never made eye contact. Laura had spoken to her heading into class and just thanked her for her help during the incident, but didn't mention anything about the ghost doctor. No one had treated her differently, so Gabby was grateful neither seemed to have said anything.

Gabby's thoughts were filled with anticipation, wondering what would signify an ASAP. It had to be some-thing significant.

The professor dismissed the class and she hurried out of the building. Ally was with Teri and although Gabby had intended to use the extra few hours from her day off work to catch up on homework and studying, she headed straight to her car and called as soon as she got to the parking lot.

Benji picked up on the first ring.

"Gabby. Glad you returned my call. Do you have time to speak?"

"I just got out of class and I'm off from work today. What happened?"

"I'm still at work but have a few minutes. I just spoke with Sheila. She e-mailed some of her findings. First, we can say that she did see surges in the network. The entire system, actually, that corresponds to the night we were present, and also on other days and times when you mentioned there was activity. I'll send the material to you before I leave today. This confirms there is something unexplainable occurring. Although that seems to be an obvious observation at this point, it is always welcome to have confirmation. One item. You said you were only aware of two security cameras, right?"

"Yes. Why?"

"Sheila found files that indicate there are ten total cameras in that office. We found video files on your boss's machine, but unfortunately, we are unable to access them. They are compressed and encrypted and can only be decrypted locally."

"What does that mean?"

"It means you must be on the computer to remove the decryption. The software we used the first time did not have decryption capabilities. I was not expecting the additional layers. It would be excellent if we could view the videos during the same surges."

"Okay."

"There's also something else that we found odd."

"Something else? Like what?"

"Sheila found several folders with different names. It's a list of first names such as 'Sharon' and 'Patricia' and a few others."

"Sounds like our personnel files, or maybe for annual reviews. I can understand why that would be there. Did you check them?"

"No, they are not encrypted, but I instructed Sheila not to view since you asked me not to invade any personal files. But that's not the odd part."

"Come on, Benji. Say what you need to say."

"The files used to check the network status. Those are hidden in some odd folders no normal person would ever dig into unless they were specifically checking for network items like we were. However, as Sheila was combing through them, she found two folders mixed in that stood out since their location did not make sense. It is possible the folders were mistakenly copied, which happens, but the way the files are organized on this machine, it is doubtful. You would have to know where you were clicking to access these folders, and they have been accessed. The two folders are 'C.M.' and 'G.M.' I assume the 'G.M.' might be for you, Gabby Mendez, but I'm not sure on the 'C.M.'"

"Cora. Cora Mendez. My mother."

"One mystery solved. The last date on your mother's folder is older, but the one with your initials was accessed more recently. These folders are also fully encrypted, but it is also the fact that they seem to have been purposely hidden in a place where they should not belong."

"What's the significance of that?" Gabby asked.

"This is never a good sign and something we have seen before. When someone wants to hide something, they will usually try to locate it somewhere that no one would normally look. If they know how to encrypt files, they'll typically do that as well. In this case it seems someone, most likely your boss, has done both."

"So now I need to access Ed's computer?"

"Yes. You would have to get directly on the machine and do it yourself or allow me access so I can do it. Then Sheila can perform her magic."

"No, they warned me. I can't let you back in my office."

"Then this is something you must do if we are to learn more."

Gabby hesitated. She thought of Ed and how long she'd known him. It was probably nothing and just an accidental folder copy or videos of their work projects.

"What do you want to do?" Benji asked.

"So Sheila will be able to get to the other documents that aren't encrypted?"

"She has only viewed the file names, but not their contents. Are you okay with digging deeper?"

"Yes, tell her to do what she can. I know it won't be much, but maybe I'll recognize the document names and can tell you what they are so she doesn't have to waste time on them. I'd hate for her to comb through a bunch of needless evaluations."

"What about the encrypted videos?"

"You can only see their name, and there's no indication of what they might be?"

"No, unfortunately. They will be meaningless unless we can view the video contents. The only way we can truly know is if you get on the machine. Can you get to your office tonight?"

"No, it would be too weird if I came in, plus my sister has a school event with one of my nieces later, so I need to get Ally. I'll be back tomorrow. Let me think about it, but let me know what Sheila finds."

"Okay. I must go. Please try to follow up with me this evening. Otherwise, I will contact you tomorrow."

Gabby had reached her car during the conversation and was sitting in the driver's seat. She started the drive to her sister's and kept thinking about Ed and what those files might be. She has always trusted Ed, even with his few odd but seemingly harmless comments he'd made to her over the years. Then she thought about it. Her mother. When Gabby was younger, Ed was helpful and kind to her, too. Could there have been something there she just wasn't seeing?

She felt her insides twist as her mind shifted to more possibilities she didn't want to consider. She called her sister.

"Hey, Gabby. Still at school?"

"No, Teri. I'm on my way."

"That's early. Everything okay?"

"I'm not sure. I have a strange question for you."

"Strange? You know I have Linda's class thing tonight."

"Yes, I know. I'm still picking up Ally. It's about Mom's diaries."

Teri didn't reply right away. Gabby thought about what to tell her. She didn't want to say anything that painted Ed in a bad light. He had done so much for them, especially giving Gabby the job and his willingness to work around her class schedule.

"Mom's diaries. What about them?" Teri asked.

"Yes. We said we would talk to each other if we ever decided to read them."

They had found Cora's stash of diaries when going through their mother's things a few months after her funeral. They agreed they wouldn't read through her personal writings at the time, since the pain of losing her was still raw.

"I want to read them," Gabby said.

"Why now?"

"I have my reasons. I don't want to lie to you, but I don't exactly want to tell you why. Not yet."

"Why wouldn't you want to tell me?"

"It's related to work. If I find anything, I promise I'll tell you, but if it's nothing, then I won't bother you with it. I really don't want to read them, but I'm looking for something specific."

"Hell, Gabby."

"You said hell!" a small voice echoed over the phone.

"That doesn't mean you can say it! Go to your room!"

Gabby heard a cry fading as Grace fled.

"Sorry. Look, that's a hel—heck of a thing to say to me, Gabs. Tell me it's important enough to read but not tell me why. I'm not sure what's worse."

"Look, you have a ton going on right now with the kids. If it's something to worry about, I'll give you every detail. Otherwise, just worry about Linda tonight."

"Okay, Gabby. Do you remember where they are?"

"I remember we put them in the storage bins, but I don't know which."

"The bins in the storage unit," Teri said. "Her bedroom stuff is on the back left, second to last stack. It's one of the green ones labeled 'Bedroom Closet.'"

Teri was the organizer and the one that required order in a house of six to prevent additional chaos.

"Okay, I'll be there shortly to grab Ally and then will go find the diaries. Are you sure you're okay with this?"

"Yes, I'm okay. It must be important if you're willing to read them. Tell you what, just go to the storage unit now and come get Ally after you find what you need. It's still early in the afternoon, and Linda's school thing isn't for a few more hours. This is supposed to be your study time, isn't it?"

Teri knew her schedule better than Gabby did sometimes.

"Yes, but this is more important right now. I'll head to the storage unit first. Thanks, Sister."

"I'll see you soon. If you have any problems finding the bin or it's not where I said it is, call me back."

"You know it'll be exactly where you told me it is, Martha Stewart."

Gabby could almost picture her sister's humble shrug.

GABBY GOT TO THE STORAGE FACILITY LOCATION. IT WAS MADE UP of twelve separate buildings, each climate controlled. She drove up to the entrance and entered the keypad code to engage the gate. Once it opened, she drove toward the rear of the location to Building 11, the second to last one on the right. She grabbed her keys and found the long unused key. She entered a second code to get into the building then moved to Unit 1012. As she turned the key and opened the upward sliding door, she was overcome with memories of her mom, Cora. After the death of Gabby's husband, she hadn't hesitated to let Gabby move back in. Teri had her family and home, and Gabby remembered feeling like a failure. Bad marriage, a widow and pregnant, then coming back to a place where she said she would never live again as an angry 17-year-old before starting college.

Gabby turned on her phone light and headed toward the back left side of the 10x20 unit. She found the stack of bins she was looking for exactly where Teri said they would be. There were three green bins stacked on top of each other. She pulled off the top two and placed them on the concrete floor. The first one was labeled "Bedroom" so she skipped it. The other two had the proper "Bedroom Closet" label. She opened the first bin, but knew it was the wrong one as soon as she removed the lid. They had organized all of her picture frames in that one. The second one was it. The diary was at the top of several documents. It was a simple leather cover with "Cora" embossed on the front. It was a Christmas gift Teri had given her one year.

Cora had always kept a diary. This was the last one. The older diaries were on the other side of the bin under a blanket. She wouldn't write daily but said if it was worth writing down, she'd note it. She always encouraged her daughters to use their own diaries and not to be afraid to record even what they deemed to be a trivial thing. It didn't always have to be a major life event.

> "What about someone reading it, Mom?" Gabby had asked her once.
> "The really private things you can write in your own language or your own codes, or simply leave names of people and events out. Once you're gone, will it matter? This helps get me through a day sometimes. Transfer the good and especially the bad on paper, and it can help you release it. Even if it's just a small comfort."
> "Can I read it someday?"
> "A diary is extremely private. When I'm gone, you can read it, but as long as the owner of a diary is alive, respect that. Unless you have permission or it's truly important like a life and death situation, let it be."

Gabby put the other two bins back and returned to her car with the diary bin. She put it in her backseat. She started the car, meaning to head to Teri's to get Ally, but she kept looking back at the bin. She had to know. And she had to know now.

Gabby turned around, popped the lid off, and pulled out a few of the older diaries. She picked up the last one and slowly turned to the front page. The earliest date was three years before she died. She checked the other two diaries below it and together they covered almost six years. Gabby grabbed one and flipped to the first entry. Her mother's penmanship had been so elegant. Gabby's was barely legible. She looked at the pages and ran her index finger gently over the page.

January 23. Had a wonderful day with the girls. Gabriella loves getting on Teri's nerves. It's hilarious to watch. I remember being the same way with my brothers. She has so much of me in her, but I'll never tell her that. Not until she's an adult, at least.

Gabby took a moment to breathe in and out as she felt her emotions rise, then continued. She took her time reading the first several pages, word for word, then got into a rhythm. She started to skim, recognizing some of the repeated phrases that she was chronicling. "Diagnosis." "Blood test." "Chemo."

She was soon able to skip the details of Cora's illness with a glance, and skip to larger sections. She skimmed through most of the diary and grabbed another one. This was older than the first.

As she reached the last year of the volume, the writing style changed. Before, the writing was smooth and spaced, like Cora had taken her time with each word. The patterns then became looser. Margins not always aligned, messier writing. Then the letter 'X' started to show up, alone. It stood out because it looked so out of place and was also in a different color than the rest of the writing on the same page. Gabby read the first entry she noticed.

I can't believe I'm saying this, but 'X' was acting strange today. It's not the first time, but he looked different. Worried he may be sick.

She flipped two more pages and there it was again. A blue 'X' in the middle of a page of black ink.

Something is definitely wrong. 'X' isn't himself. Maybe I should speak to him to see if he's okay.

She went on to find more entries scattered throughout the next few months. She skipped through until the tone changed.

Either he's dying or he's not the person I thought he was. 'X' is making my insides twist when I see him. I swear I caught him staring at me through the blinds in his office. I will speak to him tomorrow.

I spoke to him today. He said he's been to the doctor, and he's being treated for some type of imbalance. He seemed embarrassed to discuss it, but I've known 'X' for more than twenty years and although he doesn't outright share his feelings, he's never kept important things to himself. Maybe he's sicker than he wants to let on. I'll continue praying for him.

Ed. This thinly veiled 'X' could only have been Ed, unless Mom kept some secret man hidden from them, but she never would. She worked for Ed for 22 years and never had a bad thing to say about him that wasn't work-related. A few times she would be upset over deadlines or stress. They worked together well before they got into business with cadavers, importing and exporting larger, difficult-to-ship items such as statues, art, and machinery. The knowledge gained from doing this a few years helped when he decided to go into the body business. They initially helped other companies set up their exhibits until he thought about making a grander exhibit on his own since nothing like that existed in Texas. When Ed decided to shift focus, he discussed it with Cora before proposing a partnership with the larger companies. He was the boss, and they weren't partners, but he never decided anything without her. She was his right hand, and they worked on all their projects as a team.

Gabby forwarded through more pages.

'X' seems to be better. Maybe I was just seeing things that weren't there. He's a good man, but he's not perfect. I have to give him that. Too many years. Too much history. I feel bad for thinking some of the things I did. But I felt them, nonetheless. I have more important things to worry about like my girls.

She held on to the diary and decided to thumb through the previous two. There were no more 'X' references. One thing did stop her—an entry from four years before.

March 14. The Big C. Just like Mom. She survived ten years with it. Hopefully I can beat it. Gabby still needs me, and even though she may not admit it, so does Teri. I need them. Too soon to leave my girls.

March 14. When she was first diagnosed with breast cancer. She didn't tell them for almost six months and even then downplayed it initially. Gabby closed her eyes as they watered and kissed the diary.

"I miss you, Mom."

She wanted so badly to just hear her mother's voice say, "It's okay, Gabby. Everything will be okay."

The words never came, but the memory of her saying that was enough.

Gabby put away the diaries except for Cora's final,

embossed one. She held it for a moment and then placed it on the passenger seat to have it next to her.

Could Ed have been doing something that her mom had picked up on? No, she couldn't picture it. She promised Teri she would share if she found anything relevant, and although she wasn't sure, it was time to go talk to her sister.

CHAPTER TWENTY

GABBY GOT TO TERI'S HOUSE A SHORT TIME LATER. THE KIDS were all getting ready for Linda's teacher's night. Teri made all of them attend school events unless they had an exam or school event of their own.

John answered the door.

"Teri's getting the little ones ready in the master bedroom."

Gabby made her way to Ally, who was in the portable playpen on her back and babbling.

She picked up her daughter and moved to the room where the girls were getting dressed. She opened the door and smiled, and Teri stopped what she was doing and moved toward her baby sister.

"What is it?"

"What?"

"I know that face."

"It's something, but I know you don't have the time and have to get the girls ready."

Teri looked at Linda and Grace and then back at her sister.

"Tonight. I'll call you as soon as we get back."

Gabby nodded, grabbed Ally's bag, and they went back home.

She spent some time with her daughter and ate dinner. She studied as Ally napped and a few minutes after 9, her phone rang. Teri was making a video call.

"Wow," Gabby said. "I'm getting an actual video chat?"

"All I kept thinking about is what you read in that diary."

"Are the kids around?"

"I got Linda and Grace to bed, and Nick and Jess are in their rooms. I told John I was calling you and not to bug me. He's watching a game, anyway."

"How did Linda's teacher night go?"

"Okay. Talks too much, but good grades. Sounds like her Aunt Gabby. Wait until they get Grace in a few years. I think she'll make both of you look like Saints."

"Better watch it with that one."

Teri sighed. "I know. So come on. Tell me what happened."

Teri was sitting up on her bed with her headboard and the bottom of a cross visible behind her.

"It's awkward," Gabby said. "I skimmed through the diaries and Mom kept referring to someone named 'X.' She was concerned about this X's behavior. Someone close to her."

Gabby paused, waiting to see her sister's reaction.

"Ed?"

"Huh," Gabby said. "That didn't take you long to guess. She didn't name him outright, but he's the only person I thought it could be. So what do you know that I don't?"

Teri sighed. "One night Mom came in upset. I was just a couple of years out of high school and going to Dallas Community College to get my basics and studying. You were already in bed or at a friend's house or something. I could tell something was wrong with her. Her cheeks were flushed, and she seemed jittery. I'd only seen her like that a few times, and the last time before that was when Dad died."

"What was she upset about?"

"I asked her, but at first she refused to say. She told me it was nothing and not to worry about it. But…"

"But you turned on Tenacious Teri and bugged her until she broke?"

"Don't call me Tenacious Teri."

"But you were, right?"

"Yes, but still, last thing I need is for one of the kids to hear and latch on to that."

"Okay, sorry. You were persistent. So what did she say?"

"She only told me a little, but I caught her at a time that she must have felt like she needed to talk. She said she had been getting some weird vibes from Ed. Said a few weeks before she caught him looking at her, and normally, she wouldn't think much of it. But on this night, she said she saw something that rattled her. She wouldn't tell me what, and I pressed her, but she just said he seemed to be doing something she'd never expected. She had indirectly confronted him, making an excuse to go to his office and address whatever it was. Maybe his reaction or something else made her feel uncomfortable enough that her opinion of him changed."

"What kind of thing would he do to make her feel uncomfortable?"

"I have no way of knowing for sure, unless you found something specific in that diary, but I'd guess he must have made an advance on her or maybe done something inappropriate."

"Why would you think that?"

"Mom was flustered. I had seen her get hit on by creepy men before, and she just took it in stride and cut them off at the knees. It had to be something big to rattle her like that. Ed is someone she trusted, and I'm sure confided in to some degree. It must have been something really uncharacteristic to make her feel that bad, but she still gave him the benefit of the doubt."

"Is that the only time she ever spoke about it?"

"A few weeks later I asked her how things were going and all she said was that she had known him for so long and thought maybe he was just going through a tough time and everything was okay. She sounded like she had just let it go. Or at least she seemed to."

"Did you believe her?"

"Yes and no. I would still see her come home slightly rattled or bothered a few times, but nothing like that one night. Maybe she was still trying to figure things out, but she never said anything bad about him to me again. Now it's your turn. What happened to make you go looking for her diary in the first place?"

Gabby explained what Benji's hacker friend Sheila had found and the options that Benji gave her.

"I don't want to invade Ed's private files, but after what you just told me, I think we need to know. I have to find out if these strange things happened, and also why he has what appears to be a secret folder with Mom's initials."

"You've worked there a few years now, Gabs. Have you ever noticed anything?"

Gabby thought hard. "I'm so busy, and my mind's either focused on my work, Ally, or school. I've never picked up on anything inappropriate from him, but honestly, I may not have noticed. He was always so good to us, Teri. I remember him bringing us snacks and taking us to grab ice cream or junk food when we were younger."

"Same here. Being older, I think I would have picked up on it, but the incident with Mom was the only time I ever had any type of negative thoughts about him. But we never would have a reason to suspect, would we?"

"No. We never did. Do you think I should go through with it?"

"That's a tough one, Gabs. I'm not sure what I'd do, but with what I know, I would lean toward saying yes and getting on that computer."

"Okay," Gabby said. "I'll set it up," Gabby said as she picked up her phone and texted Benji.

"I'm ready to proceed with my boss's computer. What do I need to do?"

Benji replied immediately. "I'll get a new USB sent to you tonight. I'll ask Jay to take it by so there's no threat of me showing up at your house."

Gabby turned to her sister. "It's set."

"I feel horrible," Teri said. "What if we're wrong?"

"There's one more thing," Gabby said.

"What?"

"There's a secret folder with my name on it, too."

CHAPTER TWENTY-ONE

GABBY HAD CLASSES THE NEXT MORNING AND HAD TO BE AT work by 1 pm. The Donor Showcase was getting closer, so she needed to complete some final touches, but it was the last thing on her mind. About halfway through her shift, she asked Ed if she could work a little later since she wanted to finish up the display she was working on.

"Of course, Gabby. Stay as late as you need to. The Donor Showcase is on Saturday!"

Ed didn't seem to think twice about it, but Gabby stood there just a few seconds too long.

"Was that all you needed?"

"Oh, no. Sorry, Ed. I spaced out a bit."

"It's okay. I'm sure you have school or Ally on the brain."

Gabby mustered a fake laugh and got back to work.

The clock hit five. The last of the staff was out by five after, but Ed didn't leave right away. Gabby could have finished the task she was working on an hour earlier but had slowed down to minimize what she had left once she'd be alone. Gabby looked back more times than she wanted to, but at 18 minutes past five, she heard Ed's door close and his keys rattle as he locked his office door.

"Goodnight, Gabby. Hope you're not here too late."

"Thanks, Ed," Gabby said, trying her best to give a smile without guilt.

Her insides twisted as Ed walked out. She'd known this man for so long and couldn't believe what she was about to do.

Gabby waited ten more minutes and kept checking for Ed to come back, but she was alone.

She made sure the front door was locked and moved toward the break room. She checked the upper rear cabinet and tried to reach the top shelf, but it was too high. She grabbed one of the chairs and stood on it.

What if he finally moved them? she thought.

She moved a few items, including cleaning supplies, plastic cups, and some napkins, and behind them all, there it was. A box with "POISON" written on it and a picture of two rat silhouettes.

She pulled the box and it jingled. Ed hadn't even tried to stuff it with something to keep it quiet.

Gabby got off the chair, opened the box, and pulled out the master ring, which held four keys. She knew one was for his door, another for the main doors, and one was a skeleton key. She wasn't sure what the fourth one unlocked.

She eased out of the break room and took one more check at the front doors. Still locked. She had her own key for the front door but was concerned about only one.

She moved to Ed's office and the first key she tried didn't work. The second one, however, slid in without resistance and turned. She left the door propped open so she could hear just in case someone did come in.

She sat at her boss's desk and flipped on his computer. Once the monitor popped up with the login screen, she took the new USB drive Jay had delivered to her from Benji. She grabbed her cell and dialed.

"Greetings, Gabby," Benji's voice answered. "I was getting nervous."

"He left a little later than expected. The keys were in the same place. I'm in his office. Are you ready for the USB?"

"Yes, go ahead and place it."

Gabby slid the drive in and the light on it turned red. She set her phone down and flipped on the speaker to free her hands.

"Okay, done. How is this different than what you did before?"

"Before, we only had to log on to the network. That software unlocked general passwords and pulled from any network machine. Now, however, we have to log in directly to run the more complex decryption software, and since this is a local administrator, we need you to click some screens and enter a password that Sheila will provide. Sheila told me this will only be a temporary password and will revert to whatever he was using so it won't fail the next time he attempts to log in."

"Okay, whatever Sheila says works for me."

The light on the USB turned green.

"I got it," Benji said. "You may want to write this down somewhere. Once you're ready, enter the following sequence. P-8-0-7-B-K-D-9-6-Pound-Pound."

Gabby wrote the sequence down on a piece of paper, then entered each alphanumeric character and pressed enter.

"I'm in."

"Excellent. That password should work until we are done, so simply re-enter it if the screen needs to be unlocked."

"Now what? Where are those files?"

Benji guided her on how to access the main folders on the

C drive. Gabby did as instructed as Benji led her into six layers of oddly named folders. Some with just numbers.

"You weren't kidding. Who would have ever thought to look in here?"

She went down one more level and saw it. "C.M." and "G.M."

"I see them," Gabby said.

She had been nervous about taking the keys and sneaking into the office to hack into Ed's computer, but that didn't compare to how she was feeling now with the folders right in front of her. She went into her mother's folder first.

Inside this folder were more embedded folders labeled by years. They went back to six years before her mom had died. She opened the oldest year. There were about ten video files inside it.

"What do you see?" Benji asked, startling her. She had forgotten he was on the phone.

"I found the video files."

"Gabby, I'm not sure what you're going to find, but be prepared for anything. Sheila said she could spend days telling me stories about the videos and pictures she's found on people's machines that they never expected anyone would see. Do you see a small lock icon on the file?"

Gabby looked at the file name, which was gibberish but numbered in sequence, and saw a small padlock shaped icon in the upper left of the image.

"Yes, I see a red padlock."

"Okay, that means it's encrypted and not something we can unlock remotely. Can you right-click it?"

"Yes, I see copy, move, and some kind of skeleton icon."

"Choose that skeleton on any file and Sheila's software will decrypt it. It will encrypt again once you log off."

Gabby chose the skeleton and another skull appeared, spinning in a circle. Once it stopped, the padlock was green.

She clicked the file and a video popped up with a play arrow. It was blurry.

"I got it."

"Okay. Don't forget, no matter what you may find, we need to find out where there might be more cameras. Those files may tell us."

"I understand. Let me hang up and go through these. I'm not sure how long it will be."

She clicked "End" on her phone screen and moved the mouse to the Play button. She took in a deep breath. "Please don't be bad."

The blurry picture adjusted. "How does it look now?" a man's voice said.

A face of someone came into view. It was a man staring right into the camera.

"It's good," Ed's voice said.

"That's the last one. Should be good to start using them now."

It must have been the first day the cameras had been installed.

The screen blinked and the next image was Cora. Gabby's mother was sitting at her desk, gathering some items. This was before they had been working on cadavers, so she was just in front of her computer. The time showed a few minutes before five. Cora stood up at one point, and the camera showed her body but not her head as she did. Then she left.

"The cameras were new. Maybe they didn't realize it would be focused on Mom."

Gabby moved on to the next batch of files. More of the same. They were spaced out by days and even weeks, but Ed had saved them. Most were just Cora working. Gabby jumped forward to the last few files in the folder. They were mostly short video clips. Some thirty seconds long, the longest no more than five minutes. None of the files were too big in size. Then she clicked on the following year.

There were more than forty files this time. Gabby checked the first few, and they were more of the same. One video focused on Cora's face for a long time.

"You were so beautiful, Mom," Gabby said.

They had been friends. Maybe he just kept them for memories. Maybe they just never got around to adjusting the camera angle.

She scanned down the list. The last four files were much larger than the rest. She opened the first one.

Cora was working on something laid out across the floor. She was on her knees and bent over, shifting to several spots, and finally moved off to reveal some kind of project she was working on. The camera moved. All the previous videos had stayed in place as if the camera had a static visual setting, but now it was adjusting and zooming in. Cora flipped to the other side of the project, and this time her chest was facing the camera. As she leaned down to detail something, the cleavage from her button-down shirt looked considerable as the camera caught the outline of her bra.

The camera zoomed in tighter, directly on her breasts. Gabby jumped and closed the video. She was breathing rapidly.

Maybe he was just lonely that day. Mom was beautiful. Maybe it was just too tempting.

She went through the last three files for that second year. These videos were much longer. She skimmed through. On the days Cora was working on the floor, the contents were more of the same. The camera would zoom in for close-ups whenever her rear or chest were in highly visible spots, then zoom out with her movements. The shortest video was a day when she wore a shirt that covered up to her neck, but he still focused on her curves with every significant move of the camera. He had to have been sitting at his desk the entire time watching her. She was on the last file when she noticed the scene changed at the end. Cora was no longer in the picture, but Ed appeared. It was a few minutes after five and he appeared to be alone. He took the base of the project, looked up directly at the camera, and adjusted it. He moved it a few inches to the right. In some frames on the previous videos, Cora was cut off if she was too far left.

Whatever justification she had granted Ed to this point was gone.

"You adjusted the camera to see better, you son of a bitch."

She moved to the next year. The first three files were the same, and the new adjustment didn't let Cora escape the screen. Gabby was angry, but in the end, she felt some relief he had only been looking and there had been nothing physical. At least not on the videos.

She moved on through the rest of the year. The remaining files were shorter and went back to her mom at her desk. Her project must have finished. The last files in the year showed some major changes.

Cora's work area was different. Her desk had been adjusted forty-five degrees so that the camera caught her from above and to the side. The entire screen was clearer. Suddenly, the camera moved again, but instead of just zooming in or out, it moved left to right and up and down, and then it went dark. It adjusted to black and white, but looked more like a photo reel negative. It took Gabby a few seconds to realize what was happening.

He had upgraded the camera. This one had newer angles and some type of filter, like a negative filter. Cora was wearing a white shirt and the negative effect acted like an X-Ray. You could see through the fabric and Cora's bra was visible. It was like he was looking at her skin. The camera moved for a few minutes, like he was trying to perfect the view.

She jumped to the next file, and it was back to normal. The

color of her shirts and sweaters were too dark for the negative to have taken effect, but he tried.

She jumped to the second to last year. She skimmed through until she found another negative video. That outfit. Gabby recognized it. Teri once got mad at her mom for wearing it publicly. It was a halter top with a low cut back but contained thicker material on the chest and was meant to be worn without a bra. Gabby remembered the conversation between Teri and her mother that morning before she left for work.

"Mom, are you wearing a bra? That back is low and I don't see a strap."

"This dress doesn't need a bra, Teri. It covers everything."

"What if it's cold in the office? Don't you think that's inappropriate?"

"Teri, you think everything's inappropriate."

Then she turned to Gabby.

"Honey, does this make your mom look slutty? Apparently Teri thinks so."

"I didn't say that!" Teri yelled.

Gabby smiled, only seeing how beautiful she looked.

"You look sexy, Mom. Professional sexy. Not slutty."

"Thank you."

This was the dress Cora was wearing on the video. The negative filter must have been Ed's Holy Grail. You could see the entire left breast from the picture. Gabby fast-forwarded and then something she hadn't seen before happened.

Ed appeared next to Cora. He was talking to her, although there was no audio. She looked up at him and was laughing, then back to her computer. Ed put his hand on her shoulders, still laughing, but as soon as Cora looked down his eyes shifted. He was trying to get a look down her shirt, hoping for a bare breast now that he knew she was braless. The camera must not have been enough for him that day. The conversation itself looked normal, and Gabby couldn't tell if Cora noticed.

Gabby could see frustration in Ed's face, and then suddenly he fell hard on the floor, clutching his knee.

Cora reacted immediately and rushed to check on her boss. As she tried to check the source of his pain, Ed got what he wanted. His eyes bulged as he looked down her dress and got the eyeful he had been hoping for. A few minutes later he limped off and Cora was back at her desk. She had a look of concern on her face. She looked back toward Ed's office a few times and then looked upset, like something had finally dawned on her. Gabby noted the date. It corresponded to the same time as one of her 'X' diary entries.

Gabby went through the last year of files. Cora never wore that dress again, but one big change was that initially, there were more videos of Ed talking to Cora, like he enjoyed seeing himself on the camera with her. She seemed less relaxed than she had before, like she was guarded.

Then the files shortened and there was a long gap. Gabby checked the date. It matched the timeframe when Cora was first diagnosed with breast cancer.

He couldn't do it anymore after her diagnosis.

Was it guilt? Were you heartbroken? Was it just infatuation? Or were you just getting your rocks off?

The video clips ended. She backed out of the folder and saw her own. She clicked on her name, but there were no year folders underneath it. Just three files. She cracked the knuckles on her right hand with her right thumb, contemplating, trying to prepare for what she couldn't. The dates were from before pregnancy. She clicked the first one. It was a wider shot and since Gabby didn't work at the desk much, she was in the background with one of the first cadavers she worked on. They had received three initially, and this was The Runner. She was just learning, and she and Cora were working on it. Actually, Cora was working on it and showing her what to do.

Gabby remembered this day. She had worked with her mother for about a year before Cora quit due to her illness. Gabby had only intended to work through her second year of grad school until she'd hopefully get an internship. She never expected to work with cadavers, but it turned out she was good at it. Mom had been patient, and so had Gabby. Her youngest daughter, who had been so rebellious and a wilder child than her older sister, had found something that held her attention. For whatever reason, the bodies fascinated her. The smooth fibers of each muscle, how they connected to each other, and how the slightest turn would change an entire facial feature. Even without skin, Gabby could imagine what their faces looked like when they were alive.

Gabby waited for the camera to move, but it was still for the first few minutes.

Finally, it zoomed. It moved toward Gabby's face and stayed there a few minutes. Then the camera shifted back to Cora. It held on her face. Gabby noticed her bone structure and the elegance of her movements.

The camera zoomed out and Cora and Gabby turned. Ed walked up to them. There wasn't any audio, but Gabby didn't need it. She remembered exactly what happened that day.

Ed walked up and put his hand on both Cora and Gabby's shoulders. There was nothing ugly about it. He was smiling.

"You both seem to work well together, even with dead bodies staring back at you. You're braver than I am."

"Thank you, Mr. Bernard."

"How many times do I have to tell you you can call me Ed, Gabby?"

Then he took a long look at Gabby as she apologized and

called him by his first name. He looked at Cora, then back at Gabby.

"You look so much like your mother."

Cora smiled and Gabby's face flushed. "Thank you, Ed. I hope I look half as beautiful as she does when I'm her age."

Then Ed walked out of frame.

The camera zoomed back in and locked in on both of their faces.

The next few files were just of Gabby. She was working on the cadavers. These videos were scattered several months apart. Then they were gone. The last one was dated right around the time Gabby got pregnant.

So Ed's Turnoffs: Cancer and babies. Got it.

She backed out of the folder and logged on to her personal e-mail. She tried to process what she had just seen as she downloaded a few choice videos to her cloud storage.

Her phone buzzing snapped her out of it. It was Benji.

"Progress?"

"Sorry, I got sidetracked. Give me a few more minutes and I'll get back to you."

She returned to the task. Check for cameras. She knew where one definitely was now. It was mounted outside his office. She dialed Benji.

"Hey, I'm still looking. Where are the regular video files you can't see?"

"Back out one level behind where the folder names are. Go under 'processed' then 'files.' There should be a folder for each camera, then within those folders there should be more folders sorted by date or a number sequence."

Gabby followed the instructions.

"I see seven different camera folders. Pretty straight forward. They're all named 'Camera' with a number after them."

She opened "Camera 1" and folders that appeared to be sorted by date.

"There are only the last twelve months," Gabby said.

"That makes sense. Video files are huge, so it probably backs up to a site and only keeps a history of a few years. Whatever legal requires. He would only backup what he wanted to keep."

She jumped into the first folder twelve months prior.

She pulled up the first camera. It covered the entryway. She knew this camera over the door. She moved on. Camera 2 was over the Baby Room, Camera 3 over the main Showroom with the cadavers. Camera 4 covered the primary hallway.

Then she moved to Camera 5. Camera 5 was the same angle that she'd been seeing. She got up and walked outside Ed's office. She moved to the main offices that now housed several cubicles, but it was a different layout when Cora worked there. Gabby glanced over at the windows. There were two light fixtures over each of the windows that faced out toward where her mom had been working on the videos. This camera was purposely hidden and based on the angles, she was sure it was located between one window and the door. Most likely as part of the ceiling trim.

She returned to the office and moved to Camera 6. Camera 6 was different. The camera screen shape was narrower, and the quality wasn't as good as the others. The angle was also lower. It had four squares in various parts of the office. They were the computer monitor cameras. He was wired into the computer monitors.

She went to the last one. Camera 7. This was a normal camera and covered the new room. He must have added it after the rest, since that room had only been built a few months before.

Gabby looked down at her phone. Benji had been waiting. She picked it up and explained what each camera was doing.

"Perfect. Let me add Sheila to our call."

There was a pause and then Benji came on. "Sheila, you there?"

"Yes," a deep female voice answered. "Are you in?"

"Uh, yes. Hi, Sheila. Thank you for your help."

"Haven't done much yet. Hopefully we'll figure out a way to help you and I'm so sorry for what you're experiencing."

"I appreciate that."

"So in a few seconds, you'll see a pop-up window. Tell me when."

A small blue square appeared. 'Do you grant Shay14 access to your machine?'

"I see it."

"Click 'Yes.' I'm going to download some of the more recent files so we can try to match them with what's been going on."

Gabby did as instructed. The windows shifted around quickly and files started copying to some new location Sheila mapped to.

"This will take a bit, so you can grab a drink or whatever unless you want to stare at the screen."

"Won't someone know I'm here doing this once they look through the files recording now?"

"I'm going to wipe out anything after 3 pm today. You okay with that?"

"Yes, and if you could, anything around that first time I put in the USB. If you find anything."

"Understood. We can get off the call. I'll have Benji contact you when I'm done."

They hung up and Gabby decided to get up and grab a drink from the break room, but instead she looked at the computer, wondering how deep and ugly this apparent fascination with her mother had been.

"If only you'd had a camera on yourself, Ed."

She looked around his office for some kind of further evidence, but nothing stood out. Then she stopped and stared at the desk. Other than grabbing supplies from the big top drawer, Gabby had never had a need to go into the other drawers in his desk.

Gabby had seen the top long drawer that held pens and notepads open before, but she had never seen what was in the lower drawer. The one with a lock.

She pulled on it. It didn't give. She looked at the key ring, picked out the one key she didn't know what was used for, and inserted it. Nothing.

Gabby opened the top drawer and pulled out a thick paper clip. Being a younger sister, she knew how to pick the basic locks on Teri's drawers when she was younger to borrow clothes without her knowing. The lock on Ed's lower drawer was simple and only required one of those small keys.

The drawer opened on her second try. There was a plastic cover over it. She inspected it and it slid it back, revealing the contents underneath. Underneath were only four items. Some tissues, a pair of latex gloves, a bottle of lotion, and a box.

She didn't want to touch the items, knowing full well what Teri had told her about Nick when he hit puberty. The lotion alone would be one thing, but this kit wasn't for softening skin. She pulled out the box and set it on the desk. It was a simple box, made of wood, maybe half the size of a cigar box. Her eyes bulged as she slowly opened it.

The box was filled with pictures. They were upside down. She flipped the first one around and it was Cora. She was wearing tight jeans and a shirt that hugged her shape. It was at some outdoor event and she was getting in her car.

She flipped the next picture. Cora was in a bathing suit near White Rock Lake in East Dallas. Gabby had been with her. She was in shape enough to wear a two-piece but had always worn a one-piece in public. The picture focused on her body. She had on large sunglasses and a hat and was lying out by the water. The picture looked high quality. Gabby figured he had a zoom lens to get that close and clear without being there.

Gabby let out a loud gasp as she flipped to the third picture. Cora was topless and in her bedroom. It looked like she had just gotten out of a shower. The outside of the picture had a blurred object to the top and left. Gabby realized it was part of a window frame and curtain. Ed had been outside her bedroom window when he took the picture.

The next picture was a different night. This time Cora was completely nude, in her walk-in closet like she was looking for something to wear. Gabby started to sob.

There was only one picture left. Tears fell as she turned it.

The picture was old. A family picture they had taken when her dad was still alive. A young Gabby and Terri sat in front, with Cora behind. In place of their father was a poorly photoshopped picture of Ed. He was smiling, wearing the same color blazer that her father had worn in the original picture.

Gabby grabbed the pictures and ran to the break room, wanting to be as far away from Ed's desk as she could.

She was sobbing and shaking. She ripped the nude photo and shoved it into the garbage disposal and flipped the switch on. She started to tear the next one and caught herself just as she was about to rip it.

Evidence. She needed to keep these. But not the nude one. No one needed to see that ever again. She needed to tell Teri. She needed to do something.

Gabby put the pictures face down, sat in a chair and cried. There had been no cameras in the break room, so Ed wouldn't get the satisfaction of seeing her break like that.

She tried to gather herself for the next twenty minutes. She couldn't believe it. Ed had always been so good to her mother, and now she knew why. He tried to turn to Gabby after she was gone, but it wasn't the same. Just as she was catching her breath, she heard her phone ringing from a distance.

She grabbed the pictures and ran back to the office, picking up on the fifth ring.

"Gabby," Benji said. "Sheila has completed her task. She wiped out the video for this evening, the first time you planted the USB and the nights Jay and I visited. She will require some time to go over it. Could take a day or two. We will get back to you as soon as we know something. Be sure to log out of that computer completely and remove that USB. Make it look the same as it was before you entered."

Gabby logged off the machine and put the USB in her purse. "I'm done. I'll wait for your call."

They hung up and Gabby stared at the open drawer below her. If she took the pictures, he'd know. She may have disturbed it enough that he would know, anyway. Did she want to give this away now and confront him as soon as possible? She wasn't sure. She thought about it some more.

No, I won't give you that satisfaction. I'm gonna nail you to the wall and I don't want you to see it coming.

She grabbed her phone and took pictures of each of Ed's photographs as well as the drawer contents. She would have to hope he wouldn't realize the full nude was gone. She had no choice.

She put the pictures back in the box turned backward and in the same order, minus the missing one. She hadn't touched the other items so left them as-is, then pulled the plastic rolling cover back over them. She closed the drawer and used the same paper clip to lock it, then tried to reposition anything on the desk she might have moved.

She stood up, adjusted the chair and walked out. Everything looked right, but she was upset and realized she might have forgotten an easy detail. If Ed wasn't looking for anything, he probably wouldn't notice. He wasn't big on observing minor details unless it was about her mom, apparently.

Gabby put away her tools and got out the door as soon as she could, almost rushing. She headed to pick up Ally from Teri's house, which worked out perfectly. She and her sister were about to have a long talk about what to do about Ed. Hopefully, for once, they'd agree on how to handle something important to the both of them, even if it meant finding a way to destroy a man they had both loved most of their lives.

CHAPTER TWENTY-TWO

GABBY CALLED TERI ON HER WAY TO PICK UP ALLY. "WE NEED to talk, Sis."

"Okay. Why don't you just stay for dinner? We can talk after."

The entire family was at home. There were no school events to rush to, so they all sat together and Gabby enjoyed the company of her nieces and nephew, but caught Teri sneaking looks at her, knowing something was wrong.

Once dinner ended, the teens went to their rooms while Teri got the little ones ready for bed.

Teri finally came out of the girls' room. John was on the couch watching a baseball game while Gabby and Ally were on the loveseat.

"Honey, will you be out here for a while?"

"It's barely the third inning. I'm planning on watching the rest of the game."

"Okay, I need to talk to Gabby in the bedroom."

"Tell you what. Grab me a beer and some popcorn and I won't go near the room until you're done."

Teri gave him a look. "Sure, I just finished getting the girls bathed and to bed, but hey, I'll get your beer."

John winked at Gabby. "This is the life."

"Asshole," Gabby mouthed to him with a smile.

Teri microwaved a bag of popcorn and handed it to him in a bowl. "There you go, King."

"That's right. You know how to treat your King."

"Just remember," Teri said as she started to hand him a beer bottle, then slammed it down between his legs, just missing any critical parts. "I'm a light sleeper and my knife is right by the nightstand."

John jumped up and smiled. "Yes, honey. Thank you. I love you. You're beautiful."

"And don't you forget it," she said as she gave him a peck on the forehead.

Teri turned back to Gabby. "Come on."

The sisters went into Teri's bedroom. Gabby was holding Ally, who was awake but keeping quiet, playing with her mom's hair.

They sat on the bed and faced each other.

"What did you find?"

"It's bad, Teri."

Gabby proceeded to provide most of the details. She told her about the cameras and eased toward the videos.

"So he was secretly recording her and you? Looking through Mom's clothes?"

Gabby nodded. "Did you ever think Ed would be capable of something like that?"

"Other than what I told you yesterday, no. I would have never suspected it would be this bad. It sounds like an obsession. But he never acted on anything? Mom wouldn't have let that go."

"I haven't gotten to the worst part."

"It gets worse?"

Gabby put Ally on the bed and handed her a stuffed toy. Ally took it willingly and played with it while her mom and aunt spoke.

Gabby took out her phone and pulled up her camera roll.

"After I saw the videos, I decided to go through his desk. There were items. Tissues, lotion and gloves. And a box."

"Oh, my God. That's a teenage boy whack-it kit. I found that in Nick's room when he was twelve and did my best to ignore it."

"I remember you telling me and I recognized it as soon as I saw it."

"I know it's part of life, but it's not like we had brothers. John said it was normal, but this? This is a grown man doing this while thinking of our mother. At work. I think I'm gonna be sick."

Teri gagged before she composed herself. "What was in the box?"

Gabby started to answer but couldn't bring herself to speak. She scrolled to the next picture and placed her phone on the bed so they could both see.

"Prepare yourself," was all Gabby was able to get out.

Teri scrolled through each photo. Gabby could see her sister processing the memories of the lake just like she had earlier. Then she reached the topless pic.

Terri gagged and ran to the bathroom. The puke hitting the toilet bowl was unmistakable.

The sink turned on, and Teri quickly brushed her teeth and returned to the room.

"I'm sorry. I just can't believe he was near the house and waited to get a picture like that."

Teri walked back to the bed cautiously, scrolling through the pictures again. She held up Gabby's phone.

"He was outside the window. What if he was watching us?"

"I don't think so. Even the more recent videos he had of me, it was like he was trying to fill whatever hole mom dying left, but he abandoned it. There was one more picture."

"What was it?"

Gabby described the fully nude picture and how she had destroyed it in the garbage disposal.

"That was evidence, Gabby! How could you shred it?"

"I couldn't stomach it, Teri. But realistically, evidence for what? That he's a pervert? What do you think?"

"He is a sick man, but he did so much for us. So much for Mom. And you."

"I know. That's why I was struggling to deal with it at first. I was even trying to justify that maybe he was just lonely, but these pictures. These pictures are something I can't forgive."

"He was so good to us when we were younger, Gabs. I still can't believe it, even with these pictures. Do you want to get him arrested? Do we destroy his life?"

"Right now I'd love nothing more than to see him arrested, but I've been thinking about it. Arrested for what? He had cameras put in his place of business. These pictures will prove he was a peeping Tom, but Mom's gone, and her diaries don't name him outright. Do you think anything will actually come of it?"

"I don't know. Maybe we tell him. Maybe we don't. I don't know. I need to think about it."

"Teri, I know he was good to us. I know he was good to Mom, but that doesn't make it okay."

"I don't know if I can destroy someone, even now. I mean, like you said, Mom's gone."

"Teri. He WHACKED OFF TO PICTURES OF OUR MOTHER THAT HE TOOK THROUGH HER WINDOW!"

Teri started to cry and covered her face.

She took a few minutes to calm herself and finally looked up. "What do you want to do, Gabby?"

"I want to destroy him," Gabby said. "Mom died not knowing this."

"But you don't know that!" Teri said. "You said in the videos she seemed cold and worried at one point, but then calmer. She never left the job. Do you think it's possible she let it go, thinking he was harmless?"

"Sister, even if all that was true, do you think she knows he was outside her window watching her naked or following us on our White Rock Lake trip?"

Teri opened her mouth and stopped. "No. You're right. There's no way she would have let that go. He crossed a line, but shouldn't we just forgive him? Mom's not here anymore."

"I still work there, Teri. You think I want to go back, knowing what I know and pretend that I don't? Do you really think I'm capable of that?"

Teri shook her head. "No."

"Besides, how can we forgive him if he doesn't ask for it?"

"You can forgive without being asked," Teri said quietly.

"NO! He needs to know we know. I want him gone. I want him in jail!"

"How? You said yourself that the odds are low anything would come from it. They were both adults and the cops or a lawyer could say Mom was lonely and liked it and let it happen. Even if we both know that's not true, do you want her memory violated like that? What about the unnecessary attention it would bring to our family? What if he says he had permission? How can we prove that? Mom's not here to defend herself."

"I don't care. I want him to know that we know. I want him fired and if he doesn't go to jail, to be humiliated. Do you want to see the videos?"

Teri stared at her younger sister for a long time, then back at the phone pictures and nodded. Gabby pulled out her laptop and pulled up the videos she had uploaded to her cloud storage. Teri's eyes teared up and her cheeks reddened. She imagined Ed standing outside their window, possibly seeing her or Gabby in their rooms half-dressed before he found Cora's room. How many nights could he have been there that he didn't take a picture? How many until he got the right one that hit his sweet spot? If only she had looked out the window, she might have been able to protect their mother.

"Stop, Gabby. I've seen enough. He needs to answer for this. We need a plan."

"Right now, I'd like to go in with a bat and destroy his office and burn the pictures."

"John can back me up, but I'm pretty sure you'll end up in jail. Do you want to risk having Ally taken away from you? Even with John's reputation, there's no guarantee they'll give her to me if that happens. Can you picture her with another family while you go through your case? And what about school?"

Gabby shook her head, knowing her sister was right.

"I have classes in the morning. I'll text Ed I have an unexpected project and can't come in. I'll come here instead, and we'll figure out a good way to handle this. I think we're both too amped up to decide this now. What do you think?"

Teri nodded a few times. "I agree."

GABBY GOT THROUGH HER MORNING CLASSES. SHE DID HER POST class assignments as fast as possible to free up the rest of her day. Benji had texted her that Sheila was working on the videos but odds were she wouldn't be done until later that night or the next day. If she found anything significant, she'd call sooner.

She finished up and went straight to Teri's house instead of heading to work. Besides Ally, only Grace was home as the rest of the kids were in school.

"Did you come up with anything?" Gabby asked.

"I have a few ideas. You?"

"Yes, but I'm hoping yours are less radical. In all but one scenario, I'm still carrying a bat."

"I talked to John after you left."

"You told him?"

"Of course. I want to be sure we can do the most damage and not get arrested in the process. If we go in there and you beat him to death, we'll both go to prison."

"So no bat?"

"Oh, no. You're taking the bat. Just make sure you don't kill him with it."

"Then why take it?"

"To scare him into not fighting us."

"I'm listening."

They spent the next hour discussing their ideas, stopping only to feed Ally and listen to a few interruptions from Grace. They wrote down some ideas and scratched out whatever didn't work. Teri, ever the planner, pulled out her laptop.

"What are you doing?"

"I'm going to make a spreadsheet. What do you think?"

"I think we need to keep this on paper and burn it as soon as we're done. No evidence."

"But we're not going to do anything illegal."

"Do you really trust that I won't do that with a hundred percent certainty?"

Teri looked at Ally and back up to Gabby. "For her, yes. You will not cross that line. Because if I go to jail and lose my kids, I'll shank you myself."

Gabby smiled. "I guess we are sisters after all. I wasn't left by aliens like you told me when I was little."

"It's almost 2:30," Teri said. "Do we get ready and do this tomorrow?"

"Why wait? Let's do this now before we lose our nerve."

Teri called her husband, and she sounded like she dominated the conversation, taking only a few breaths between speaking. She walked back into the room.

"John will be here within the hour. He'll watch Ally and Grace. The bus should be dropping off Linda shortly. Nick and Jess can help once they get home from school. John insisted on going in case things got out of hand, but I promised him we wouldn't let it get that far. I intend to keep that promise. Understood?"

Gabby nodded.

They spent the time before John's arrival gathering what they needed. They were ready to go by the time he got home. John took a long look at his wife.

"I know I can't change your mind, but I don't want to be bailing either of you out."

Teri looked back and nodded.

"Now go nail the bastard."

They didn't say much on the way to the office.

They entered. Everyone was scattered in their offices and cubes, but no one was in the Showroom. Gabby and Teri walked straight toward Ed's office, and Gabby walked in without knocking. Ed was sitting at his desk and looked up.

"Gabby, I was wondering where you were today. I was concerned since you hadn't called. Teri? Wow, this is a wonderful surprise!"

Ed stood up.

"Don't get up, Ed," Gabby said. "We need to talk to you, but first I need you to send everyone home."

Ed's face turned as if he hadn't heard her clearly. "Send everyone home? Why would I do that?"

Gabby held up her phone, flipped to a picture, and slid the phone across the desk. It was the lake picture.

"Now, Ed."

He looked down and slowly sat back in his chair. He reached for his phone and hit a button.

"Marcy? Please send everyone home. You, too. I think everyone's been working hard and want to give them a paid afternoon off."

He hung up. Gabby looked back and saw Marcy and the rest of the staff head out the door. Marcy was the last one out.

Teri tossed the long duffel bag she had walked in with on the desk and unzipped it.

Gabby held her stare on Ed for a moment before opening her mouth.

"I saw the videos, Ed. I saw the pictures, too."

Ed's forehead was already wet with sweat. "What do you want?"

"How could you, Ed?" Teri said, raising her voice. "How could you do that to Mom?"

"I didn't. I mean, I didn't mean to—"

"Cut the bullshit, Ed," Gabby yelled. "Don't give me you didn't mean to. You didn't mean to what? Sneak up and take pictures of us on a family trip to White Rock Lake? You didn't mean to install secret cameras to watch her? To watch me? Did you accidentally find yourself at our house with a camera taking naked pictures of her? Did you watch me? Or my sister?"

"No, no! Never!" Ed yelled as he started to cry and get up out of his seat.

Gabby reached into the duffel bag and pulled out a blue aluminum bat. "Sit down, Ed. Before you end up in jail for the rest of your life, you need to tell us everything."

Ed jumped back in his seat. "Please, no. I don't want to go to jail. I'm sorry. I just loved her. I never hurt her. I swear!"

"You don't think this would hurt her?" Teri said. "Knowing what you did? Are you sure you've never looked at my sister all this time she's worked here?"

"I would never do that to you or Gabby. You know I love you girls."

"Love us?" Gabby said. "What about the videos of Gabby?"

"She just reminded me of Cora. She looks so much like her. I thought maybe she might make me feel better after Cora died. It wasn't the same. Gabby, I'm sorry. I love you both like you were my own daughters."

"You have the nerve to say you love us after what you've done to our mother?" Teri said. "Would a normal person ever try to secretly videotape someone they claimed to love as a daughter? You sick piece of shit."

Ed started to cry hard. "I'm sorry. I loved her. I loved your mother."

"So you show that love by stalking her and replacing our dad in a family picture?" Gabby yelled as she swung the bat and smashed some items on Ed's desk. Ed jumped back and was shaking.

"I'm sorry. I'm so sorry. I loved her, but I know she didn't love me. I thought maybe after your dad died she might, but she never did. I would never hurt her. I would never hurt any of you."

"Did she know?" Gabby asked.

"She had to know I liked her, but she never said anything. She never knew about the videos, and she never knew about the pictures. Please, I'm sorry."

Ed started to sob uncontrollably. Neither of them had ever seen him do anything but smile. Gabby put the bat down and the sisters looked at him. This sick, pathetic, broken and lonely man.

Teri put her hand on Gabby's shoulders. "That's enough,

Gabby. He may be sick, but I believe him. He would have never hurt Mom."

"It doesn't change what he did!" Gabby yelled.

"No, but remember what he's done for our family. He didn't have to hire you, and he did. Yes, he may have had an agenda, but think about it. Can you really blame him for falling in love with Mom?"

Gabby took a few breaths, looked up at her sister and then back at a sobbing Ed. She slowly handed Teri the bat.

"Okay, Ed," Gabby said. "I'd be lying if I didn't say before yesterday, I loved you for taking care of my mom and being there all these years. I loved you like an uncle for being good to me and Teri. That's why I'm so pissed. Why we're pissed. Before we walked in here, I wanted to see you in jail or dead. Instead, I'm going to tell you what's going to happen."

Ed heaved and tried to calm himself. He wouldn't look up and covered his eyes with his palms. "Whatever you want, Gabby."

"I want you to resign. I have the videos. If you get another job, you better promise you will never do anything like this. Remember, Teri's husband is an attorney with connections. I'll find out where you are and where you're working, and I have friends that will figure out anything you do with a computer or camera. Do you understand?"

Ed nodded, his hands not leaving his face.

"We never want to see you again. Whatever good you did for us is meaningless now. I'm sorry you're lonely and I'm sorry that you fell in love with someone that would never love you back, but that doesn't excuse what you did. We will follow up and if we find out you do this to someone else, I will show up with those tapes and pictures and destroy the rest of your life. I'll make you an internet star. You need to be gone before I come back to work tomorrow and you'll leave instructions that I'm to keep my position. Are we clear?"

"Yes," Ed mumbled. "I'm sorry. Never again. I'm sorry I hurt you both."

Gabby turned to her sister. "Anything to add?"

Teri had tears in her eyes, mixed with anger and sadness. She shook her head.

"We're done here, Ed. Goodbye."

Gabby pulled a crowbar from the duffel bag and walked around the desk to where Ed sat. He pulled back in his chair as Gabby slammed the crowbar into his bottom desk drawer and ripped it open, breaking the lock. She grabbed the box with the original pictures. She used the crowbar to toss the tissues, lotion, and gloves out.

"I'm not touching this disgusting kit."

She slashed the crowbar across the top of Ed's desk, knocking down most of the items. She grabbed his nameplate and held it up.

"My mom gave you this one Christmas," Gabby said as she threw it across the room. "You don't deserve it."

The Mendez sisters walked out of the room without looking back. They got into the car and both held each other, shedding tears of anger and adrenaline until they settled down.

"Did we do the right thing?" Teri asked. "What if he does do this to someone else?"

"No," Gabby said. "You were right. He's a lonely coward, but I don't think he'd ever hurt anyone. I meant what I said about following his whereabouts. He has to live with not only losing Mom, but losing us, too. The punishment would never be enough, but I don't think he'll ever shake it."

The boss had been dealt with. Gabby was certain they would never see him again.

CHAPTER TWENTY-THREE

GABBY AND TERI RETURNED TO TERI'S HOUSE AND UPDATED JOHN on what had transpired.

After spending some time to let their adrenaline settle, Gabby decided to get Ally home. Gabby needed to process everything and didn't want the kids around. She had Angie and Ree to share her problems with, but she'd already put so much on them and this was a deep family issue. Teri had John to lean on, but right now, Gabby only had her Ally.

They were home for about an hour, which Gabby spent replaying all that had happened in her head and hoping they had done the right thing, when Benji called.

"Gabby, I just had a long conversation with Sheila."

"And did you find anything?"

"Yes. Yes, we did."

"What is it?"

There was silence for a few moments. "I'm not sure it's something we should discuss on the phone. It's really something you have to see. It's something I want to see. Sheila wants to show us both. It's important."

Gabby started to wonder what it could be that neither wanted to discuss it.

"Okay, Benji. That's fine. When?"

"Are you free tomorrow night?"

"I think I can be. Where?"

"Sheila says we can meet at her place if that is agreeable. If not, somewhere neutral, but not at your home or work, especially with what happened during my unwelcome visit. Also, you might not want to bring Angie or Ree into this. Not until we know what Sheila found."

This can't be good news, Gabby thought.

"It's okay. I won't lie to them if it comes up, but they'll understand. Her place sounds good."

"I'll call or text you with a time tomorrow. Sound good?"

"Yes, that's fine. Benji, should I be worried? This sounds bad."

"She only told me a fragment," Benji said. "I am still trying to process and decipher her meaning, but it may be best if we both heed her words that it would be best to see it for ourselves. She has never invited me to her home, so I expect it must be something big. However, what has been happening to you is already a grand event. She does love to put on a show, so that may also be part of it."

"Thank you, Benji. I'll wait for your call tomorrow."

GABBY WENT TO HER CLASSES THE NEXT MORNING. SHE WAS scheduled to work at 2, but wasn't sure if she could just stroll in after what happened with Ed. She kept wondering if he might just call their threat and stay. What if it escalated into a big disturbance? How far would he take it? How far would they?

She was still rattled and had a hard time concentrating on

the day's lectures, but made it through her first two classes. Benji texted her during her lunch break before her last class.

"We shall meet at Sheila's home at 6:30 tonight. Will that work for you?"

Gabby quickly replied yes. Benji sent her the GPS location pin.

Gabby got through her last class and thoughts of what they may have found overshadowed whatever worries she had about Ed.

It wasn't until Gabby was pulling into the parking lot that she felt butterflies in her stomach. She didn't see Ed's Lexus in the lot, but sometimes he took a cab or ride share if he didn't feel like dealing with traffic.

She walked into the office and made it a point to wave at Marcy, who wore a concerned look on her face and motioned for her to stop. Marcy came out of her office and met Gabby in the hallway.

"I don't know if you heard, but I have some bad news."

"What is it?"

"It's Ed. He came in early this morning and said he had resigned, effective immediately. He grabbed a few things from his office and just walked out. He wouldn't even let me throw a quick goodbye lunch."

"Did he say why?"

"He said he got a great job offer in California and couldn't give the details yet, but…"

"But what?"

"He looked sad. Wrong. I mean, if it was such a great opportunity, why wouldn't he be more excited? After all the years here, just can't imagine why he would leave like that."

Gabby looked at Marcy for a moment. "You've been here a few years. You worked with Ed and my mom, who were here the longest, right?"

"Yes, of course. I'm about to hit eight years."

"You never noticed Ed being off or different in all that time before today?"

Marcy's forehead crinkled. "What do you mean?"

"I don't know. If he looked sad or off, was it the first time?"

Marcy thought about it. "You know, a few years ago, when your mom was first diagnosed, he seemed really down for a few days. I had never seen that part of him. I know they were close, but that's it. He was always great with me. Other than a few times we had to work long hours, he was the best boss I've ever had."

Gabby smiled. Marcy was an attractive woman and younger than Cora, but she seemed to have no ill will toward him. Maybe it was just her mom. It didn't change anything, but it made her feel better thinking he may not have been doing that to multiple women. Maybe he never would again.

"I wonder how long it'll take to replace him," Gabby said.

"I don't know. I called the Corporate office, and they said they'd start looking for someone internally and expand if necessary but needed at least a couple of weeks to start the process. They were caught off guard, too, and weren't happy he didn't give more notice. They still made him a counteroffer, but he said he had already made up his mind and thought it would be a nice change."

Gabby nodded and smiled back at Marcy. She got back to her work. The mood in the office was somber. Besides Marcy and Ed, Gabby didn't see the others often since they were either in their office or working on their own projects while she worked on the Showroom or ER with the bodies. But today, everyone was walking in and out of their workspaces, making small talk. Gabby figured everyone was just trying to cope with the day's news.

Gabby walked by Ed's office and looked in. She saw his bottom drawer was still pulled out, empty and still bearing the scars from her angry crowbar attack. The rest of his desk had most of the items still on it. He had taken the nameplate that Cora had gifted him, but left the lamp, nice pens, and almost all the other trinkets he'd gathered over the years.

Gabby took in a breath, satisfied for the moment. She started to feel a little sympathy but quickly shut it down.

He pleasured himself with secret pictures of Mom, Gabby. Don't forget that.

That was enough to end any regret.

She returned to her work but didn't accomplish much for the day. She walked out two minutes after five and headed to Teri's house to update her about Ed and spend time with Ally until it was time to head to Sheila's.

Gabby arrived at Sheila's place about five minutes early. Traffic wasn't too bad, and the GPS instructions were solid. Sheila had a nice one-story house that was a little more than 3,000 square feet. It had a security bar gate entrance before the walkway and the front was aligned with several flowered azalea shrubs. Sheila's front door was painted red and when she answered the doorbell, Gabby smiled. She was expecting all black leather for some reason, but Sheila was in a blue skirt and top. She looked like a soccer mom except for her long, jet black hair and dark purple lipstick.

"Hello, Gabby. I'm Sheila," she said as she extended her hand. "Please come in."

Gabby entered the long hallway into an open living room, although it was the oddest living room she'd ever seen. Around the entire back, side walls and on both sides of the entertainment center that took up almost half of another wall, were plants and trees with different kinds of fruits and vegetables growing from them. The colors were mixed and gave the room a fake greenhouse look with way too many bright colors inside.

"Wow, this is colorful, but beautiful," Gabby said, adjusting to it.

"She is like Poison Ivy from the comics," Benji said, appearing from the kitchen. "With a much wider array of color choices."

Sheila laughed. "I'm into natural items. I study Wicca but am not a Wiccan, but I do enjoy learning about how different plants and herbs work together to help feed and heal. I'm far from a hippie, just curious."

"She is not kidding," Benji said. "Two years ago she asked if I had any knowledge on how to keep a potted ficus alive."

"That's when I was just getting into this," Sheila said. "Back then I was into origami and in place of all these plants were mostly tables of origami art. When I get into something, I get really into it."

Gabby didn't know what to say as she tried to take it all in.

"Not what you expected, I take?" Sheila said. "It's okay, you can be honest."

"No," Gabby said. "Not at all. When I hear paranormalist, I think of someone like Benji wearing mostly black and trying to let out an aura of mystery. No offense, Benji."

"None taken. I own it."

"I'm not a paranormalist by choice, really. Or a hacker. I was raised with both. I come from five generations, at least, of women with special senses to the paranormal. The hacker thing was more from my dad. Second generation computer geek."

"What do you do for a living?"

"Computer consultant during the day, and the paranormal stuff at night and weekends. I enjoy it. And, obviously, a devious hobbyist dedicated to whatever I'm into at any given moment. I understand you have a little one and you're a widow?"

Gabby nodded, not sure how to react.

"Please don't take offense," Sheila said. "I don't mean to make you uncomfortable. I'm pretty open about my life. I have two kids, but they're with their dad tonight. Married once, but wasn't for me. Plus he was a cheating prick. I don't have time to put up with crap like that. Life's too rewarding and too short to live in misery. I am currently only dating younger men. First, because it's way more fun than I expected it would be, and as a bonus, it pisses him off."

Gabby laughed at her openness, losing herself and almost forgetting why she was there.

"It is a true pleasure to meet you," Gabby said. "As happy as you sound, I know I'm here for a darker reason."

Sheila's smile softened but didn't go away. "Yes. I know. Are you ready?"

"How prepared do I need to be?"

"Whiskey or scotch?"

Gabby looked at her. "That bad, huh? Scotch, then."

Sheila walked over to her kitchen and came back with a bottle of scotch and three glasses. She motioned for Gabby to sit in the center of her long couch. Benji sat next to her and Sheila poured them each a drink.

Gabby started to get nervous as Sheila walked up to her entertainment center and pulled out a laptop. She flipped on her TV and hit a few buttons on her laptop until the display mirrored onto the 70-inch screen mounted on the wall.

"It's easier if you see this. I put together the clips of the times we saw a spike in activity. I won't say anything at first, so just watch for now. It's less than eight minutes. You might want to take a big swig before I begin."

Gabby wasn't much of a hard liquor drinker, but she downed her entire glass. Sheila poured more once she put it down. "Just in case."

Gabby took in a breath.

"These won't all be chronological," Sheila said as she hit play.

The first video was when Gabby first saw the reflections on the computer screen. She was working on one of the displays and then she jumped back, obviously scared. She was focused on the figure and turned her head back to the computer. That was when the reflections appeared to be everywhere.

The next video was the night Benji and Jay were in the office. It sped through several moments of Benji setting things up and walking around and talking. The camera started to glitch as Benji spoke. Sheila paused it again and pointed to three spots. The first was a reflective frame, the second a stapler, and finally, one of the computer monitors. Each item was facing a different angle, yet all had something reflecting off their surfaces. The same something.

Sheila pressed play and the video zoomed toward the monitor. It was a yellow, slitted eye with some type of scaly muscle around it. Almost like one of the cadavers.

The video resumed. The camera glitched a few times and Gabby saw a reflection or some kind of movement each time it did. This continued until the camera went black. It resumed and the same scene replayed, but this time it was from a different angle from a different camera. At this angle, as Benji moved at what appeared to be the same time the first camera went out, this camera caught something unmistakable. The right side of Benji's shirt collar flipped up and then down, as if an unseen hand had flicked it up. There were a few more minutes of video until it finally faded out.

Gabby looked at Benji, but he was staring at the floor. She looked at Sheila, and she made full eye contact and smiled.

"I don't understand," she said. "I did all that?"

"No, dear. Not even close," Sheila said. "Benji is the

stronger paranormalist. Tell her, Benji. And make eye contact."

Benji looked at her. "Sheila helped point out what I did not see. I can only tell you what I felt that night. I took detailed notes after I got home and dosed myself with ibuprofen after getting knocked around and almost stabbed by the flying dagger. The sensations I get in person cannot be replicated in a video. I can tell you what I felt that night I was there. I felt something was all around me, but it was thin and not a heavy presence."

"What does that mean?"

"Think about a heavyweight boxer like Mike Tyson or George Foreman versus the lankiest, skinniest guy you knew in high school. I'm sure your memories hold someone."

"Jamie LaVoie. He was so skinny if he stood sideways behind a small tree we couldn't see him. We called him Stick."

"Exactly. It is like that. I've sensed heavy presences before and they typically loom big and dark. I felt the dark sense, but not the heavy presence. It was as if whatever was there was flimsy and barely leaving its mark, just like a shadow. Or—"

"A reflection."

"Yes, a reflection. I couldn't feel anything but the darkness, not a physical thing. It was definitely present. You saw the echoes of it, especially in that monitor, and I expect the only reason that was clearer than anything else is because I made it angry. It did not want me there. The moment when I pretended to hurt you and own you was the most intense."

"There's more, Gabby," Sheila said. "Prepare yourself."

The next scene was when she saw the eyes of the displays all reflecting back at her. Her head was turning side to side as she looked at all the cadavers. She remembered seeing the reflections just before the eyeballs popped out.

But that's not what happened in the video. Gabby was on the floor, trembling, but then stood up, walked up to the figure nearest her and reached into its eye sockets. She yanked both eyeballs out and tossed them to the floor herself.

She moved slowly toward the other cadavers and repeated the process, reaching in and pulling without even flinching. She didn't appear to be agitated, just moving with a purpose.

After the last cadaver, she moved back to her original position. The screen paused.

Sheila walked up to the TV and pointed to one of the small framed wall paintings without saying a word. Gabby noticed the eyes in that reflection, then Sheila resumed play. On the video, Gabby sat in her position for a minute, then started yelling. This is what she remembered. Screaming as the eyes were on the floor, but in her memory they flew out of the heads as she stared at them from a distance. She never pulled them out.

Sheila let the video keep going as the rest of the scene played out like Gabby remembered.

"How?" was all Gabby could get out. She looked back at the screen and then to Sheila and Benji. "I don't remember that. I did it. I did it all."

"It wasn't you, Gabby," Benji said.

"I did that! Are you trying to say that's not me in the video? Or it's whatever you sensed?"

"Both," Benji said. "You carry no memory of doing what we just witnessed, obviously, but you do recall the slight reflections and lights bouncing off the glass and smooth surfaces. There is no doubt you extracted those eyeballs, so whatever this thing is, it appears to have invaded your mind and you did all that subconsciously. Your exhaustion, coupled with all that has been occurring, may have contributed to it as well."

He paused, trying to find his next words.

"Or it just made me do it," Gabby whispered. "Oh, my God. If it can control me, I could be a danger to everyone around me. I could hurt…"

"Do not jump to that conclusion yet," Benji said. "I do not believe you are capable of harming your daughter. That night, whatever that was, surrounded you. When you are frightened, that fear can be used against you, especially when you are alone without distractions. It would require tremendous concentration just to make you drop an object, but to have that kind of power to get you to stand up, walk around and physically extract eyeballs from multiple skulls? That takes some power. It also requires that you be so completely focused and fearful that it could capitalize on it and cause you to perform its bidding. Odd question, but were you maybe compromised that day?"

"Compromised how?"

"Drinking, drugs, medication."

"No, I've never had a drink during or before work. I have to keep my mind clear for my classes. I drink the few times I go out with my friends or with my sister, but haven't been drunk in years. No drugs or meds either."

"Then one last question. Darkness. Have you been introduced to anything dark recently? Or anyone, for that matter, that would be considered a dark or troubled person?"

Gabby's thoughts immediately jumped to Ed.

"Those tapes," Gabby said. "Did you find anything unusual with me or possibly with my boss? Something non-supernatural, I mean."

Sheila shook her head. "I didn't have time to go through every minute of the files, but nothing that stood out. I concentrated on the times that I received from Benji. What's the deal with your boss?"

"I don't want to go into detail, but I just found out he

wasn't a good man. He did some horrible things to my mother. He took pictures and video without her knowledge. Other than my mom and my husband dying within the last two years, this is something dark that I wasn't aware of until now."

Sheila moved and sat on the opposite side of Benji, leaving Gabby between them.

"So much trauma in such a short time," Sheila said. "Death. Betrayal. Even sorrow is a form of darkness that can be taken advantage of."

"Advantage of? How do you mean?"

"Just as there is good in this world," Benji said. "There is evil. Things we see in humans, and things we cannot see. Things we may not understand but are there. Spirits, entities, cursed places."

"I never bought into anything like that," Gabby said. "Do I think there are things we don't understand? Yes, but not like that. At least not until now. So darkness or evil. You're saying all these bad things that happened to me caused this?"

"No, just that it is a possibility," Benji said. "Some darkness and entities are attracted to pain and suffering. You have had more than your share recently. How long ago did these incidents with your boss happen?"

"It started several years ago and lasted until my mom was diagnosed with cancer. I had no idea who he really was until I had access to the videos and his desk. My sister and I just confronted him yesterday. We forced him to quit."

"You don't have to give details," Sheila said. "This lingering darkness from this man has festered for so long and was there without you even knowing. Whatever this is that's happening to you, he could have been the doorway. Then the sorrow and death could have made you a prime target."

"A target for what? To scare the hell out of and play with?"

"That is not something we can know," Benji said. "I do know something was present at your workplace and it seems to be pursuing you, your friends, and your family. This has happened multiple times now in your house, in your office, and while out in the open. That is not common."

"What, that it's following me around?"

"If it is a spirit, usually they attach to a location, such as an old house or building. Some attach to people, but the fact that it seems to be following in so many places and at the same time protecting you like it did when I claimed you were mine is the unusual part. It must be strong or have something strong to attach itself to in order to do what it has been able to thus far. You have never had anything like this happen to you? Maybe when you were little?"

Gabby shook her head. "Never. Teri would scare me, but it was just stupid things like jumping out from behind a door. What do I do?"

"There's only one thing we can really do," Benji said. "We must perform a type of seance. Find out what this entity is and what it may want. We know it desires to haunt you and protect you simultaneously. Maybe we can rid it from this world. I am willing to try, but not at your office again. Whatever it might be, it already caught my scent there and would have an advantage. The next logical place would be at your home."

"My home?"

"Yes, it is the place where you feel safest. If Sheila agrees, I would welcome her help. I am the stronger medium, but she is by far the smarter one. She can read patterns and use logic to figure out things I may not see."

"Yes, I'm willing to help," Sheila said. "We need to do this sooner than later."

"Will it just be the three of us?" Gabby asked, her voice trembling.

"I'd suggest bringing people you care about. They'll help protect you, especially if you have a bond with them."

"Ree and Angie," Gabby said. "My sister needs to take care of Ally, plus I don't think she'd be able to handle stuff like this. She's strong but would probably die of fright if this happened to her."

"That sounds like an excellent plan and it is probably best if we leave out your sister," Benji said. "We require a focused audience, so I will also ask Jay to skip this. The only time he attended one of my seances, he was more terrified than my client. I do not believe he will mind. Sheila, are you available tomorrow?"

"Yes, I can get my ex to take the kids one extra night. He knows about my side work and won't mind."

"Great. How about you, Gabby?"

"My work Showcase is tomorrow night," Gabby said. "I've been working on it for months, but none of that matters right now."

"Then please call your friends and find out if they are able to participate tomorrow evening."

Gabby texted her friends, and both agreed they were fine for the following night but asked for details and why they hadn't heard from her all day. She would catch them up later.

"Then we are confirmed," Benji said. "I am sorry you have to endure this, Gabby, but we will do our best to sort this out and rid it from your life. I'm the best chance you have, at least in this city."

"He's not just boasting," Sheila said. "Probably the best in this part of the country."

Gabby felt a little better but was still scared. She knew getting back to her normal life was what she needed. She wondered how she could ever get past knowing she pulled out those eyeballs without even realizing it.

"I have to do this. This time it was dead bodies I pulled

eyes from. What if I try to do that to someone I love next time? My God, what if I do that to Ally?"

Then Gabby lost it. She started to sob, thinking of the unimaginable possibility of hurting her own daughter.

"It shall not come to that," Benji said. "The love you have for your daughter is stronger than you know."

CHAPTER TWENTY-FOUR

ANGIE AND REE GOT TO GABBY'S HOUSE AN HOUR EARLY TO HELP her prepare and to find out what they missed. Gabby told them everything about Ed and her mom. She hesitated before continuing.

"I'm almost afraid to tell you the next part," Gabby said.

"Why?" Ree asked.

"I'm worried you'll be afraid of me."

"That's just not possible, Gabs," Angie said. "Spill."

Gabby gave them the details of her visit to Sheila's house, beginning cautiously, but then hurried to tell them the rest before she lost her nerve.

They both hugged her.

"I could never be afraid of you," Angie said. "And I'm so sorry about Ed."

Ree put his hand on her shoulder. "Ed. Hard to believe, but you have us and Ally, so the hell with him. And scared of you? Come on. How could I ever be more afraid of you than I am of Angie? Have you seen how she looks in the morning? If you pulled out my eyeballs you'd be doing me a favor."

Angie punched him in the arm but welcomed the smile on Gabby's face.

"I don't know what I'd do without you both. I should have never been worried about telling you."

There was a knock at the door as Benji and Sheila arrived.

Without hesitation, the paranormal pair took over the coffee table in the middle of Gabby's living room.

Gabby returned to the kitchen to finish preparing the food she almost let burn when she was speaking to her best friends. Once Benji and Sheila were done with their setup, the five of them sat at the table to eat.

"Nice meal," Benji said.

"You said it would be good to eat beforehand since it can be draining."

"Yes, plus I thoroughly enjoy free food. It is never a bad idea to have sustenance in your body prior to a seance. The ceremony can weaken your senses and cause nausea. The fact that you are an excellent cook makes it that much more welcome."

"What exactly are we going to do?" Ree asked.

"He's a little nervous," Angie said, doing her best to hide her own fear.

"I would be concerned if you weren't," Benji said. "Fear is our defense mechanism, and I am hopeful everyone's senses are on high alert. At Gabby's work, I had no idea what we were dealing with, and this spirit ignored me until I pretended to harm her. This time I am going to try to make contact directly without baiting and maybe ascertain what it desires both from Gabby and its overall purpose."

They finished the meal and moved to the coffee table. Sheila sat on one long side with her back to the entertainment center that housed Gabby's flat screen TV, Angie and Gabby sat directly across from her, and Ree sat alone at the shorter end to Sheila's right. Benji flipped the main living room lights off and then took his seat next to Sheila.

"Gabby, please sit directly across from me."

Gabby switched places with Angie.

"Are you going to get possessed or something like that?" Ree asked, his voice trembling.

"Nothing so dramatic. It will be more like mediation than a crystal ball. We must all try and sync our emotions and maintain calm. It will boost my senses. It will boost all our senses if we do it correctly. I will tell you what I feel or hear and between Sheila and I, hopefully we will pick up something. Should any of you feel, sense or hear anything yourselves, just allow it to happen. This is all about channeling energy."

Sheila nodded. "The love you and Angie share with Gabby is critical. Benji and I have a bond with our senses, but that pales in comparison to the emotional bond people can form with each other. That energy will help amplify Gabby's energy, which we will try to amplify even further to attract whatever this is without making it angry."

"Just do as I say and try to remain as calm as possible," Benji said. "I have done this many times, but no two seances are the same. Most often it takes just a few minutes to yield results or end in failure."

Benji placed one large candle in the center of the table.

"I thought there weren't going to be any crystal balls?" Ree said.

"The flame serves a dual purpose. If any of you are distracted, simply use the candle to calm yourself. In the event something is present, the flame may dance to announce its arrival."

Benji lit the candle.

"Has anything bad ever happened during one of these seances?" Ree asked.

"Define bad."

"Scary demons try to kill you. Stuff goes flying around trying to kill you. Basically anything that might end in a horrible death."

"On two occasions. Once an object on a shelf fell and left a minor cut on my thigh. During the second incident, a few light objects went airborne for a few seconds, then fell to the floor harmlessly. Nothing I would consider a major event."

"But what about all the stuff that's happened to Gabby already?" Ree asked, his voice shaking. "And to us?"

"This is why I asked Gabby to bring you here. The stronger the bond, the stronger the protection."

Ree nodded, trying his best to calm his nerves. Angie had a concerned look on her face and made no attempt to hide her worry.

"Let us begin. Gabby, are you ready?"

Gabby nodded.

"One thing the movies do get right," Benji said. "We need to hold hands. Please do not let go until I instruct you to."

Benji extended his hands and took Sheila's to his left and Ree's to his right. The chain of hands continued from Sheila to Angie to Gabby and ended with Gabby and Ree slapping their palms together to complete their not-so-perfect circle.

Benji raised his joined hands and lowered them, and the rest mimicked the movement. "Everybody take in one big, deep breath and then remain quiet."

"Do we need to close our eyes?" Angie asked.

"Leave them open. Be attentive to everything, even if it seems insignificant. Now, deep breath."

He led them with a big inhale and everyone followed suit. Collectively, they let out a long exhale.

Benji stared at the candle and started to hum. It was soft and low, but a steady tone. Gabby looked at him while Ree stared at Angie.

"I know you are here," Benji whispered. "I can feel your presence, but you are attempting to hide. Please, do not conceal yourself. I am not here to harm Gabby. I only wish to speak with you."

He returned to his humming.

"Come out. Speak with me. Speak to us all. Gabby is here with her friends. They desire that you join them. To become part of their own circle."

The candle began to flicker and Ree, Angie, and Gabby gasped. Ree started to get up, but Angie pulled him down.

"Stay still!" she whisper-yelled at him.

He calmed down as the candle flame danced.

"Yes, please continue," Benji said. "Come out. Come closer so that I may hear you. What is it you seek from Gabby? Do you desire her? Do you want to bring her harm—"

Benji let out a sharp gasp.

"Hold…" He gasped again. "Hold your advance. I only wish—"

Benji gasped again as the candle started to flicker.

"Why?" he gasped.

"Benji?" Gabby yelped.

"He's okay," Sheila said. "It's strong. He just needs to adjust."

Benji took in several short breaths before exhaling. The floor started to vibrate underneath them, like a stereo with the bass turned up too loud.

"Thank you for allowing me to see you," he whispered, still short of breath but calming himself. "Why are you here? What do you seek from Gabby?"

The floor started to buzz harder and the ceiling fan above them started to rattle.

"I am Gabby's friend. I can relay a message to her if you wish. Is it desire that compels you?"

Benji gasped again. His eyelids closed, then popped open, revealing red and bulging eyeballs.

Their connected grips around the table tightened. Ree started shaking, and sweat trickled down his face.

"What's happening?" Angie asked. "Is this normal?"

Sheila turned to Benji. Gabby saw her face and then felt chills run up her arms and down her spine.

"Sheila?" Gabby said.

Benji's head snapped back, and he stared straight up to the ceiling.

"Benji!" Sheila said, trying not to yell.

Benji let out short, rapid breaths. "Then why?"

The table flipped up and smashed Benji's face, catching Sheila's shoulder as it rose. The vibration they'd felt crescendoed into the rattle of an earthquake and Gabby's flat screen formed a small web of cracks as the table came back down and landed over Benji, knocking him on his back.

Gabby and her two closest friends screamed. They leaped up to pull the table off Benji and looked up as a loud popping noise emanated from the entertainment center. The cracks on the TV screen expanded. Gabby finally saw a clearer reflection of what she had only seen partially in her office. The yellow eyes and musculature that she had witnessed before now had a full mask of facial muscles and a long mop of hair draped down its shoulders. It sneered.

"Do you see that?" Angie asked.

Ree ran back and let out a high-pitched squeal. Gabby couldn't move.

They were all seeing it.

Benji sat up, his nose bleeding. Sheila tried to help him to his feet, but the TV flew off the entertainment center and shattered over his head, knocking him back to the floor.

"Stop!" Gabby yelled. "Stop this!"

The television then lifted into the air with Benji rising

underneath it. His body flew sideways as a sudden roar of wind threw him across the house and into the window on the other side of the kitchen. The window shattered as Benji smacked into it and bounced back, slamming hard on the floor with a loud thud.

"Benji!" Sheila screamed as she ran toward him.

Sheila flew forward as an unseen force lifted her off her feet and sent her flying, landing on the broken table. There was a swooshing sound and something crackled. The candle, which had been thrown when the table flipped, was now on its side. It still emitted a flame. The corner of the throw rug under the coffee table where the candle had landed was on fire.

Ree stood frozen in fear while Gabby ran to the kitchen to grab the fire extinguisher from under the sink. Angie helped Sheila to her feet and pulled her from the flames as Gabby raced past her to try to put out the fire.

As Gabby struggled to focus on the extinguisher instructions, the flame shot up in the air toward Ree. He didn't move, but Angie rushed over and pushed him aside, leaving him with only a singed arm. Gabby pulled up the extinguisher and hit it. The flame went out quickly and then everything stopped.

The vibrating was gone and everything stopped moving. Gabby and Ree rushed to check on Benji while Angie checked on Sheila.

"Sheila's out cold," Angie said. "But she seems to be breathing fine. I don't see any visible injuries."

"Benji's breathing," Gabby said as she fell to her knees beside him. "Ree, help me flip him."

Benji was face down, but together they turned him over. He was bleeding, and a bone was sticking out of his lower calf. Ree fled to the kitchen sink and threw up.

"Benji," Gabby said. "Benji, are you okay?"

She shook him as Angie arrived and examined the rest of his body.

"He might be in shock," Angie said. "We need to call an ambulance."

"Benji," Angie said as she put her hands on his face. "Benji, open your eyes."

Benji's eyes slowly opened. "Gabby. The spirit. It is a big, dark spirit, but it is not alone. It is connected to something far stronger, but whatever it is, it wasn't here in your house. Gabby, the doorway. Your boss was not the passage through it. It was the deaths. The deaths surrounding you."

"What do you mean?" Gabby asked.

"You are the doorway, Gabby. This spirit. These entities. They arrived here through you."

Benji's breathing became labored. Angie moved to the other side of the room to call 9-1-1.

"Benji," Gabby said, trying to hide her panic. "I'm sorry, but how did it come through me? What does it want?"

Angie returned and put her hands on Benji's face and forehead.

"I do not know," Benji whispered.

"But how can I be the doorway?"

"Something about you. Something dark you are either unable to see or something secret you have locked deep inside. If it came through you, darkness was the only way. Your trauma alone could not have been enough to do this. It must be something deeper and darker, or a combination of events. Is there something you have yet to tell me? Something you have yet to tell anyone? Look inside and try to determine what it is you are holding on to so you can come to terms with it."

Tears started to fall down Gabby's face.

"Gabby, you must be careful. I still have no clear vision on what it desires, but this other, stronger being it is connected to..."

Benji's eyes started to close.

"Benji! Stay with me. The stronger thing. What about it?"

"It's more dangerous," he said as his eyes opened. "More cunning. More to fear. Although it may not have been present here tonight, the reflection spirit was thinking about it and they were communicating."

"How am I going to save my family and friends if something this strong is around me?" Gabby asked. "How can I protect my daughter?"

"In the Heavens above, the angels, whispering to one another can find, among their burning terms of love, none so devotional as that of 'Mother.'"

"What is that supposed to mean?"

"A poem by Edgar Allan Poe. Even he knew what I tried to tell you last night. The love of a mother is one of the strongest weapons you will ever wield. Let it guide you."

"I think you're more damaged than you look."

Benji looked down at his leg.

"This is definitely the worst, most violent thing that has ever happened to me in all my paranormal experiences."

"I'm so sorry," Gabby said. "I never thought anyone would get hurt."

"Do not concern yourself," Benji said as he winced and took in sharp breaths. "The pain is numbing now. I can barely feel anything. Besides, I may have a decent reputation in the paranormal community, but this will make me legendary."

It was the last thing he said before he passed out.

"Gabby," a groggy voice said.

Sheila was standing up, dirty and dazed but coherent.

"Sheila!" Angie said. "Sit down! The ambulance is on its way."

"Is Benji okay?" Sheila asked.

"No," Gabby said, still kneeling by Benji. "He passed out and his leg is broken. Bone splitting broken."

"What did he say to you, Gabby?"

"He said there are two spirits or beings. The reflection one that has been tormenting me from the start, and another, stronger one that wasn't here. They were communicating. He also said my boss wasn't the doorway."

"Then who?" Sheila asked.

"I am the doorway."

"So what is it that you're keeping from us?" Sheila demanded.

Gabby's tears came down harder. "I can't."

"Gabby, tonight was bad. I've never been through anything like this. Benji risked everything to do this for you. You need to tell us what happened. It may help us get rid of it if you can find a way to cope with whatever it is you're hiding."

"Leave her alone," Angie said as she put her arms around her best friend. "She doesn't owe you or Benji anything."

"No," Gabby said, pulling away from Angie. "I need to come clean."

"What are you talking about?" Ree asked.

"Benji was right. There's something I've never told anyone. Not even you, Angie."

"It's okay, Gabby. What is it?"

"Michael."

"What about that bastard?"

"The night he died…"

"Yes," Angie said, a look of concern coming over her. "He beat you that night and you were pregnant. You defended yourself and his drunk ass fell through the glass table. Isn't that what happened?"

"Yes, that is what happened."

"Then what, you feel guilt because he died during a fight?"

"No, Angie. That's just it. He sat there bleeding and I swear I thought he was dead, but before the police or ambulance got there, as I was crying and bleeding from the fight, he moved. Blood spit out of his mouth and he started to breathe again."

"Gabby, maybe you should stop," Ree said.

"No! I have to get this out. He spit out blood and he started breathing. He had just kicked and punched me in the stomach. I was afraid he was going to get back up and finish what he started. I fully believed he was going to kill me if he had a second chance. I saw him breathing and then he looked up at me with this evil grin. I grabbed my stomach and thought there was no way the baby could have survived. That just consumed me with rage and my only thought was protecting Ally. I picked up a shard of glass from the broken table and as soon as he raised his head, I slammed the glass through his throat. It stayed stuck inside without breaking, and as he struggled, I stood up and lifted my foot, then brought it down with all the force I could and smashed the glass in deeper. Then I watched until he stopped breathing for good. He was defenseless at that point. I could have run away, but I didn't. I murdered the son of a bitch. I killed him."

No one spoke for the next few seconds as Gabby broke down into Angie and Ree's arms.

"It's okay," Angie whispered. "You feared for your life and for Ally's. No jury in the world would convict you, and this will never leave this room."

Angie looked up at Sheila. "Never leaves this room, right?"

Sheila took a moment to process and didn't realize Angie was looking directly at her. "No, of course not. I don't know your history, but if that man was willing to risk killing your unborn baby, in my eyes, you were fighting for two lives. Angie's right. No jury would convict, but it won't come to that, because as she said, it will ever leave this room. Not through my lips."

Ree reached out to grab Sheila's hand. "Thank you."

"There is something I don't understand," Sheila said. "If you were the doorway, then what does it want? It hurt Benji and it tried to hurt me, but it won't hurt you. There are sometimes spirits who become infatuated with a living human, but I didn't get that sense. Even though my abilities are nowhere close to Benji's, that's something that's usually easy to spot."

A cell phone went off. Gabby looked over, realizing it was hers, but she buried her head back in Angie's chest.

"I don't want this darkness around me anymore," Gabby said.

Another phone started to buzz. Angie reached into her back pocket.

"It's Teri," Angie said as she moved to answer. "Hello?"

"Angie!" Teri screamed, then there was muffled movement.

Gabby heard the yell and snatched the phone from Angie's hands.

"Teri? Teri, what's wrong?"

"Gabby! Something's here! It's tearing my house apart! Hurry!"

The phone cut off and Gabby jumped up. "Something's attacking Teri. We need to get over there now!"

CHAPTER TWENTY-FIVE

GABBY GRABBED HER PURSE AS HER BEST FRIENDS STARTED FOR the door. They heard a loud siren getting closer.

"Sheila, can you please stay with them until they take Benji?" Angie said as Gabby and Ree rushed out. "And get out before the police arrive. If they do get here, just tell them whatever you have to."

"I got you covered," Sheila said. "Place was ransacked, Benji walked in and was attacked, but no one saw them since they wore masks. Gabby had to rush out due to a family emergency."

"That was quick," Angie said.

"Not my first time. We have to come up with quick stories to replace 'An evil spirit did it,' even if it's the truth. As soon as they take Benji to the hospital, I'm heading to you. Just text me the address and I'll be there as soon as I can."

Angie nodded as she passed the EMTs on their way in.

Gabby, Ree, and Angie jumped in Angie's car.

Angie screeched into Teri's driveway and Gabby was out the door before she came to a complete stop. The front door was open and Gabby flew through with her friends right behind.

The living room looked worse than Gabby's. Debris was everywhere, and the couch and love seats were flipped upside down. Screams were coming from the rear of the house.

Gabby ran toward the sound and saw the door of Teri's master bedroom opening and closing. Nick's door, the last room down the hall, was in the middle of the hallway, pulled off its hinges.

"Teri!" Gabby screamed as she saw a scattered mess of mattress and clothes when she entered the master bedroom.

"Gabby!" Teri yelled from the direction of Nick's room.

The trio ran toward the room and Nick was pressed against a wall, being held by an unseen force with his legs three feet off the carpet. His sisters were in the closet.

Its doors were open and Grace and Linda covered their ears as they screamed. Teri stood in front of her daughters with her arms outstretched, trying to form a protective wall.

Jess ran toward her brother.

"Leave him alone!"

Nick's body jumped forward and then slammed back against the wall. Jessica's head flinched sideways like something had punched the side of her face. She fell.

"Mommy!" Grace and Linda screamed.

Jessica ran back into the closet and Teri turned toward her sister.

"Gabby! Help us!"

Nick fell from the wall and something in the room moved. A shadow headed toward Gabby and passed through her, zipping down the hallway.

Nick's room was calm. Teri ran toward her son and held him. "Are you okay, Nick?"

"Yes, I'm okay, Mom."

Gabby let out a sigh and looked back at the girls. Jess was carrying Grace and Linda had her arms wrapped around her older sister's leg.

"Teri, where's Ally?!"

"I put her in the bathtub in my bathroom to protect her!"

Gabby's face dropped and she rushed out of the room.

"Everybody stay here," Teri yelled as she ran out to follow Gabby.

Gabby got to the master bedroom first and leaped past the overturned mattress. Teri almost knocked her down as she rushed into the bathroom and pulled the curtain so hard that it tore, sending the shower rod flying. Ree and Angie ran in behind them, wondering why the sisters were staring downward and not moving.

Ally's stuffed rabbit sat alone in the center of the tub.

"Where is she!" Gabby screamed as she grabbed Teri by the shoulders and shook her. "Are you sure she was here?"

Teri couldn't answer as she stared at the rabbit. Gabby picked it up, but Ally wasn't underneath. She ran out of the bathroom and started to flip the mattress over. Everyone else joined in. Ree helped her move the mattress, and Teri and Angie went through Teri's huge walk-in closet and started flipping clothes and shoes around. Nothing.

They all rushed out of the room and started tearing through the living room. Teri stopped in front of Nick's open doorway and screamed at her children. "Check all the rooms for Ally! She's not here!"

The entire family minus John, who was at work and had no idea what was happening, moved frantically through the house.

"She's gone! She's not inside!" Gabby yelled.

"Mom!" Jess yelled from the hallway. "The garage!"

They rushed to the garage, but Ally wasn't there.

"They took her!" Gabby yelled. "My baby! Why? WHY?"

Teri called 9-1-1. Gabby was gasping as she frantically ran to the backyard to continue searching and then headed around the house to check the front yard. Sheila pulled into the driveway as Gabby was checking between Teri's trees.

"What's wrong?" Sheila asked as she hurried out of her car. She was holding Benji's bag.

"Ally's missing! Help me!"

They both looked around the front yard and behind the bushes, but there was still no sign of Ally.

The police arrived within ten minutes and Sheila headed inside to tell everyone just to say someone in dark clothing came in so they wouldn't be treated as suspects. She wanted to ensure their stories would match up with the story she had prepared to explain Benji's injury at Gabby's house.

Teri spoke to the police initially and told them Sheila's story and that Ally was missing.

Gabby was in Teri's bedroom, sitting on her reading chair and sobbing while Angie held her.

Sheila walked in while Teri was speaking to the police.

"Gabby, I might have a way to find Ally."

Gabby looked up. She couldn't get any words out, but her red eyes begged to know more.

"You're the doorway," she whispered, not wanting the officers to hear. "I might be able to use that connection to track her."

Gabby's sobbing slowed as she looked up at Sheila. "How?"

"The seance. The reflection spirit or demon or whatever it is, was there with us while something else was here and took the baby. Whatever these things are, they were intelligent enough to distract us while they apparently took Ally. I don't know if they did it to get to you or if Ally is who they wanted all this time. Either way, we have to find her, and if you're the doorway, maybe I can sense something through you while everything is still fresh."

"Please. If it'll help, do whatever you have to."

Sheila nodded. "We need to keep the police out of this room for a few minutes."

"Get Ree," Angie said.

Sheila stepped out and Ree returned with her.

"What's going on?" he asked.

"Sheila thinks she might be able to track Ally through Gabby," Angie said. "We don't know how long the police will be here. Can you use your expert ability to annoy other human beings to keep them from coming in?"

"I will wield my power to its maximum effect," Ree said. "Let me know when you're done, but I swear they won't interrupt."

Ree walked out and Sheila locked the door. She set Benji's bag on the floor and reached in. She pulled out a small vial of some type of reddish liquid.

"We need to lay that mattress back down," Sheila said.

She helped Angie set the mattress back on the bed frame.

"Please sit," Sheila said, motioning to the bed. Gabby moved from the chair to the edge of the mattress. Angie sat next to her, still holding her tight.

Sheila sat on the other side of Gabby.

"What are you going to do with that?" Angie asked, squeezing Gabby a little harder.

"It's okay, Ang," Gabby said. "Whatever we have to do."

"This is a cinnamon essential oil. It should help increase my ability to connect with you and break through any mental or supernatural barriers."

Gabby nodded.

"Can you get me a small towel?" Sheila asked Angie. Angie moved toward the bathroom and returned with a teal hand towel.

Sheila poured a few drops of oil onto her hands and rubbed them together. She used the towel to dry her left hand. She placed her right palm on Gabby's forehead and moved it around until she found whatever spot she was looking for. "I need to put my other hand near your heart. Skin on skin increases the odds of making a connection."

"Don't ask. Just do it," Gabby said.

Sheila placed her left hand underneath Gabby's shirt and laid it on Gabby's chest. She closed her eyes.

"Gabby," Sheila whispered. "I need you to think about the spirit. Think about when you saw its reflection at your office the first time. Think about tonight at your house. Think about that shadow you saw tonight. Try not to think of anything else. Just take those images and keep repeating them in your head. Take a few big breaths."

Gabby did as she was told. On the fourth breath, the images of the reflections she saw in the Gymnast's eyes alternated with what she saw in her living room during the seance.

"I got it," Gabby said.

"Yes, I can sense something. Now, don't stop. Keep going and don't think of anything else. Keep repeating these memories and images in your head, no matter how disturbing."

Gabby continued. The pictures in her head repeated over and over. More time passed than she expected, but she kept going, thinking Sheila would interrupt her soon.

"Quick, think of your husband. Think of stabbing him in the neck with the glass. Every detail. Tell me when you do it."

Angie started to say something, but Sheila stared her into silence.

Gabby shuddered, but did it. She pictured the scene again vividly. Michael. He was bleeding and starting to move as Gabby cradled her stomach, hoping her unborn baby was okay. She felt phantom pain as she recalled cutting her hand as she lifted the largest shard of glass she could find and drove it into his neck. It made a wet, popping sound. Michael gasped and even as blood started to spurt from his neck, he managed to pull himself up a few inches. Gabby lifted her shoe and slammed it down on the protruding glass. The shard shattered as her foot came down on his neck. It was as satisfying a memory as when it actually happened.

Gabby gasped. "I did it. He's dead."

"Now think of Ally! Picture her and only her!"

The words came on so suddenly and with such authority, Gabby jumped and all she could think of was Ally.

Sheila gasped and gasped again without exhaling. Her mouth opened and Gabby felt something inside her pulse with heat as Sheila's hands let go.

"I see it," Sheila said. "The spirit that's been haunting you. Benji was right. It does have a partner."

"Where is she, Sheila?" Gabby yelled.

"She's definitely not here, but there's something else. The partner is also a dark spirit, but neither of them is capable of carrying another human out of here. Maybe strong enough to toss around, but there was someone else here. Someone corporeal. Not a spirit."

"Another person was here?" Gabby asked.

"Yes. They must have a human helping them. It's just a faint whisper of another presence, but still living."

"Where did they take her?"

"They're out of range. Ally was in a vehicle with this other person. They traveled in a northwest direction after leaving the neighborhood. They have to be at least a few miles out by now if I can't see them. The signal weakens the further away they are."

The doorknob turned and there was a frantic knocking.

"Dammit, Ree," Angie said as she got up to answer it.

It was Teri, with Ree right by her.

"Let her in," Ree said.

"Gabby, I just went with the police next door to the Jamison's. They have a doorbell camera. Tammy just came over and she gave me her phone. Look!"

She pulled the phone up and there was a clip from the doorbell camera. Teri pressed play. A car was parked and waiting on the street. It was too dark to make out the driver's face, but Teri pointed at the windshield.

"It's a ride share!"

A short shadow ran back to the car and appeared to be holding something. The car took off, but there was a darkness around the plates, like they had been purposely blocked.

"That's who took Ally," Gabby said.

"The reflection spirit attacked us at your house while the darker spirit attacked your sister's family here," Sheila said. "Both distracted everyone long enough for the person to grab Ally. We need to head out and hopefully get closer so I can get a better read."

"The police have notified all emergency services to be on the lookout for Ally and should be issuing an Amber Alert soon," Teri said. "But they don't have enough information on the car. They want to talk to you, Gabby."

"We need to get out of here and find Ally," Gabby said.

"Just head out there and go full drama queen like Ree when he doesn't get to pick where we eat," Angie said.

"I'm way ahead of you."

Gabby walked out to the living room to face two waiting officers. The one on the left held out his phone, revealing a still image of the car Teri had shown her.

"Ma'am, does this car look familiar at all?"

"No, it's too dark and I don't know any ride share drivers. And if you have that car, why are you still here?"

Gabby's voice rose a pitch. "Go find my baby! She's not here and you see someone took her. GET OUT OF HERE AND GO FIND HER!"

The officers tried to calm her down. "Ma'am, we still need to process—"

"Process what? She's not here! Tell you what? You stay here and I'll go find her myself!"

Gabby ran outside and as the officer tried to chase her, Terri grabbed the officer, gently, by the shoulder.

"Officer Grant, she can't do anything else. Let her go. Her friends will watch her. I'll stay here. She wasn't here when it happened. My family was."

The officer looked back as Ree, Angie, and Sheila rushed out after Gabby. They all jumped in Angie's car. Sheila and Gabby took the backseat.

"Head northwest," Sheila said. "Keep going until I tell you."

After a few miles, Sheila placed her hands back on Gabby. "Just close your eyes and think of Ally. I already recognize what to look for in these entities, but just think of Ally and only Ally."

Gabby concentrated on images of her daughter. Her birth, holding her fingers, and feeding her, and rocking her to sleep.

"Head more to the west," Sheila said.

Angie turned in that direction and after about five more miles, Sheila instructed her to go North.

"Gabby," Ree said. "Aren't we heading—"

"Work," Gabby said. "This is the way to my work."

"Are you sure?" Angie said. "It could be anywhere."

"No, it has to be the Donor Showcase. It's tonight. Over thirty current and potential donors were invited for a private preview of the new exhibit I've been preparing."

"Wait," Sheila said, pulling out her phone. "I'm still wired to the live cameras at your work."

She hit a few buttons on her phone and her eyes widened. "What time does it start?"

"9 pm," Gabby said.

"It looks like several donors arrived early," Sheila said.

"Why would they take Ally to my work?"

Sheila looked at Gabby and back at her phone.

"This is where it first appeared to you, right?"

"Yes, I think so."

"Power. If this is where they were first able to break out, then it may be where they generate the most power. You work with dead bodies. That may fuel them even more."

"Fuel them for what?"

"I don't know. Maybe a bigger purpose. Typically, they are just looking for a doorway to enter our plane or are drawn to something they're attracted to. Evil, strength, power, beauty, or just life. Strong negative emotions. These are the most common reasons, and we figured it was just attracted to you. But why take the baby and involve your friends and family?"

"Jealousy," Ree said in almost a whisper.

"What did you say, Ree?" Gabby asked.

"Could they gain strength from or feel jealousy?"

"Why would these things be jealous, Ree?" Gabby asked.

Ree looked at Angie, who wouldn't turn.

"When Ally was born, we saw you less. And for just a brief moment, and I mean brief, I admitted to Angie that I was jealous of her. Yes, I know, she's an innocent baby, and you were happy, but it changed things. I was being a childish jerk and I got over it."

Ree looked over at Angie. Gabby looked in the rear-view mirror to see Angie's eyes. Angie sighed. "That same night I told Ree I understood. I was a little jealous, too. This was just a one-time thing and lasted a few weeks. We love Ally and now that we're part of her life, it was stupid to even bring up. Please forgive us. You know she's like our baby, too."

Gabby nodded. "I get it. Do you think that could be part of it, Sheila?"

"I'm sure it added to it and makes sense after how they attacked Benji. Jealousy is one of the seven deadlies and a major emotion, so they could feed off that as well as fear. Your Boss could have been jealous of your family and not having your mother. Also, your sister's family. Could they have been jealous of her, too? Even slightly?"

Gabby didn't want to think about it.

"You said you've spent less and less time with them this last year," Angie said. "I know your nieces and nephew love you. And I know you wanted to fix that."

"And my sister was always jealous of my freedom and closeness with my mother," Gabby whispered.

"Then it's highly possible all these emotions, your boss, and the deaths of your mother and husband could have combined and formed an even stronger dark energy that attracted them to you, and then they fed off that darkness. The jealousy was the bonus that helped them expand to your friends and family. All to gain more strength."

"That means they might be even stronger than we realize," Gabby said. "Ally could be in real danger."

"Yes."

"How sure are you that they're heading to my work? What if we're wrong?"

"How far away are we?" Sheila asked.

"Ten more minutes the way Angie drives," Ree said.

Sheila placed her hand back on Gabby's chest and closed her eyes. "Think of Ally, but think of your work, too."

Gabby pictured the first time she brought Ally into work with her. She remembered everyone fawning over her, even Ed. Her thoughts started to shift as Ed came in, but she brushed it off and he disappeared. She pictured her other coworkers.

"Hurry," Sheila said to Angie.

"Are you sure that's where they're headed?" Gabby asked.

"Not headed," Sheila said. "They're already there."

CHAPTER TWENTY-SIX

Angie floored it and hit 120 miles per hour on the longest stretches of road. They reached the parking lot and rushed through the front doors, flying up the stairs instead of waiting for the elevator. They entered, a group of three women and one man, unkempt with the sweat of fear and adrenaline covering them all. Almost every member of the board and potential donors were there, dressed in semi-formal wear. Everyone was in the Showroom where Gabby had spent the last few months preparing her Thespian Display Project. Many were observing the displays while they waited for the presentation to start from the stage located in the far back side of the Showroom.

Marcy was at a front table and stood up, looking back to check if anyone could see Gabby and her ragtag group.

"Gabby, what's wrong? And why are you dressed like that and who are these people? This is your project. I thought you would be here an hour ago."

"Marcy, I'm sorry. I can't explain right now, but this is important. There's something I need to search for. You didn't see anyone unusual come in tonight, did you?"

"You mean besides the four of you?"

"Is everyone here in the main Showroom?"

"Yes, Nancy Richards, the company CEO, flew in from New York and is going to deliver the big pitch in a few minutes."

"I'm sorry I can't explain, but please, I need to run into the other rooms to look for something. Will you keep the main people out? It'll probably be better if they don't see us."

"I agree with that. Just hurry, Gabby. You know how important tonight is. This could provide our funding for the next three years. I know this wouldn't be possible without you, and it's been a whirlwind since we lost Ed, but I can't let you hurt our chances."

"I agree. Just tell them the other rooms are getting some final touches. I'll duck in through the Baby Room and hopefully we'll be gone before anyone notices we're here."

"I don't know…"

"Marcy! I'm not asking and I'm not leaving. I'll scream if you'd like so everyone will head this way."

Marcy's eyes bulged.

"Come on," Gabby commanded as she turned around and entered the main door to the Baby Room and closed it behind her.

"Oh, this isn't good," Ree said.

He looked up and saw the room was darker than normal. The cylindrical and glass box displays of the babies in various stages of pre and post birth development looked brighter, as if they had been cleaned and the lighting adjusted for the evening's event. Two displays showed a full skeletal structure and another displayed bright, colored nervous systems. The box displays were tougher to view, as they were filled with babies who had been stillborn, others that were born but died later, including 18-month-old conjoined twins, and a few others with open torsos that revealed their internal organs.

The gentle lighting gave each baby a faint glow, making them hard not to stare at, no matter how badly you didn't want to.

"We need to start in the back," Gabby said. "Maybe these spirits didn't realize all these people would be here and are avoiding the crowd."

She moved past the Baby Room and led them to the Reading Room. Informational displays made up the majority of the space. Most held smaller sections of bodies with explanations of various adult body parts and how they are preserved. The room was brighter and primarily used during guided tours. They looked around, but the room was empty.

Gabby led them to the door into the next room. "This is the final room on this side of the building," she said. "The Archives and also Major Body Repair."

The area was long and held tables, long shelves, and a smaller office in the rear. Gabby flipped on the lights and they rushed toward the back.

"This might be the perfect area," Gabby said. "Other than when I'm doing major long term repairs, no one comes back here too often."

"What exactly is in here?" Angie asked.

Gabby moved cautiously as she spoke. "Spare parts and anything damaged beyond what we can repair. Plenty of areas where they could stash Ally."

"I don't want to see any more bodies," Ree said.

"Where is she?" Gabby said, trying hard not to panic.

"Ally," Angie said. "Focus on Ally. Ree, go with Gabby. Sheila and I will take the far end. We'll cover more ground."

Everyone nodded and they moved. Ree was behind Gabby and they scanned through a few long sections of shelves with boxes and various items before it broke into a larger, more open area. A body in a clear plastic cover was on its back on one of the metal tables.

"This looks like a morgue," Ree said.

"Perfect place to hide," Gabby replied.

She looked around the covered body, which was damaged and unusable, and moved her hands around the arms and legs and checked behind the plastic, clearing every possible area where Ally might fit.

On the opposite side of the room, Sheila and Angie were going through a few lockers. None had locks, and they opened and closed each of the forty compartments that adorned part of a long wall, but only found a mix of supplies.

Ally and Ree searched through more body parts. Ree jumped back and yelled as Gabby lifted a severed head and checked behind it but still found no signs of Ally. After a few minutes, the two groups met in the middle.

"Nothing?" Angie asked.

Gabby and Ree shook their heads, and Gabby rushed back out to the Reading Room.

"There are drawers underneath most of these display cases where she might fit."

They moved to each wall and display distributed throughout the room to verify their drawer contents, but there was still nothing.

"The Baby Room," Gabby said. "We have to check more closely. The only other rooms are on the South and East sides of the building. There's Ed's office, the main work room with all the cubicles, the supply room, and the ER. But all of those are visible from the Showroom. Someone would have noticed."

Gabby broke into a fast walk and returned to the dark Baby Room.

"Can you turn these lights on?" Ree asked. "It's hard enough to see."

"No time," Gabby said. "The primary control is in the main office, and I don't think Marcy will be willing to help if we ask. Use your phone light if you have to."

They moved slowly, taking their time to check the darkest shadows. The room contained seven columns, five of which were positioned like the five dots on dice, with the two additional columns located to the left and right of the center. Each column contained informational plaques as well as displays, which gave the room a maze-like feel.

A voice boomed.

"Welcome to all of our esteemed colleagues. We appreciate your attendance and hope what you've seen so far…"

The presentation was starting.

Gabby moved toward the glass cylinder displays that contained the more developed fetuses. She lifted each cylinder and checked around them. Each cylinder sat in a nook with at least a foot of empty space behind it, all big enough to hide Ally.

"Ally?" she called out.

Panic started to set in as she turned back toward the others. "Why isn't she crying?"

"She could be asleep," Angie said from across the room.

Gabby knew that tone. She was trying to be positive, but Gabby was growing desperate.

"Where is my baby?" Gabby said aloud without yelling. The speech going on in the other room was loud enough that no one would be able to hear her.

Angie was checking the glass box displays against one wall and Sheila was doing the same on the adjacent wall. Ree was checking the middle displays near the center column. They were moving at a frantic pace when Sheila let out a loud gasp.

The other three turned to look at her.

"What is it?"

Sheila turned toward the center where Ree was and rubbed her temples.

"Something's here. In this room."

"Why are you looking at me?" Ree asked. "What do you see?"

"I don't see anything," Sheila said. "I sense it. Something is here. And it's right next to you."

Ree moved back as he looked around. "There's nothing here!"

They all moved near Ree. Sheila glanced at the display nearest him and started to look around frantically.

"What is it?" Gabby asked.

"It's here. Right here."

"There's nothing!" Angie yelled.

Gabby looked up toward the center column of the room. One she had passed by for years.

"This column," Gabby said. "Something's different. Something's wrong."

She stepped closer. "It's too big. Thicker than normal."

Sheila moved and reached up to touch the column, then flew back and smacked against one of the displays. She squealed in pain.

As they stared at the column, its shape started to shift, dissipating into a dark cloud. The cloud seemed to replace part of the solid outer column trim. The cloud cleared, exposing a shelf in the center of the column about five feet high.

Ally was sitting on the edge of the shelf. She was seated and her eyes were open, but she didn't make a sound.

"My baby!" Gabby yelled and rushed toward her daughter.

One of the glass box displays, which sat on four wooden legs like a table, shifted and blocked her way. Gabby got the wind knocked out of her as her stomach slammed into a display corner, shattering part of the glass.

Another box display shifted and then another,

surrounding the center column and forming a barrier between Ally and her mother.

Gabby jumped on and over the display directly in front of her, landing in the gap behind it. She reached Ally and as she was about to grab her, she saw her daughter's eyes and stopped.

Her eyes had slits like a cat's. Just like the reflection that had been haunting and taunting her.

Then the cylinder displays exploded. Shattered glass and fluids shot out and rained across the room, gifting them all with small cuts to their exposed skin but missing their eyes as they reflexively closed them.

As Gabby wiped and opened her eyes, she looked up to make sure no glass had struck Ally, then screamed as she took a step back.

Ally, who loved to run, but still didn't have the greatest sense of balance, stood rigidly on the column shelf. She leaped off the small ledge and landed perfectly five feet down on the floor, something she should not have been able to do at her age. She stared at her mother during the entire jump. Ally smiled as all glass enclosures shattered simultaneously.

The room went quiet for a second, then filled with wet popping sounds. Something moved toward Gabby from the shadows of the floor. A baby's head appeared, staring at her from its empty eye sockets. Its tiny, partially formed arms pulled it forward, slopping over the spilled fluids with each movement.

Then the rest came into view. Each fetus, fully formed baby, and even the bone and nervous system babies, started to slither toward Gabby. The ones without legs used their arms if they had them or their noses if they didn't. Even those that were preserved at just a few weeks old made their way forward. The entire tiny army created a cacophony of slushy movement as they approached their target.

Angie, Ree, and Sheila moved next to Gabby as the babies formed a circle around them.

"Ally?" Gabby's voice cracked as she said it.

Ally's eyes looked up at her with no emotion or recognition.

She lifted her hand and pointed. "Hello, Mother."

Ally had never called her anything but Mama and typically it was in choppy two or three word phrases like "Mama" or "Go Mama." She sounded much older and not like herself.

Gabby screamed as the long dormant fetuses moved forward and Ally took a slow step toward her.

CEO Richards' voice on the microphone cut off mid-speech. "Sorry, there's still some work in the other rooms that's a little loud."

She continued, raising her already amplified voice to talk over whatever was happening in the Baby Room.

Then they all screamed, with Gabby's voice being drowned out only by Ree's higher pitched squeal.

The babies didn't stop. They were coming slowly and with determination.

"What do we do?" Angie said as her body trembled. "Sheila?"

Sheila's knees were locked in fear and she tried to open her mouth to respond but only felt the sting of her sweat invading her eyes.

"Ally!" Gabby spat out. "We need to get Ally!"

She moved forward and kicked at the larger fetus in front of her. It made a plopping sound as Gabby's foot landed. It flew in the air and across the room, splattering against the wall.

Then the babies stopped. They moved in unison and seemed to all lift their heads and turn toward the direction of their fallen brother or sister. The four adults all screamed in terror as the dead babies rose and hovered in the air and then flew directly at them, landing across their faces and bodies.

The second trimester fetus landed on Sheila's face and squeezed its arms around her, blocking her mouth and making her gag and fall to the floor, choking. When the third trimester fetuses hit Ree, he cried in terror and fell, passing out cold.

Angie's reflexes were quicker. She ducked and threw a block with her forearm, knocking the babies headed for her aside, but three of the smaller ones still landed near her face and the goop left from the two-month-old that hit her in the eye blinded her. She clawed at her eye to get the goop out and started screaming as it fell through her lips.

Their screams were unmistakable now. Someone was banging on and pulling at the Baby Room doors as Gabby shook off the fetuses that had struck her and continued toward her child.

Then the crowd in the Showroom started to scream.

The doors to the Baby Room flew open and two women in beautiful black dresses ran by on their way to the exit, shrieking with a man in an elegant suit right behind.

The babies shifted their attention, rushed out the doors, and invaded the Showroom.

Gabby turned and Ally was gone.

"Where did she go?" Gabby yelled.

Sheila got her bearings and pointed to the doors. "She must have gone with the other babies."

Angie slapped Ree and he came to. She pulled him up, and they followed as Gabby and Sheila exited the Baby Room.

As the four entered the Showroom, they realized why everyone had been screaming.

The Body Parade displays were moving. Each thespian display's body was shaking and their heads were turning in every direction, moving toward the person closest to them. Some of the patrons ran past the approaching displays, but many were frozen where they stood.

Every one of the displays had their faces decorated like Sugar Skulls. The faces were similar to the Day of the Dead designs Gabby experienced with The Runner and The Diver that first day. However, each display was unique with its own distinguishing colors and design. Some had their entire face covered while others were only partially or half decorated.

Then someone started laughing.

"You really had me!" an older man in a tux yelled up toward the stage. CEO Richards, sporting a pale face as she stood at the microphone, looked down at him, expressionless.

"These are amazing effects," the man in the tux continued. "I haven't been this scared in a long time!"

Then a few others let out a collective gasp and started laughing, too.

The Gymnast, in its reverse bridge position with the book still on her stomach and the prop sword in her hand, was the display nearest tuxedo man. The display creaked as The Gymnast's head turned even further and her leg lifted, pulling free from the steel bars running up her legs to support her upside down position. Her arm ripped free and her entire body flipped over. She stood up and her right hand reached for tuxedo man's throat. His bald head turned red and his face turned a dark shade of purple.

The man's wife, wearing a white sequined dress, screamed as The Gymnast's free hand pushed her back, knocking her into a woman directly behind her.

The other figures followed The Gymnast's actions and broke free from their bases, slinking toward the person or groups closest to them. One woman yelled and let out a groan that echoed throughout the entire room.

Nancy Richards screamed into the microphone and fell on

the stage in fear as The Diver, no longer resembling its distinguishing Olympian pose, approached her.

"What do we do?" Ree said.

"We need to save them!" Angie said. "Ally might be in the middle of it all!"

"Wait," Sheila said. "Gabby, the cadavers. The babies. They're just distractions. We need to stop the spirits to save Ally!"

"Can you stop them?" Gabby asked.

"I think I can create a Devil's Trap."

"A what?"

"Just trust me. Get whatever weapons or tools you have and save everyone you can. Just give me time to set it up in the Baby Room."

Gabby nodded and led her two best friends across the Showroom to reach the east supply room. It didn't contain the larger tools like the ones in the Archives, but enough for makeshift hand-to-hand weapons. Gabby opened the tool drawers and pulled out blades, hammers, screwdrivers, and whatever else she could find that might be useful. She handed Ree a screwdriver and Angie a hammer. She stuck a few tools in the waistband of her jeans and took a scalpel for herself. One of the same tools she had spent months using to make repairs and put this event together.

The patrons that made it to the front doors were banging against them, but the doors wouldn't open and the glass wouldn't shatter. A menacing growl came from behind the stage. Gabby looked up and saw the face of the yellow-eyed, dark spirit that had been plaguing her all this time, laughing and glaring, its image reflecting off the marble back wall. Its face was eight feet high. The muscles on its skeletal face were torn and hanging, and it had long, silver hair down to its shoulders. Everyone in the Showroom screamed even louder.

Gabby turned and ran toward The Gymnast, who was still

choking the bald tuxedo man. The wife was yelling at the attacking cadaver to stop while trying to pull herself up. If The Gymnast could hear her pleas, it wasn't letting on. She saw a younger couple bracing themselves against a wall. The Cyclist, now free from its bike display, crept toward the couple. Gabby tossed them a spare hammer.

"Fight back!" she yelled at them.

As she moved toward tuxedo man, she tripped and fell over one of the developed fetuses and the scalpel slipped from her hand. She looked back, but the baby ran from her.

She crawled to grab the blade, then pulled herself up as soon as she had it in her grasp. She approached The Gymnast, who was now on top of the fallen man, still choking him with one hand while striking away his wife with the other as she tried to intervene.

Gabby moved on her tiptoes, trying to stay quiet, and when she was only a foot away, she sliced her scalpel across the ankle of The Gymnast, easily cutting through the boneless structure and separating the foot from the ankle.

The Gymnast turned, but Gabby was already slicing at the wrist that was choking tuxedo man. The wrist split apart, but not enough to loosen the hold of the two fingers still around his neck.

The cadaver released her grasp from the wife's shoulder and took a big swing at Gabby. The blow connected against her jaw and knocked her sideways. Gabby saw flashing lights as she regained her balance and then jumped up, pulled her arm back, and punched the protruding scalpel into the face of the cadaver. Her hand and weapon sliced straight through The Gymnast's cheek, exiting the other side with an eyeball skewered on the blade.

The cadaver leaned back as if in surprise, but didn't even wince as the eyeball fell off the blade onto the floor.

Gabby realized if the display bodies were being

controlled, they probably couldn't see or feel anything. A stab wasn't going to cut it.

She took a few steps back and checked Angie and Ree.

"Go for their limbs!" she yelled. "I don't think they can feel. Forget their eyes or trying to stab them. Take away their hands and feet. Rip them apart!"

Angie took her hammer, flipped it around and slammed its claw into the throat of The Runner, then pulled with her entire body. A sharp tearing sound followed as half of The Runner's neck ripped apart. She sent another blow that completely decapitated her enemy. The Runner continued to move toward her, headless, so Angie lowered her body and started swinging at the legs.

Ree had a harder time using the screwdriver in his hand against The Swimmer, but with no bone structure on the cadaver, he managed to slice into its shoulder and the entire right side of the neck and pectoral muscles easily tore free.

Gabby moved closer to The Gymnast and threw a hard kick, forcing her off balance enough to cut and separate both arms from her torso and then kicked the knee. Gabby concentrated on the same leg she had already removed the foot from and sliced at the knee until The Gymnast fell and could no longer advance toward her. Once Gabby determined it couldn't easily inflict any more damage, she looked up as tuxedo man's wife was performing CPR on her husband. Gabby looked at his purple lips and knew it was a futile attempt, but she wasn't going to stop her.

Gabby stifled her desire to cry out and took a quick look around for Ally, but there was still no sign of her. Another yell for help made her turn. CEO Nancy Richards was seated on the stage, supporting her body with her arms behind her and inching backward as The Diver approached her across the stage. Gabby ran up and cut into its foot, but The Diver ignored her and leaped at the CEO, taking a solid two-handed grip around her throat. Mrs. Richards was choking and Gabby tried to get at the attacking display's arms, but it kept squirming and moving from side to side with such speed that she couldn't cut through enough flesh to stop it. Gabby looked around the stage and reached for the microphone stand, then stood up and moved behind the attacking body. The Diver was on top of Mrs. Richards, who didn't appear to have much fight left in her. Gabby lifted the stand and slammed its heavy metal base through the center of The Diver's torso. The stand grazed Mrs. Richard's stomach, but at this point, Gabby was more concerned about saving her life than possibly breaking her ribs.

The microphone stand tore a big round hole through the cadaver's body, with only a small chunk of muscle staying attached. The Diver held his grip as Gabby was able to move close enough to smack one arm with the microphone stand base enough times to break it free.

Gabby dropped the mic stand and jammed her foot into the cadaver's back and pulled its head toward her until it slowly separated from the shoulders like yarn on a mop, with individual muscles tearing free with each pull.

Gabby pulled the one remaining hand off, and the CEO started to cough. She was okay.

Gabby turned back. The couple she had handed the hammer to were on the floor, panting as they continued to hack at The Cyclist, even though they had already ripped it to shreds.

Ree had destroyed The Swimmer, and Angie was screaming with fury as she hammered the last of The Runner, which didn't have enough complete body parts left to identify what it had been originally.

There was a loud crashing noise. The front doors finally released and the crowd, who had almost crushed each other trying to break the doors down, raced out. The only other people left in the Showroom besides Gabby and her best friends were the CEO, tuxedo man and his grieving wife, another dead man near Ree, and a woman sitting against the rear wall with her neck snapped sideways.

"Do you see Ally anywhere?" Gabby yelled.

Angie and Ree shook their heads. None of them had seen her in the midst of the carnage.

Gabby looked up at the ceiling and the walls. "Where are you and what have you done with my daughter!"

She scanned the walls, framed art, and the glass doors where Ed's office used to be for any sign of the Reflection Spirit, but there were no more reflections. Gabby stepped off the stage as CEO Richards got up and grabbed Gabby's arm.

"I don't know what's happening, but thank you, Gabby, for saving my life. Right now, I need to get the hell out of here and you should, too."

She limped off the stage and joined the others out the front doors.

Angie and Ree looked up at Gabby.

"Where are the babies?" Angie asked.

Gabby stared at her and ran to the Baby Room. "Ally!"

The three reached the room. The door was closed.

Gabby pulled the door open and rushed in. Sheila stood near the center column, her hair flying around from an unseen gust of wind. There was a small shadow of a person near the column, doing something they couldn't see in the darkened room. On the side of one of the walls, there was another column of darkness, like a tornado trapped inside a cylinder. The twisting darkness was groaning and screaming.

"Sheila! What's happening?" Gabby screamed over the noise.

The air around the dark cylinder and around Sheila was spinning, and she looked like she was struggling to stand.

Sheila turned to the three. "I trapped one!"

They stepped closer to the cylinder of black air and saw some kind of writing underneath it. The Devil's Trap. Whatever that was, Sheila had been successful.

"Are you okay?" Angie yelled.

"Help me!" Sheila yelled. "The other one is still loose and I can't move!"

They neared the center of the room and then saw why Sheila was stuck. She was surrounded by the babies, but Ally wasn't among them.

"Where is Ally?" Gabby asked.

"She's here behind the center column," Sheila yelled. "Something's with her."

Gabby rushed forward and kicked the babies blocking Sheila. She couldn't see through the small shadow as the babies moved in closer. Gabby sliced her blade downward and cut through the fetuses grabbing her leg, but they were so small it didn't do anything to slow them down.

Ree and Angie moved to either side of Gabby, and the babies formed a circle around them. They stood with their weapons out.

"What do we do?" Ree asked.

"We have to get to Ally," Angie replied. "Do whatever you have to."

The babies rushed them. As they flung their weapons forward, the babies overwhelmed them. Four pulled themselves up to Gabby's face, and even without teeth, they gnawed and bit at her face and nose.

The other groups did the same to Angie and Ree. Ree gagged as one of the babies rubbed against his mouth and tried to smother him with its head.

Angie was trying to scream, but her mouth and nose were being covered, too.

The majority went harder at Gabby. Six babies, only two of them fully formed, were grasping at her head and neck. One of the larger babies shoved its arm into Gabby's mouth, reaching in up to its elbow while the other fully formed one covered her eyes. Gabby felt her mind going black, but she couldn't pass out. Not now.

Ally, she thought to herself.

Gabby tightened her grip on her scalpel. The scalpel. Her tool. Her livelihood. The thing she was so precise with.

She raised her scalpel up, not thinking about hitting her own face, which would have been easy to do with her vision blocked. She felt the blade pop into the baby choking her and she kept lifting her hand, pushing the scalpel up through the baby's torso until her own hand reached the baby's neck. She twisted and pulled, splitting the fetus in two. It fell as Gabby repeated the step with the second baby. The arm cut free but was still down her throat. She reached with her free hand and pulled it out, puking when she caught her breath. The remaining babies were smaller and underdeveloped. Gabby knocked them loose and stomped down on the fetus in front of her, then leaped over the babies behind it.

She moved toward Angie and took out the larger babies until Angie was able to fight off the rest. She moved toward Ree and did the same.

"Try to free Sheila," Gabby said. "She might be the only way to stop this. I'm going for Ally."

Angie and Ree moved.

Gabby turned back toward Ally and the babies she'd leaped over earlier were stacked behind each other, forming a wall of flesh between her and her daughter. With most of the larger babies destroyed, the wall was only a few feet high.

Gabby looked behind them at the center column and saw her daughter. The something that was with her was the human shadow. Whatever had picked up Ally and entered the ride share at Teri's house was holding her daughter, but didn't seem to be hurting her. It actually appeared to be trying to soothe her. Ally was looking straight at the shape's face. As Gabby stepped closer, she saw that it was a young girl with long hair, but surrounded in darkness that made it difficult to distinguish any facial features. Her eyes were glowing yellow, too. Gabby reached over, but something grabbed her hand. She looked to her side and from the surface of the shiny marble column, she saw the reflection of the spirit's yellow eyes and they seemed to be struggling as they held her in an invisible grip.

"Angie! Ree! Help me!"

Ree and Angie were knocking the few swarming baby remnants out of the way, pulling on Sheila, but they still couldn't free her. They heard Gabby yell and ran toward her, bypassing the babies still trying to form a barrier between Ally and the young girl. They saw the column reflection with its unseen grip on their best friend.

"Help me!" Gabby screamed. "That girl is doing some-thing to Ally!"

Neither the girl nor Ally paid them any mind. Ally's gaze was fixated on the young girl's face, and then Ally's eyes started to glow yellow, matching the shade of the young girl's.

Gabby punched at the column, but her knuckle cracked as she struck hard marble. The reflection didn't flinch.

Ree and Angie tried to rush the girl, but the same invisible hand that was holding Gabby back pulled on them as well, preventing them from stepping forward.

Ree turned to Angie. "Break that marble. You have the hammer!"

Angie slammed her hammer against the reflection on the marble and a small chunk cracked. The reflection didn't move and held its invisible grasp on Gabby.

Ree looked around, knowing his screwdriver wouldn't do much damage, then grabbed one of the box displays, now devoid of all its glass, leaving only its wooden frame. Ree grabbed one of its thick legs and shook it from side-to-side until it broke free.

Ree lifted the wooden leg and smashed it against the marble column as Angie continued striking it with the hammer.

The small chunk Angie had created broke into bigger pieces. Angie continued to slam the hammer down and Ree kept pounding it until larger pieces tore away more easily.

The grip on Gabby's arm eased, and she saw the eyes still staring back at her from the column. She pulled the hammer from Angie's hand and in a frenzy, started to hack at the column over and over until the column's only lighted portion that could hold a reflection was gone. The force holding her back was lifted, and she ran for her daughter. Gabby reached out to pull Ally from the girl's grasp, but her hands stopped and her nose scrunched as if she had run into a glass door. This time it wasn't an unseen hand pulling her back, but more of an invisible wall only inches from shadow girl and Ally.

A guttural sound filled the Baby Room. Gabby glanced around and saw the Reflection Spirit looking back at her in every piece of remaining display case glass still standing. Parts of the walls also held the reflections, but the Spirit's face took up the entire glass rear wall. Its yellow eyes were locked on Gabby and it hissed at her, revealing a spiny tongue emerging from its maw.

"Destroy it all," Gabby said. "Wherever you see that monster's face."

Gabby kicked the display nearest her until all the pieces of glass fell. Ree and Angie followed suit. Gabby rushed toward the larger wall, where the reflecting spirit was still hissing and bearing a sinister grin.

Gabby hurled the hammer at the Spirit's wall face and it

spun in the air, flipping over itself three times before it struck dead center and the entire glass wall came crashing down. The face screamed as the wall shattered.

The fetuses stopped their attack as the wall fell, freeing Sheila from confinement.

Gabby turned back and rushed toward Ally as Angie knocked down the last of the display cases. The protective wall was down and Gabby reached for Ally, but the young girl's arm flung out and struck her. The girl's gaze never shifted from Ally's eyes as Gabby lost her balance and fell to the floor.

Angie and Ree almost got to her, but the girl reached out and knocked them back in a swift, too fast to see motion.

Sheila headed toward them. "Let's do this together!"

The four stood side-by-side and rushed the shadowy girl. Just before they reached her, there was a bellowing scream behind them that stopped them cold.

They turned, and the twisting shadow spirit Sheila had captured in her trap was no longer contained.

The fetuses congregated where the shadow had been confined and seemed to be clawing at the floor. A dark, misty cloud hovered above them.

"What just happened?" Ree screamed.

"They broke the Devil's Trap," Sheila yelled. "Benji said there was a stronger presence. That was it."

"What does that mean?" Ree said, his voice quivering.

"It means that I have no doubt these are full fledged demons. Stronger and more evil than we realized. An old darkness."

"Can you trap it again?" Angie asked.

"I don't know. Be careful and I'll try. Move!"

The cloud came down on them and its scream was so loud it pierced through their brains and they fell as they cupped their ears. Once the scream died, Gabby punched at the

Shadow Demon, but her arm went straight through its gaseous form. Angie and Ree also tried but met nothing solid. The Shadow swirled around them, toying with them as they tried to strike.

Sheila ran back to grab Benji's bag, still by the broken Devil's Trap.

The Shadow shifted and a tall figure formed behind Sheila, knocking her forward. Her head smacked against the wall and she fell, unconscious.

Gabby, Ree and Angie regained their balance as their heads cleared and they stood next to each other, placing themselves between the Shadow Demon and the young girl, who was still carrying Ally.

The Shadow shifted back to a cloud and swept against the three of them, striking their bodies within a second. They fell and tried to get back up. They looked at each other and saw that each was bleeding from their faces and heads.

"I never even saw it coming," Ree said. "How are we supposed to stop that thing without Sheila or Benji?"

"She's my daughter and I have to save her," Gabby said. "Or I'm going to die trying, although I can't ask either of you to do the same. Leave now. Try to get help."

"I'm not leaving your side," Angie said.

"Well, then, I'm not letting her be the only martyr," Ree said. "Still trying to make me look bad, even here at the end. I do love you both, in case you didn't know."

"We know," Angie said. "And we love you, too."

The Shadow cloud spun around the young girl and Ally then rose to the ceiling.

It was circling. Stalking its prey.

"We need something more than a screwdriver and a hammer," Angie said. "And the only one of us who knows how to catch that thing is out of commission. Any ideas?"

"No," Gabby said.

"I wish Benji was here," Ree said. "I'm sure he'd know what to do."

Benji. Gabby recalled Benji's quote and the words from some poem by Poe. "The love of a mother is one of the strongest weapons you will ever wield. Let it guide you."

The Shadow Demon turned back to them and this was no reflection. Its face was pure shadow, and it had black eye sockets. It smiled, revealing sharp white teeth, red eyes, and a twisting pink tongue. As it stepped toward them, it walked on reverse-hinged legs.

The temperature in the room dropped.

Gabby grabbed Angie and Ree's hands. The demon got closer, revealing scattered pieces of black flesh hanging from its form.

"Time to die," the demon said, filling the room with the deep bass timber of its voice.

"No!" Gabby yelled as it stepped closer. "You can't have her. She's mine!"

The demon maintained a slow pace toward them. In one swift motion, it whipped its arms forward and Gabby felt her hands empty as Angie and Ree were knocked to either side of her, landing hard.

Gabby turned to see each of her friends on the ground in pain. She had to help them.

No. Ally is what matters. Only Ally.

Gabby looked forward as the Shadow Demon took another step and was only a foot from where she stood. She closed her eyes and thought of Ally, concentrating on her like Sheila had shown her earlier. Something filled her head and her chest. She didn't know what it was, but she felt a calming peace as Ally consumed her thoughts and allowed her to ignore the threat before her. She thought of her mother Cora, consoling her and Teri when they were little and they cried. Then she thought of Teri cradling Jess when she first had her heart broken. She remembered the day Ally was born. She held her and all the guilt and pain she had endured over her marriage disappeared, leaving only the love she felt for the tiny life she had brought into the world. That was the moment she finally understood what Cora had meant when she told her daughters they would never truly know love and pain until the day they had children of their own.

I'm with you, Gabby. I will always be with you, just as you will always be with Ally.

Gabby opened her eyes at the sound of her mother's voice.

Cora stood before her, bathed in gleaming light.

"Mom? How? Is this a trick?"

"The darkness around you provided a path," Cora said, "but it is the power of your light that brought me here. Power from the love that I took with me to my death that still lives in you and Teri. Power you pulled from your innermost being. Power that can save my granddaughter."

Cora smiled as she started to fade.

"Mom, please, don't go!"

"Save her, Gabby."

Gabby wanted to stop her. She wanted to hold her and ask her so many questions, but she knew what she had to do. She nodded as her mother disappeared.

Gabby turned toward Ally, picturing herself holding her tight and feeling her heart beat against her chest.

She didn't hear Ree and Angie scream as the Shadow Demon raised to its full seven foot height and stretched out its thin arms, bearing them down as its mouth opened to rip into Gabby's head.

The moment the teeth landed on Gabby's flesh, a shimmering light formed around her. Instead of a gnashing bite, she felt a surge of energy inside her spread and leave her body. She opened her eyes, and the Shadow was facing her, its red eyes moving rapidly within its dark sockets as if in confusion. She sensed fear as the light she seemingly produced turned a deep shade of blue and expanded past her, enveloping the demon. The fear, however, wasn't hers. The demon screamed, this time in pain rather than an attempt to terrify its prey. Gabby pounced. She jumped at the creature before it could react and this time it remained solid. She wrapped her arms around its body and squeezed. The Demon shuddered and twisted in agony but couldn't break her grasp.

Gabby raised her head and stared into the demon's eyes. "Time to join your brother."

She thrust her fist into the Shadow Demon's chest and it cracked as her arm passed through without resistance.

Blue light shot out from within the hole Gabby's fist had created and passed through Gabby and slammed into the young girl. The girl didn't flinch as she absorbed the burst, closing her eyes as she soaked it in.

Gabby felt the Shadow Demon's body give way, and it dissipated in her arms, bellowing one last time. She stared at the emptiness before her, then flipped around to find her daughter. The young girl was still holding Ally, then raised her up, still maintaining their gaze as the blue light consumed her. The girl's eyes glowed brighter and then the light around her faded. She turned toward Gabby and gave her a soft, almost friendly smile. Then the girl turned back to Ally, pursed her lips, and took in a long breath.

Gabby broke into a run and rushed toward the girl. "Get the hell away from my daughter!"

The girl finished her deep inhale and shifted her gaze back to Gabby.

"It's okay," the girl said, with a high-pitched voice that sounded like it belonged to a much younger girl. "She's my new Kitty now. You can have her back."

She kissed Ally on the cheek. Ally's yellow eyes faded, returning to their natural color just as Gabby reached them.

Gabby swung at the girl and this time there was no barrier. The girl's head snapped back, then Gabby grabbed Ally, who was still staring at the girl, and pulled her into her arms.

Ree and Angie rushed the girl, but she stepped sideways and they both fell forward. The girl didn't react. Instead she looked back at Gabby and Ally, then calmly walked to the door. The darkness surrounding her lifted as she exited the Baby Room and turned toward the front doors. Before they lost sight of her, the girl stopped and turned to look at them, revealing a soft face that didn't look evil or monstrous. She appeared to be an almost normal, but slightly disturbed child, no more than eleven or twelve years old.

Then the young girl smiled wide. The smile turned more into a sneer, and she winked before stepping out of view. Any temptation they had to follow her was gone when Ally suddenly squealed.

"Hi, Mama," Ally said.

Gabby fell to her knees with her daughter in her arms and began sobbing. Angie and Ree joined her on the floor, holding their best friend as their own tears fell at the sight of Ally's pale face. She looked weak and hungry, but the love in her eyes as she looked at her mother was unquestionable.

Gabby held her tightly and repeated, "Thank you, thank you, thank you," directing her gratitude to God and every person and force that intervened to help them stop the demons and get her daughter back.

"I think it's over," Gabby said. "They wanted my baby, but she's mine. Forever mine."

Gabby shut her eyes and felt the pain and worry inside her disappear, leaving only a sense of peace.

"Thank you, Mom."

CHAPTER TWENTY-SEVEN

THE POLICE SHOWED UP MINUTES LATER. SHEILA WOKE UP WOOZY and was treated for a head injury, but before leaving for the hospital, Gabby let her hold Ally.

Sheila took a long look at her and Ally gave her a weak hug.

"It was all worth it," Sheila said. "I'm glad she's okay."

The aftermath was chaotic, with no one able to explain exactly what had occurred. Most were unwilling to say that the cadavers came to life at first, but when no one could come up with an explanation, one broke and several more agreed that the bodies and babies had somehow reanimated, killing three people.

By the time the police were done interviewing, they reached an early conclusion that there had to have been some kind of leak from the chemicals used in the bodies or in the Baby Room that caused them to react and attack one other. Unofficially a mass hallucination that led to three deaths.

Gabby had Ally checked by an EMT. Ally was dehydrated, but otherwise, her vitals were okay. The EMT suggested taking her to the ER so they could give her some additional fluids and monitor her for a few hours.

Once the EMT's let them go, the police had questions about why they were there after Ally's earlier reported kidnapping. Their synchronized story was that Gabby received an anonymous phone call that her baby was at her former daycare, so they rushed over and found her safely in front of the doors. Gabby knew there were no security cameras inside the main doors and bet the crowd of people at the event would be enough to explain how it would be easy for someone to sneak in and out. Gabby said she didn't care to pursue the incident now that she had her daughter back.

Gabby, Angie, and Ree didn't alter the story, and they were able to leave quickly after Gabby kept insisting she needed to get her baby to the ER.

By the time they arrived at the hospital, the news of the events had reached the media. Ally was admitted within minutes. Everything checked out and after running fluids in her, she was released two hours later. Angie and Ree never left Gabby's side.

Once they left the hospital, instead of going back to Sheila's to retrieve their cars, they headed to Gabby's house. Gabby called Teri on the way, who had already tried calling her multiple times, to let her know Ally was safe and she would give her the details later.

Angie contacted Sheila, who said she was staying overnight for observation, but other than a mild concussion and a few minor scrapes and bruises, she would be okay.

Once they got back to Gabby's, Teri was waiting. They took turns watching Ally as they each took showers and cleaned up what they could. The mess wasn't as bad as Teri's house, but they took extra care to remove broken glass and furniture so no one, especially Ally, would suffer any additional injuries.

Teri stayed late and only left after Gabby assured her they'd be fine. Teri already had the kids and John cleaning up at home. As exhausted as they were, Gabby, Angie, and Ree stayed up late and eventually all fell asleep around 3 am. Angie and Gabby slept in Gabby's bed with Ally between them. Ree tried to join them but didn't fit, so he slept on the floor at the foot of the bed. None of them wanted to sleep alone.

Gabby tried to sleep in, but she kept waking up to check on Ally and by 7 am decided it was pointless and got up. Teri returned early with her family, who all wanted to see Ally. Even John dropped by before heading to work.

Sheila called mid-morning to say she was okay and had just been released. She also told them Benji's leg surgery went well, but he would be in the hospital for a few more days.

Gabby missed her classes the next two days and wasn't sure if she still had a job to go to. The repairs would be significant, but after what happened and the lawsuits that she was sure would follow, she fully expected Body Parade, at least their branch, wouldn't survive. She felt for everyone's jobs, but it was something she would worry about another day and another time. Her professors reached out to her and told her to take as long as she needed and she could make up her remaining work over the summer if necessary.

Gabby didn't care about her job or her classes. Her only concern was not letting Ally out of her sight. Angie and Ree both used their trauma of being present at the widely publicized events to get time off work and not leave Gabby alone. The only time they left was to get their vehicles back and pick up food. Teri was also spending part of each night with her sister and niece.

Even with the help, Gabby dragged Ally with her playpen into the bathroom when she showered. She wanted to be able to see her face. She no longer felt the demons or darkness around her, but there was still an impending sense that Ally would disappear if Gabby let her out of her sight.

Gabby had been avoiding all reflective surfaces, fearing the possibility a yellow pair of eyes staring back and waiting. On the third day, she was still raising her hand in front of her face as she passed the dresser mirror in her bedroom, something she'd been doing every time she passed any mirror in her house. In her effort not to look up, she focused on a picture of Cora on her dresser.

Mom.

Mom wouldn't let this take her over. She'd be strong. She'd face reality.

Gabby lowered her hand and glanced at her reflection. The bags under her eyes were deep and her still-healing face was pale. She saw Ally's reflection as she lay in the bed next to Angie. Her little face was pale, too.

Stop it, Gabby. She's fine. Baby steps.

Teri's kids came by each night, and this third night was no different. They rushed in and Grace and Linda hustled past their auntie and right to Ally. After a few minutes, it was Grace who spoke the thoughts Gabby had been avoiding. Words she assumed everyone around her was saying and thinking, but only discussed when they were away from the house. The words she knew Angie and Ree had been texting each other, given away by their awkward and guilty looks when she saw them doing their best to act normal.

"Something's not right with Ally," Grace said.

"Grace!" Teri scolded. "That's not a nice thing to say after everything that happened to her. Now what do you say to your aunt?"

"I'm sorry, Aunt Gabby. But she doesn't look the same."

"Grace!"

Grace shrugged, but Gabby sighed and her shoulders dropped.

"It's okay. I keep ignoring it and hoping it's just me. Maybe it's part of the trauma of whatever that girl did to her. She seems fine, but Grace is right. She's not the same. She's not smiling as much, and she's still pale. I'm sure you've all noticed and are just trying to be kind and not say anything."

Everyone shifted uncomfortably.

"It's okay. Thank you for trying."

Angie put her hand on her shoulder. "Maybe it was just the trauma."

Teri was holding Ally, and Gabby grabbed her phone and walked to the living room. She returned a few minutes later.

"I just spoke with Doctor O'Brien. Her answering service called her once I explained Ally had been kidnapped and how it related to the Body Parade incident, which the person I spoke to knew about. They called her immediately. She said she'd meet me at the After Hours Pediatric Care in twenty minutes."

"Do you want me to come with you?" Angie asked.

"You and Ree haven't been home in days. Go get some rest. I'll let you know how it goes."

"We'll be back tonight," Ree said.

"No, sleep in your beds."

"I can stay with her tonight after I go with her to the doctor," Teri said. "If that's okay, Gabby?"

"You have to be exhausted, too."

"Believe it or not, I got some rest after we got the bulk of the house clean up finished this morning."

Gabby smiled at her older sister. "You sure it's okay, Teri? What about the kids?"

"I have two babysitting-capable teens. Are y'all okay staying here until me and Aunt Gabby get back?"

Nick and Jess nodded.

"Go, Mom," Jess said. "We'll be okay."

Angie and Ree vowed to return first thing in the morning.

The sisters drove Ally to her appointment. Gabby brought Teri into the doctor's office with her.

Doctor O'Brien examined Ally and repeated a few checks before having a nurse come in to draw blood.

"Why are you checking her twice?" Gabby said.

"Her vitals are fine," the doctor said. "But her face is too pale and her eyes look tired, like's she's been awake for days. Her reflexes seem slower than her last checkup. Her heart rate's a little slow, but she may just be drained from the events. I compared everything with her results from the ER the other night and nothing looks wrong, but she's still exhibiting physical signs of dehydration. I'd like to give her an IV again and run her blood for some additional tests. Things we don't normally look for."

"That doesn't sound good, Doctor O'Brien. We've all noticed she's not acting like her normal self. You sound concerned."

"Don't worry, Gabby. I just want to cover all bases. I just don't like that what I'm seeing on her face doesn't seem to match what the instruments are telling me. I will get a rush on our lab and should have results first thing tomorrow. I'll try my best to get them to do it tonight, but the After Hours lab is only minimally staffed."

"Yes, of course. Thank you, Doctor."

The doctor smiled. "Let me go talk to the lab. I'll be right back. I may need your help for us to get an IV in."

She left the room and Gabby picked Ally back up. "What's wrong with you, baby?"

Teri put her finger in Ally's hand, expecting her to grab it like usual, but she left her hand open and didn't even try to grip it.

The doctor returned and together they hooked Ally up to an IV. She barely reacted as the needle penetrated the back of her hand, staring at the injection more in curiosity than pain.

"The lab will have the results soon."

Gabby and Teri sat in the room as Ally slept. The doctor administered a sleeping agent to keep her from fussing, but based on her indifference to the needle, it almost didn't seem necessary.

Two hours later, the doctor came in.

"I have the results. Nothing abnormal. Everything is fine. Maybe I was just being overly paranoid. I've never had a patient kidnapped before, and I keep thinking about my own son. He's almost four now and he might be able to tell me what happened if he went through the same thing, but Ally is still so little. Who knows what she may have gone through or how she reacted to it. Without the ability to convey what happened, it may manifest in unexpected ways."

"There is one thing," Gabby said. "During all the chaos when people were running around and screaming, there was a point before I got her back when she said 'Hello, Mother,' like she was much older. She's never spoken that way or used the word 'Mother.' It's always just been 'Mama.'"

"Not unheard of. The stress of wanting her mommy could have been enough to make her try other words that she's maybe heard but never expressed verbally. Maybe 'Mama' wasn't working and she thought 'Mother' might."

"What do we do?"

"Just take her home and continue to observe her. If nothing changes in the next two or three days, or if for any reason she gets worse, call back. I will leave instructions for the front office to make you an appointment immediately, no matter how booked I am. Do not hesitate."

"Thank you," Gabby said, hugging her even though she knew it wasn't appropriate.

"I'm a mom, too, and this is new to me. I can only imagine what you've been through."

CHAPTER TWENTY-EIGHT

GABBY SPENT THE NEXT THREE DAYS AT HOME. A FEW OF HER classmates texted their sympathies and were happy Ally was safe. Even Barry texted an apology about avoiding her and how he acted on their first and only date. A few classmates offered to send her their class notes. Gabby thought about trying to get back to her studies so she wouldn't get too far behind but couldn't bring herself to take time away from her daughter.

Gabby's worry grew with each passing day. After Ally's IV treatment with Doctor O'Brien, she gained some color, but her demeanor hadn't changed. She was napping more than normal and in longer spurts, but Gabby would spend the time either sleeping alongside her or staring at her and making sure she was breathing.

Teri, Angie, and Ree had continued to call and come over every day or night, but Gabby told them to go home the night before. Sheila had also been checking in daily. Benji had called that morning to see how she was and let her know he was being released. Other than being in a cast and some physical therapy over the next few months, he was going to be fine. Gabby knew he wanted to hear the first hand details, but she couldn't bring herself to relive that night yet. Benji understood, and she promised to speak with him soon, but her concern for Ally was her priority. Gabby hoped getting back to a sense of normalcy and spending some time alone with Ally might help.

Gabby had her new television set on Ally's favorite cartoon. Normally, Ally would stare at the colorful dog and smile and drool all over herself as she moved along with the motions on the screen, mimicking the dog's running and habit of sticking out his tongue. She hadn't done that since the kidnapping. Neither the cartoons, the ceiling fan, nor her favorite stuffed pink unicorn held her attention. She'd let out a weak smile but otherwise stared into nothing most of the time.

At around 3 pm, Gabby picked up the phone and called Doctor O'Brien. She brought her in an hour later.

This time Ally's fluids and vitals were all normal. Dr. O'Brien returned with the results and sat next to Gabby.

"Gabby, everything seems fine, but something isn't right. I don't think it's physical. Give her no more than another week. If nothing changes or you have to bring her back in, call my colleague."

She handed Gabby a card. It read, "Doctor Jill Rosas, Child Psychologist."

"A Child Psychologist? She's not even two years old!"

"Dr. Rosas specializes in babies and toddlers. Trauma in children is hard to gauge. Whatever she experienced was new and scary for her. Her body is trying to figure out how to cope, but children are strong and resilient. I'm sure she'll be fine eventually, but if necessary, I think this doctor can help."

Gabby had taken the words to heart and was struggling to stay positive. Ally normally woke up once or twice a night, but in addition to more frequent naps, since the ordeal, she

had slept soundly until dawn. She was calmer and less play-
ful, and Gabby did her best to rationalize it.

Later that night, Ree and Angie came over with pizza after
Gabby told them about the doctor visit.

"We're here to cheer you up!" Ree said. "Brought some
wine!"

Gabby smiled. She was still exhausted, and she knew it
showed.

"Thank you, guys. Not sure if I'll be great company, but
thank you."

"Do you want us to watch her while you get some sleep?"
Angie asked.

"No, I wouldn't be able to, anyway. I'll just worry what
she's doing."

"Then let's sit here and watch an action or spy flick," Ree
said.

"That sounds good."

Angie got plates and drinks together and they sat around
the living room while Ree found a recent Bond movie. They
ate and watched, but Gabby was paying more attention to
Ally, who was propped up next to her, fixated on the movie
but not reacting to the action or sounds before her. Gabby
hoped an explosion or loud noises might phase her and even
turned up the volume at one point, but Ally didn't flinch.

Just as the movie was about to begin its final fight, Gabby
burst into tears.

Ree muted the TV and her two best friends hugged her
and said nothing, giving her the time and space to release
what she needed to.

"I don't know what else to do," Gabby said. "Maybe those
demons and that little girl damaged her mind."

"Maybe the psychologist isn't such a bad idea," Ree said
without much conviction.

"A psychologist for my baby. It just doesn't seem like it'll matter, but I'm willing to try anything. I just don't know what to do. What if she never gets better?"

Angie pulled Ally onto her lap. "Gabby, I'm sure she'll be fine. She just needs time—"

The doorbell rang.

"You expecting anyone?" Ree asked.

"No," Gabby said. "Can you check it? Unless it's Teri, I don't want to see anybody."

Ree nodded and moved to the door. He checked the peephole but didn't recognize the person.

"It's some guy. Looks pretty young."

"He's probably selling something," Angie said. "Get rid of him."

"Okay. I'll take care of it."

Ree spoke through the door. "Can I help you?"

"Yes. I'm looking for Gabriella Mendez Alfonso."

"What's this about?"

"I really need to speak to her directly. If my suspicions are true, I think I might be able to help her."

Gabby looked up. "It's one of the crazies. How did they find out where I live?"

The story about the Body Parade was all over the news, but there was a growing group of people who didn't believe in the story being broadcast. There were conspiracy theorists saying it was a cover up of a serial killer or a terrorist organization. A few others claimed the bodies had come to life in some demonic cult ceremony. That wasn't too far off the mark, and Gabby had received several phone calls asking about the various theories. She was surprised at the first few but then started blocking numbers she didn't recognize.

"Look," Ree said. "Whatever you think you know, you need to leave. This is harassment and I will call the police if you refuse."

"My name is Ricky Luna," the young man said. "If that

doesn't sound familiar, look up 'Ricky Luna' and 'Stone Creek.' I'll wait."

Ree looked back at Angie and Gabby.

"I know that name," he whispered as he rushed back to the couch and started to type madly on his phone.

"Oh, my God," Ree said. "It's that video from a few years ago. Remember the one with the downtown massacre where that boy looked like he was floating and killing people near San Antonio?"

Gabby shook her head. "I don't remember any of that."

Ree flipped his phone around and showed it to them. It was a shaky video of a teenager floating in the air in the middle of a downtown street with police cars being tossed around like toys. Whoever posted the video paused the action and pointed out some kind of shadowy figure near the boy.

"I do remember you talking about this," Angie said. "We argued about it because you thought it was real and I told you it was a total fake."

She looked a little closer at the video. "This was almost two years ago."

"Ricky Luna," Ree said. "That was the name of the boy. He was arrested but found not guilty and put into witness protection or something like that. Crazy people burned his house down, thinking he was some evil devil worshipper."

Gabby hadn't said anything yet but was focused on the video. It was too shaky to tell if it was real or fake, but hard to believe that had happened out in public.

Just like it would be hard for anyone to believe what happened at the Donor Showcase or anything that has happened to me over the last few weeks.

She got up and walked to the door.

"Gabby, what are you doing?" Angie said.

Gabby ignored her as she looked through the peephole. "That's you in that video?"

"Yes," he said. "I know you have no reason to trust me, but if you've experienced anything even close to what I did, I think you'll want to hear what I have to say."

Gabby looked down and then back through the peephole. The young man raised his arms and turned in a circle. "I have nothing on me but my phone, keys, and wallet. Please, I think we might be able to help each other."

Gabby turned back to her friends. Angie was shaking her head, but Ree was nodding.

Gabby unlocked the door.

The young man with unkempt hair and light stubble walked in. He had on a plain black tee-shirt and jeans and had a slight but solid build.

"What's your name again?"

"Ricky. Ricky Luna." He offered his hand and Gabby shook it.

"Ricky, if that's you in the video, why would you want to see me?"

"Can I sit down? I'll explain myself, I promise."

Gabby motioned for him to sit on the recliner and introduced her friends and Ally, who was still sitting on Angie's lap. Gabby sat at the end nearest the recliner.

"So, Ricky. Did you come all the way from San Antonio to see me?"

"Actually, I lived in Stone Creek, just outside of San Antonio and where that video was recorded. My family was relocated from Texas after everything happened. My mom and sister are in an undisclosed location but doing better."

"So all that stuff on that video," Angie said. "Was that a massive fake for attention, or did that really happen?"

"It was all real. A few months before that night, some weird things happened to me and my family. I'm going to be blunt with you and as insane as it sounds, I expect you won't think it's that far-fetched. It all started after I bought what I thought was a cool sugar skull. Soon after that, my grandmother died. That's when the sugar skull seemed to come to life and two demons invaded my world. They found a doorway to my family through my mother, who was a drug addict at the time. These demons tried to take her over but realized they couldn't control her due to how severe her addiction was. Instead, they changed their focus and used her to get to me. In the end, I was overtaken and during that night of the video in downtown Stone Creek, the girl I loved since we were kids was killed. I know now it wasn't my fault, but it happened through my own hands."

"I've seen multiple videos many times and from several angles," Ree said. "You never touched anyone."

"No. These demons gave me the ability to move things with my mind. They waited until I was weak enough and took me over. I fought as hard as I could, but once my Ellie died, I lost all control. It's only because of my sister and best friend that I made it through that night without more people dying."

"These spirits," Gabby said. "What were they like?"

"One was strong. He was dark, tall and scary and his body could shift from solid to black smoke. It made me see things that weren't there. It haunted my house and made me hurt my friends. We couldn't really fight it since we couldn't touch it. At first, we all thought it was this one Shadow Demon, but in the end, we realized there were two of them. The other demon wasn't as strong, but it reflected off surfaces and helped the Shadow drive me mad enough to almost kill."

Gabby gasped.

"I take it that sounds familiar?"

Gabby nodded.

"In the end, it was only with the help of my grandmother's academic partner that we were able to fight them off. We thought we had destroyed them, but they escaped and disappeared. I haven't seen them again since."

"What have you been doing all this time?" Ree asked.

"I spent the first several months helping my sister adjust to how drastically our life changed. I could never depend on my mom, but the best thing about this experience was when the demons took her over and then decided to break me down until they could transfer themselves out of her and into me, they gave her a shot of instant rehab. She hasn't relapsed yet, but I still fear that she will and the demons will return someday to get their revenge. The image of Ellie dying is something I still can't get out of my head. Not one night has gone by that I haven't woken up, sometimes screaming, at the thought of killing her and all the others that died that night. A few months later, I got back online with my new alias and couldn't resist looking up all the videos and opinions from the rest of the world about what happened that night."

"It was all over the internet for months," Ree said. "Those videos fascinated me. You have millions of views on some of them."

"Yes, that's when I realized people were searching for me online. I thought most were from Stone Creek and wanted to find and kill me, but I discovered many were these insane conspiracy people wanting me to lead them and give them some of my dark power. Eventually, a group connected with me that knew about these types of supernatural events. I knew that the only way I was going to be able to move on was to find out why these demons came after me. I need to stop or destroy them in order to protect my little sister, Myra, in case they ever decide to return. I think it's the only way I'll be able to truly live again. After a long conversation with my family, I decided to take time to try to find these creatures. I've been following them around the country for almost a year now with the help of this group.

I've been to California, Wisconsin, Ohio, and New York in just the last few months. Most of the events I've followed have turned out to be nothing, but I've come close a few times. Then I heard about what happened at this dead body exhibit a few days ago, and it just seemed too familiar. So now I'm back in Texas for the first time since we left. One of my contacts even got me some video, and I think I'm on the right path. That's why I wanted to speak to you. I just want to be sure."

Gabby didn't say anything for a minute. "Be sure of what?"

"That these are the same demons that destroyed my life and somehow came into yours. Does anything I've said make sense to you?"

Ree's head was already nodding before Gabby could answer.

"I don't know you, but some of what you've described is almost exactly what I've seen. What we've all seen. You mentioned that sugar skull that came to life. The first time the displays at the exhibit where I work moved, two of the displays were decorated like sugar skulls. Also, the reflections of yellow eyes and a shredded face. I work part time at this exhibit and the reflections were everywhere. We didn't experience anything like your Shadow Demon until that night of the Showcase Donor event. I can't move things with my mind, but I know there was something there. Something that got to me, my friends and my family."

"Please, tell me what happened that night, and don't leave out anything. It's important."

Gabby started to describe the details of the Donor event, and Angie and Ree joined in to fill in some additional pieces. When they got to the part about describing Ally's eyes, they all stopped talking.

"What is it?" Ricky asked. "Please. Everything."

Gabby sighed and stared at Ally, who was still and looking at nothing as Angie still carried her.

"My daughter. When I finally got to her, this young girl was holding her. Her eyes were yellow like the Reflection Demon, and then Ally's eyes turned yellow, too. She was able to stand and run and even speak in ways that her little body isn't developed enough to do yet. And it was only during that brief time. She had never moved or spoken that way before and hasn't since."

"The young girl," Ricky said. "You'd didn't recognize her at all?"

"No. A camera from my sister's neighbor's house caught a small shadow, which I'm sure was her, taking Ally from the house. We never saw her face except for that time she was with Ally and then when she left."

"How old was she?"

"I'm not sure. I'd guess maybe eleven, no more than twelve."

Ricky hesitated.

"So the Shadow Demon is coming at you, and this girl was holding Ally. How did you stop them?"

"I'm not exactly sure. I felt something inside me. After Ally was kidnapped, a woman, a paranormalist hacker, taught me how to concentrate on Ally and certain events to block out everything else and form a connection that helped us track her. Benji, the main paranormalist who helped me, told me the bond I have with my daughter was stronger than I realized. I used that same method to concentrate on Ally. Then, my mother appeared. She told me the inner power that I found in that exact moment helped bring her to me. Power that came from her love as a mother and my love for my daughter. She told me to use it to save Ally. Mom disappeared, then some kind of heat and light emanated from within my body when I focused on saving and protecting

Ally. Benji spoke about the strength of a mother's love, and somehow I was able to feel that and use it to save her."

"Save her how?"

"When the Shadow Demon made its final move to kill me, I was able to punch straight through its solid form. It screamed and then just disappeared."

"And the girl just disappeared, too?"

"No. A blue light shot out of the demon after I hit it. It went through me and surrounded Ally and the girl, but it didn't seem to hurt her."

"What did she do?"

"She looked like she was inhaling the light or something around her. She took in a deep breath and then just walked out," Gabby said.

"What did the girl look like?"

"She was covered in a dark mist for the most part," Gabby said. "But right before she left, that cloud lifted and she turned to us. We got a clearer look, and she had long, straight hair and a pale face. Nothing that really stood out. And another strange thing is that she didn't seem upset."

"How do you know? Did she say anything to you?"

"She smiled at us. She said that Ally was her new Kitty and that we could have her back now."

Ricky's hand rose to cover his mouth. His eyes glossed over.

"What is it?" Gabby asked.

"A few days before I bought the sugar skull. A young girl came to our house in the middle of the night," Ricky said. "We're pretty sure she was a ghost, but corporeal. We think she was the recruiter that noticed my mother and made her the initial target, but she was much younger than eleven. Maybe this young girl you saw was the same one, only older, or another ghost that served the same purpose as a Recruiter."

"A recruiter for what?" Ree asked.

"A doorway. A candidate with a means to let the demons into our physical world. Someone with a darkness that they could exploit to gain access to people."

"But we never saw her before that night of the Showcase," Gabby said.

"I only know how she got to my mother and gave the demons someone to exploit. Maybe she didn't have to hunt you down and found a way in without you realizing it."

"I was the doorway," Gabby said. "I thought it was my pervert boss at first, but I've had death surrounding me the last couple of years, along with a dark secret I hadn't shared with anyone. The paranormalist is the one who saw the connection, and I know for certain it was me."

"It doesn't matter how," Ricky said. "The important thing is that you're all safe. There's also something else. She said your daughter was her new Kitty. The girl I met that first night was dressed in a bathing suit. She was looking for her Kitty. Later, she and the demons attacked me in a dream while I was on a bus one night. She reached for me and said she had found her 'Kitty.'"

"What does that mean?"

"That there's no doubt we both faced the same demons and somehow our experiences are related, even though it seems they came for us for different reasons. Reasons I don't fully understand yet."

"So what now?" Gabby asked.

Ricky turned and faced Ally. "I have one more thing to ask. Can I hold your baby?"

Gabby looked back and Angie tightened her arms around Ally when she did. Gabby reached out for her daughter.

"It's okay, Angie."

Angie took a moment, then handed Ally to her mother.

Gabby sat her on her lap. "This is Ally."

Ricky reached out and gently touched Ally's cheek before extending his arms. "May I?"

Gabby slowly lifted her daughter and let the new stranger hold her.

Ricky cradled her in his arms. He touched her face and looked deeply into her eyes. He started to rock her gently, still gazing into her, then he shuddered.

He handed her back to Gabby.

"Please don't be upset about what I'm going to say. And I will preface this with there is no way for me to be sure if what I say and think is true. You may have been the doorway, but I think you were right. It was Ally they were after. I don't think the power you emanated to make the demons disappear came from their darkness. You may not have gained telekinetic abilities like I did, but I think since you were the doorway, you had some power stored within triggered by the love and need to protect your daughter. Just like your friend Benji said."

Ricky stared at Ally's face as she sat on her mom's lap and paused.

"What?"

"Gabby, she may be physically okay right now, but something's off. She hasn't been herself since this happened, has she?"

Gabby, Ree, and Angie stared at each other but didn't reply.

"That's what I expected," Ricky said. "This isn't going to be easy to hear, but you have to hear it. You saved her body, but the demons took some, maybe even most, of her soul. I think what you did saved her physically, but by then they had taken enough of what they needed to leave and not return for another fight. You stopped Ally and your friends from being killed, but what's left of Ally now is incomplete. I think that's what they were after and they got it. That blue light? Once you seemingly destroyed the Shadow Demon, I think he used your power and redirected it to the girl, and that power gave her the ability to take Ally's soul."

No one spoke. Gabby couldn't process what he'd just said.

"There's one more thing. Her body is weak and it's still here. But—"

Ricky hesitated.

"But what?"

"She's not going to survive long. Not like this. Not without an intact soul."

Gabby stood up with Ally in her arms and yelled. "No! That's not true! You need to leave. Get out of my house right now!"

Ricky raised his palms in a resigned motion and stood up, walking silently to the door. He turned.

"I'm sorry. One more thing and I promise I'll leave. The time is critical to get her soul back. I have to talk to my people and hope they can figure out where the Demons are headed now, but I'm leaving in the morning no matter what. I didn't just come here to upset you. I came to confirm what happened, and now that I have, I only have one last question."

Gabby was breathing hard but didn't reply. She was trying her best not to break down.

"Ask it and go," Angie said. "Please."

"Do you want to come with me? One thing your friend Benji got right. A mother's love. A real mother's love, I should say, is a powerful, powerful thing. I've been doing this solo for a while now, but if I had a mother as strong as you that was hell-bent on saving her baby's soul instead of worrying about her next fix, I think I'd have a much better chance at saving your daughter and stopping these demons before they can accomplish whatever it is they're planning to do. I don't expect an answer right now, but you do need to decide by morning. I'll be back tomorrow at 10 am sharp. I'll ring your doorbell twice and wait. If after five minutes no one answers, I'll leave. If you decide to come with me, be ready. Get someone you trust who will watch Ally with their life. Whether you believe me or not, I'm going to try to stop these demons and save your daughter's soul in the process. It could be weeks or even months, but now that they have Ally's soul, I think they may be easier to track. If you choose not to go, I promise to contact you if I am able to save her."

Gabby was speechless. Ree and Angie's mouths were open, too.

Ricky gave them a gentle nod, then walked out the door.

The three friends stood staring at the door for another few minutes until Gabby finally sat on the couch and held up her daughter, looking directly in her face.

"Gabby," Angie said. "You can't seriously be considering this?"

Ree didn't say anything.

"Gabby?"

Gabby pulled Ally into her chest and started to cry. Angie held her. Ree stood still.

"I knew you wouldn't leave her. I'm sorry he said such awful things. I'd be upset, too."

"No, Angie," Gabby said. "I'm not upset because of what he told me. I'm upset because I know he's right."

"You can't be serious?"

Gabby looked at Ree. "You agree with him, don't you?"

Ree looked up and took a quick look at Angie, then nodded. "Yes."

"Really, Ree?" Angie said. "Gabby, please. No!"

"Call Sheila and Benji," Gabby said. "See if they can do a video chat. Tell them it's important and I need to see their faces."

Angie did as Gabby asked, and they were all on within

minutes. Gabby told them about Ricky's visit, using Angie and Ree to make sure she didn't miss any details.

"I know who that kid Ricky Luna is," Benji said after processing. "I know his story. What he said about the possible power transfer makes sense."

"So by trying to save Ally I gave them exactly what they wanted?"

"I believe you would have all died otherwise," Benji said. "Had you not stopped them, they would have had no reason to leave any part of Ally behind."

"My thoughts," Sheila said. "If he's wrong, nothing changes. But what if he's right? Is it worth the risk?"

"So you both think he's telling the truth and Ally's missing her soul?"

"I do," Benji said. "When Ricky's story broke, I just knew it was true. I know some of the people who have been in contact with him and they're reliable."

"I have to agree with Benji," Sheila said. "That young man is on a mission to save his own mind and family. I see no advantage or reason for him to lie to you."

"Yes," Benji said. "He may need you more than he let on."

"Why would he need me?"

"Would you give your life for your daughter?"

"Yes," Gabby said without hesitation.

"He would give his for his sister," Benji said. "Of that I have no doubt."

Gabby stared back at them for a few minutes without saying anything.

"Okay," she said. "Thank you for your help. I need to go."

They hung up and Angie turned to her. "You can't do this, Gabby."

Angie looked at her best friend's face and knew the decision was already made.

"I have to," Gabby said. "I need to talk to Teri, but can

either of you help? If Ally isn't in immediate danger, she should be low maintenance."

"What about school?"

"Being part of the lead story in the news for a few days helped. My professors gave me a pass with the semester almost over and I can make it up in the summer. I think they'll even let me go into the fall, but none of that matters right now, Ang. Without Ally, it means absolutely nothing."

Gabby spent the rest of the evening arranging things with her sister and her friends. She woke up early the next morning and at exactly 10 am, the doorbell rang.

Teri, Angie, and Ree were all by her side when she answered the doorbell and let Ricky in.

She had two bags and not much else.

"I'm glad you changed your mind," Ricky said, motioning toward Ally. "May I hold her again?"

Gabby held out Ally and Ricky took her.

"My sister Myra is the most important person in the world to me," Ricky said. "I promise you I will try as hard to save Ally's soul as I would if she were my own sister."

Ricky gave Ally a kiss on the cheek. "And I'll watch over Mommy, Ally. She'll come back to you. I promise."

He handed her back to Gabby.

"I got a solid lead already," Ricky said. "We need to go."

He grabbed Gabby's bags and headed out to his car.

Gabby held Ally tight and looked at her sister and friends.

"I don't know what I'm getting myself into, but I have to be sure. I know you all love Ally like she was your own, and I'm so lucky and proud to have you all as my family. I'll keep in contact and I don't know how to thank you for helping me with this."

Ree started to get emotional and just gave her a hug and a peck on the cheek. "I love you. You know that, right?"

"I love you more," Angie said.

"I get it. I'm still number two," Ree said, trying to smile as Angie hugged her.

"We got this, Sister," Teri said. "If it were one of my kids, I'd be doing the same thing. I'm proud of you."

Gabby held up Ally. "Mommy loves you, kiddo."

She handed her to Teri.

"I thought you'd be a mess by now," Angie said.

"No. No more crying. Now that I know what's wrong with her, I need to save her soul and heal her. Otherwise, nothing we did matters."

Gabby kissed Ally one last time, then walked out of her house to travel with a young man she had just met. They got in the car and drove off, both on a mission to stop two demons and save a soul. They gave each other a knowing look.

"Do you think we'll succeed?" Gabby asked.

"We will," Ricky answered. "Or die trying."

There was no other possible outcome.

BONUSES

Get a NOVEL, NOVELLAS, SHORT STORIES, and exclusive content, all for free.

I enjoy engaging with readers. The first few years of my career, most of that time was spent at book events and classrooms when I primarily wrote MG supernatural books.

With YA/Adult books and short stories now in my catalog, I will occasionally send newsletters about new releases, special offers and general news relating to my work.

If you sign up to my mailing list, I'll send you several freebies, including:

1. YA novella *Our Possessions,* a prequel to the *Sugar Skull.*
2. YA novella *The Conductor.*
3. MG novel *Lobo Coronado and the Legacy of the Wolf.*
4. MG short stories *The Dead Club: Short Tales,* a prequel to the *The Dead Club.*

Get your free Starter Library here:
manuelruiz3.com

ACKNOWLEDGMENTS

Rudy Montalvo
Vincent "Vinny" Giles

Two of my closest friends who served as police officers for
most of their lives. They never flinch when I call to ask
unusual questions, such as:
"So, first of all, my wife is okay, but if there's a dead body in
your house, who shows up first, last, and where is the body
sent?"

Thank you both for your service, dedication, and friendship.

Imagine Exhibitions

To the person who went above and beyond to find the right
people to answer my questions about how to repair dead
body exhibits. I never got a name, but am so grateful for the
help.

My Reader Team
David Riskind
Michael Sawyer
Mari Molina
Belynda Chapa
Pam "PMoney" Marino
Daisy Ruiz

AUTHOR'S NOTE

I've had a few odd things happen to me during my life. Just like in the first book, there are several scenes in this story that are based on some of those actual events.

The car blowout the night of the concert did happen. My wife and I, just before we were married, were traveling to our hometown late on a cold night and it was pitch black, so I was flipping my headlights on and off to scare her. We were about to reach a bridge when I said, "Wouldn't it suck to have a blowout right now?" The moment I finished my sentence, that's exactly what happened. After an almost 2-mile walk in the cold, a worker at the only open gas station we reached told us about newlyweds who had died on that same bridge and the numerous car stalls, blowouts, and crashes that had occurred there since.

The chapter about the day out with the nephew and nieces is based on a weekend when my wife and I hosted her younger sister and three first cousins. We took them to the movies, then brought them to our house for an overnight visit to play games, eat junk food, and just hang out. While picking up some food, the total came out to all sixes. Then later that night, while getting ready to watch movies, the VCR counter stopped on all sixes after rewinding. That was followed by a piece of an old ceramic heater breaking off and falling to the floor, setting it on fire, and then our gas stove shooting out a huge flame while making popcorn. This book's version of the events was updated with modern gadgets, since some readers may not know what a VCR is, but this entire chapter was based on that one crazy weekend.

And yes, we all slept in the same bed that night.

A big challenge for this second book was deciding to follow the demons instead of Ricky and the characters from Book 1, but that's where the story took me. At this point, you know how it ends and how it sets up the events for the series finale.

I truly loved writing that last chapter. I hope you enjoyed Gabby's story and are ready to take the final ride in Book 3.

Please feel free to contact me for any feedback or just to say hello!

ABOUT THE AUTHOR

Manuel Ruiz is a life-long Texan with a passion for reading, video games, and music. He works in IT, plays in an 80's band, and owns way too many toys. He writes teen and adult fiction, usually with a supernatural twist, and loves to keep his readers on their toes.

Manuel lives in Central Texas with his family where he spends time giving the characters in his head something fun, dark, and interesting to do.

To find out more, please visit :
www.manuelruiz3.com

ALSO BY MANUEL RUIZ

MIDDLE GRADE

The Dead Club Series

The Dead Club

Grey is an eleven-year-old boy who is curious, a loyal friend and just realized that he's dead. He is joined in the afterlife by a tomboy, a baseball player, a beauty queen, and a science geek and together they learn that Purgatory is broken and are soon thrust into a frantic search to discover what has unleashed chaos in the Underworld.

Councils and Keepers

The Dead Club survived their first afterlife adventure, but the fallout left cracks in the Underworld that have awakened something much, much worse.

The heroes will need more than their growing powers to face an enemy linked to the Oracle's past with the ability to return the Underworld back to its darkest time.

Underworld Rising

The Dead Club is fractured. Ancient enemies have returned to demand vengeance on the Oracle and Underworld Council. The heroes are desperate, planning for war without the Oracle or Grim Reaper while facing the possibility that one of their own has turned against them.

All hope rests on a shattered Dead Club as they prepare to fight the final battle that will determine the fate of the Underworld.

Lobo Coronado

Lobo Coronado and the Legacy of the Wolf

Lobo Coronado is about to have the most exciting day of his mundane life. Kidnapped by night shadows and introduced to his long-lost grandfather, he is transported to another realm where he meets a queen, a vampire scribe and a little angel with a big attitude problem. Lobo learns that an unknown enemy with a demon army and ties to his late father is endangering multiple worlds. Teamed with his new companions, this Freaksome Threesome must work together to unleash the full potential of Lobo's famous bloodline and prevent the annihilation of Earth and the Celestial Realms.

YOUNG ADULT

The Sugar Skull Series

The Sugar Skull

17-year-old Ricky wants nothing more than to finish school, win the hand of his best girl, and get away from his troubling home life. But when two seemingly unrelated things pop up -- a curious midnight visit and the arrival of an enchanting sugar skull -- his world turns upside down. It's soon clear that the skull holds secrets far more dangerous than any high school adversary ... and its sights are set on Ricky's soul.

The Sugar Skull is the first in a 3-book series, inspired by actual events.

The Sweet Skull

Gabby just wants to raise her baby, finish grad school, and excel at her job working with cadaver exhibits. However, when the bodies start moving on their own, it sets off a chain reaction, and Gabby's life unravels.

Secrets are revealed. Ghosts manifest. Fear builds. Gabby struggles to find a way to stop the relentless chaos.

Darkness is coming. Gabby will do anything to protect her family and her sanity. Will darkness prevail, or can she stop it before it's too late?

Made in the USA
Middletown, DE
11 October 2022